THE IMPROPER PROPOSAL

At last Quentin had asked her to marry him. At last Theo had felt Quentin's lips on hers. It was only when he was about to repeat the kiss even more ardently that she drew back and gently said, "We should go and speak to my mother."

He dropped his eyes. "We must wait. I wish my aunt to become accustomed to the idea gradually."

"You did not speak to her first?" asked Theo, in shock. "Do you take me for a lightskirt?"

"It will only be for a little while," Quentin pleaded. "I cannot live without you. Please say you will be mine."

The words were intoxicating. "Yes," she heard herself saying softly, and closed her eyes for another kiss.

It was not disagreeable—though it was dangerous. . . .

CAROL PROCTOR was born and raised in Harlingen, Texas. She attended the College of William and Mary in Virginia, where she received her B.A. in English, with a minor in European History. She earned her Master's degree in scriptwriting from the University of Texas. After working in broadcasting in various parts of Texas, she married and now has a young son. She currently lives in Fort Worth, Texas, and her favorite pastimes include gardening, fishing, and music.

THEODORA'S DREADFUL MISTAKE

by

Carol Proctor

A SIGNET BOOK

SIGNET
Published by the Penguin Group
Penguin Books USA Inc., 375 Hudson Street,
New York, New York 10014, U.S.A.
Penguin Books Ltd, 27 Wrights Lane,
London W8 5TZ, England
Penguin Books Australia Ltd, Ringwood,
Victoria, Australia
Penguin Books Canada Ltd, 10 Alcorn Avenue,
Toronto, Ontario, Canada M4V 3B2
Penguin Books (N.Z.) Ltd, 182–190 Wairau Road,
Auckland 10, New Zealand

Penguin Books Ltd, Registered Offices:
Harmondsworth, Middlesex, England

First published by Signet, an imprint of New American Library,
a division of Penguin Books USA Inc.

First Printing, October, 1992
10 9 8 7 6 5 4 3 2 1

 REGISTERED TRADEMARK—MARCA REGISTRADA

PRINTED IN THE UNITED STATES OF AMERICA

BOOKS ARE AVAILABLE AT QUANTITY DISCOUNTS WHEN USED TO PROMOTE PROD-
UCTS OR SERVICES. FOR INFORMATION PLEASE WRITE TO PREMIUM MARKETING
DIVISION. PENGUIN BOOKS USA INC.. 375 HUDSON STREET. NEW YORK. NEW YORK
10014.

to Ed

Deo optimo maximo

Chapter One

When she opened her eyes, Theodora felt once again as if she were awakening into a nightmare. Such a reaction might seem extreme to anyone else viewing the modest and quietly furnished room. To Theodora, who was used to lofty ceilings, spacious apartments, and magnificent furniture covered with silk and damask, the bedroom she now occupied seemed hardly better than a prisoner's cell.

She closed her eyes and reopened them, but it did not help. No trim maidservant appeared to open the curtains and wish her good morning with a smile and a curtsy. No crackling fire sprang up in the hearth. There was no saddled mare and no groom waiting for her below.

She gave a sigh of despair. She was about to follow her usual practice of wishing that she were dead, when a sudden idea altered the direction of her thoughts. She sprang out of bed, threw on her wrapper, and hardly noticed the chilliness of the floor as she put on her slippers. She snatched the bell by the bed and rang it forcefully, waited a moment, sighed, and rang it again. No response was forthcoming. She rang it once more and waited. After another moment or two, she dropped the bell disgustedly on the table and made her way out of the room.

"Peggy!"

There was no answer. Shaking her head, she began up the narrow staircase, calling as she went.

"Peggy!"

She had reached the top of the stairs and was about to turn down the hall, when a figure suddenly materialized. It was a large, elderly female, wearing an old-fashioned mobcap with her stiff black gown.

"Miss Theodora! Such a rumpus as you're making. You should let your poor mother have her sleep, at least. It's little enough to grant her."

7

"Did you press my mull gown, Peggy, as I requested last night? Is it ready?"

Peggy gave a sniff as she made her way past her questioner and began down the stairs. "I pressed the jaconet instead." Ignoring the girl's cry of dismay, she continued, "And a good thing, I did, too. It will rain again today, and there is no sense in soiling your fine new gown." There was a great deal more that Peggy might have said upon the subject, but she was interrupted by the faint tinkling of a bell.

"There's the viscountess. I *told* you that you would wake her."

Despite her gruffness, Peggy was obviously not a person to shirk her duties. As soon as she had finished answering the viscountess's summons, she returned to Theodora's bedroom with the despised jaconet in her hands.

In a short time, she had brushed the girl's hair into order, arranging the tousled curls and pinning them artfully on one side of her face.

Theodora frowned at her reflection in the mirror. "If I attend the ball at the Upper Rooms on Monday, do you think that you could contrive something a little different?"

"We'll have to see how the viscountess is faring by then."

"The Simpsons might take me."

Peggy gave a sniff that was perilously near a snort. "We'll see what your mother says to that."

"I am going to Laura Place this morning. Their copy of the *Lady's Magazine* was to arrive yesterday, and we want to look at the new fashions." She scowled at the dress on the bed as Peggy began to lace up her corset. "That is why I wished to look other than a dowd."

"Fine feathers don't make fine birds," observed Peggy sourly, but Theodora was oblivious. As she began to help the girl into her frock, she commented, "The viscountess wishes you to come to her chamber as soon as you are dressed." Busy with her work, she paused for a moment, then continued, "I suppose you'll not be accompanying her to the Hot Bath today."

A twinge of self-reproach pricked Theodora, but she replied indifferently, "No, for I can be of little help to her there." She salved her conscience by adding, "But I will go to the Pump Room with her tomorrow morning."

"Hmph." The scorn in the syllable well expressed Peggy's opinion on the matter, but as she took a step back to survey her charge, she merely remarked, "You look well enough. You'd best put on your boots, though, for it is certain to rain."

Theodora caught her lower lip between her teeth in order to hold back a retort.

Satisfied, Peggy nodded. "I'll go downstairs and see that Cook has breakfast ready for you."

Theodora shook her head. "No, I don't wish to take the time this morning." Seeing the martial light that sprang up in Peggy's eyes, she added hurriedly, "Perhaps I can ask Mama if she wishes for some tea. Even though she has to fast before going in the Hot Bath, I should think it would be permitted."

As soon as Peggy had left, Theodora, with an expression of distaste, dropped the brown kerseymere pelisse she had been holding obediently. She crossed the room and opened a door of the tall mahogany clothespress. She removed a short, light blue jacket of a twilled silk, trimmed with scalloped binding. Ignoring her handmaiden's dictates, she selected kid slippers in the same shade of light blue. She hesitated for a moment between a rather dashing woodland hat of lemon-colored chip and a cottage bonnet of white chip that framed the face most becomingly. Deciding to be practical, she selected the latter, for while the ribbon upon it might not benefit from possible rain, the ostrich feather upon the other would surely be ruined.

Her toilette complete, she made the way down the hall to her mother's room and tapped gently upon the door.

"Come in."

Her mother was even paler than usual, she thought, and the lines beneath her eyes were etched more deeply, evidence that she had passed a bad night. She had on her dressing gown, though she was sitting in bed, propped up as usual upon her pillows. Despite her illness, she was still a remarkably beautiful woman, the prematurely graying hair only serving to emphasize the great dark eyes and chiseled features. Theodora could not help giving an inward sigh. Why did she have to take after her father, instead?

"My dear." Her mother held out a frail, bony hand, and Theodora crossed the room quickly to take it. "How smart you are looking! Is there a special occasion today?" she asked, her eyes taking in every detail of her daughter's appearance.

"Oh, no, Mama," said Theodora with an assumption of carelessness. "I just mean to go visit the Simpsons—the new *Lady's Magazine* was to arrive yesterday, and we wish to read it together."

Something altered in her mother's countenance, but she said quietly, "How nice for you not to have to depend upon finding it at the library. Shall you want a chair to go to their house? It is quite a distance, is it not?"

Theodora forced herself to smile. "Oh, I wouldn't be so extravagant. It is not too terribly far, after all—only in Laura Place. And it is such a large, fine house, too. You will have to pay a call there with me when you are feeling more the thing."

The Viscountess Westmoreland gave a worried frown. "That new spencer of yours is so becoming, my dear, but are you certain that the sarcenet will be warm enough? It is not quite April, after all. You might be warmer in your pelisse."

Theodora had no intention of putting on her much worn pelisse. "I shall be fine, Mama, thank you." Remembering her words to the servant, she added, "Would you care for some tea? I can tell Peggy when I go downstairs."

"That would be lovely." The dark eyes examined her with a troubled expression. "Do you know if John Debenham planned to call today? I should hate for him to find only an invalid here."

Theodora could not help flushing slightly. She could hardly tell her mother that she was anxious to be out of the house simply in order to avoid meeting Debenham. "I am sure that I do not know," she said, and stooped to kiss her mother. "I had better be going. They may be waiting for me."

Her mother squeezed her hand, but held on to it for another moment. "Theodora . . ."

"Yes?"

"It seems that I am forever asking something of you . . . but could you be kind to John? He and his father are not tied to us by blood, but they have been so good to our family. We owe our present comfortable situation to them, you know."

Theodora's throat constricted. "I know." She was not

grateful in the slightest for having to forgo expensive new gowns, smart new bonnets, her horse, their carriages, and a thousand other luxuries. Most bitter of all to her was the necessity for being uprooted from Westleigh Abbey. How could she be grateful for having to leave her childhood home?

Her mother released her hand. "I shall not keep you, then. You will be wanting to join your friends." She smiled at her daughter. "I hope that you have a most pleasant time."

The lines under her eyes were darker, weren't they? "Mama, I . . . I hope that I did not awaken you this morning."

She smiled again, reassuringly. "No, my dear. I was already awake, I had rather a bad night, but I expect the bath today will soon put me to rights."

"I hope so, Mama." She paused before going out the door. "I will have Peggy bring up the tea."

"Thank you. Be sure to take Molly with you."

As she stepped out into the street, Theodora was conscious again of a feeling of guilt. It was nothing new to her; she had experienced it ever since arriving in Bath. To add to her gloom, the skies were gray and it looked as if Peggy's prediction might well come true.

"Don't you need a wrap, miss? I think it might rain."

Theodora was suddenly angry. Why here, even the lowest of the servants felt free to speak to her familiarly. "No, I shall be perfectly comfortable," she said icily, trying to repress a shiver as a sudden gust of cold air tore at her skirts. "We had better be off."

She had taken no more than four or five steps when she saw that she was too late. A familiar high-perch phaeton in green, picked out in gold had turned the corner of George Street and was beginning up Gay Street toward them.

"Confound it!" she remarked feelingly. There was no possibility for escape. She proceeded on her way rather more slowly than before.

The driver, though he would not have been so vulgar as to signal or cry out, obviously had spotted her, for in another few moments, he had checked the horses and soon pulled them up to the curb. His groom jumped down from the rear seat and ran to the horse's heads. Still retaining the reins in his left hand, with his right the driver removed his tall beaver hat from his head and doffed it politely.

He was not a tall man, being of just the medium height, though he was powerfully built. Neither was he conventionally handsome: his nose had been broken in some pugilistic endeavor, and he had rather too much determined chin to fit anyone's notion of male beauty. His clothing, too, was undistinguished, being of a plain, though expensive cut. His shirt points were only moderately high, his cravat was tied very simply, and his person was unadorned by fobs or pins or any other form of jewelry. It was true that his deep-set gray eyes were compelling, but Theodora thought that a small point compared with his other inadequacies. It never failed to astonish her that other ladies were so much less perceptive than she.

She was not given time to pursue this train of thought, for now Debenham spoke. "May I offer you a ride, Miss Westmoreland?"

"No, thank you. I am merely going to Laura Place this morning." She tried to fix a pleasant expression upon her face.

"Don't be pigheaded. That's a long walk. You'd better ride."

Despite her promise to her mother, Theodora could feel herself stiffen. "Thank you so much for your *courtesy*, but I prefer to walk," she said frostily.

He gave a derisive snort, called to the groom, and after handing the reins to him, sprang down from the carriage. Ignoring Theodora for the moment, he issued his instructions, "Take them up to the Circus, then drive back down and find us. We are headed toward Laura Place." As the servant complied, starting the horses off, Debenham turned to Theodora and remarked, "Can't keep the animals standing about on such a raw day. Wouldn't want them to catch cold."

Theodora was less than pleased at having this other companion on her walk. "Really, there is no need for you to go to the trouble—"

She was not permitted to finish, for eyeing her, he remarked abruptly, "Speaking of catching cold, you'd better go back and put on your pelisse. You're likely to freeze in that."

At that moment a blast of cold air nearly took her breath

away, but still Theodora remarked haughtily, "I shall be quite warm enough, as long as I am permitted to continue with my walk."

He seemed about to speak, then shrugged instead. "Please yourself." He offered her his arm and, despite her irritation, there was no polite way to refuse it. They set off in the direction of Barton Street, the maid following behind.

"I like your bonnet," he remarked.

"Oh, I thought you had seen it before," she answered in a tone calculated to show her indifference to his opinions.

"P'raps I have. All I know is that I like it much better than that silly one with the feather on it."

She nearly gasped aloud with indignation. A sharp retort hovered on her lips, but she remembered her mother's words, and with some difficulty remained silent. Her escort was seemingly oblivious, for now he glanced up at the skies in some concern. "We're certain to have some rain soon. I hope Will pushes the horses along. You'll have to ride with me, you know."

"I certainly am *not* going to ride with you. I enjoy walking—it is such pleasant exercise." Her teeth were chattering as she spoke, but her chin was held defiantly high.

"You're going to walk to Laura Place, in the rain, in those?" Her kid slippers had not escaped his notice.

"Yes, I am." To forestall his next remark, she added, "And I consider that what I wear is no one else's concern."

His eyebrows drew together, but he ventured no reply.

They paced along in silence for several moments. Theodora thought vindictively that it would serve him right if it did start to rain and marred the finish on his shining top boots. It was what he deserved for forcing his presence on her—she certainly had never asked for his company.

"Going to visit those mush—those acquaintances of yours?" he asked.

He had been about to call her friends "mushrooms." How dare he? It was true that their family's fortune had come from trade, but they were sweet, charming girls, nonetheless. And their father had recently been knighted, after all. She opened her mouth to speak, then clamped it firmly shut. It was no business of his!

"Yes, I am," she retorted sweetly.

"I s'pose your mother knows about it?"

"Of course she does. She even told me to have a most pleasant time."

Fortunately for Theodora, her self-control was not to be exercised for much longer, for at that moment, the phaeton appeared beside them.

Debenham acknowledged his groom with a nod of his head, before turning once again to Theodora. "You'd better ride—it will be a long, cold walk otherwise."

This gracious invitation only strengthened her resolve. "Some other time."

He still retained her arm. "I'll walk the rest of the way with you, if you like."

Such a sacrifice was clearly against his own inclinations, and for the first time since seeing him today, she smiled. "That *is* kind of you—but Molly is all the company I need, thank you."

He shook his head as if despairing of the female sex, released her arm, and bowing curtly, soon resumed his place in the carriage. In another few seconds, the phaeton was bowling down the street.

"How perfectly odious he is," said Theodora to herself. She glanced at her maid, to be certain that she had not overheard, but all she could see was that same look of dumb admiration in the girl's eyes. How entirely ridiculous!

Happening to notice the dark clouds gathering above them, she resumed her walk with a renewed vigor. Hardly any time had passed before a fat raindrop landed squarely on her nose. Luckily, she had thought to bring her little silk umbrella. She unfurled it and continued walking. The raindrops were thickening. She tried not to notice.

"Miss Westmoreland?"

Really, she had almost had enough of this maid. "What is it?"

"Shouldn't we find shelter until the storm passes?"

What a poor-spirited creature. "You see that we are already to Trim Street. There is hardly any distance to go, now."

Some twenty minutes later, a bedraggled Theodora stood dripping upon the Aubusson carpet in the drawing room of the Simpson house. Miss Julia Simpson, the younger of the sisters, was busy chafing Theodora's hands in order to warm them. The elder, Isabel, a tall and elegant girl of nineteen, had efficiently stripped Theodora of her bonnet and spencer, and handed them to a maidservant. She looked up to observe her sister's activities, and commented dryly, "Do' stop that, Julia. What Theo needs are a few moments in front of the fire."

The younger, a plump and pretty girl of seventeen, immediately desisted, though she could not help following Theo over to the fire and remarking, "Oh, your poor bonnet and your pretty spencer. I hope they are not utterly ruined. You should have let us sent the carriage for you, you know, you really should have."

Her sister scowled at her meaningfully as she responded, "I'm sure dear Theo would have let us, if she had had an inkling that it might rain."

Beginning to be warmed, Theodora at last could speak, "Yes, actually Debenham offered to drive me here in his phaeton, but I refused."

The sisters exchanged significant glances. They had known Theodora scarcely three weeks, but already they had shared the most intimate secrets of their hearts. The mere mention of Debenham's name conveyed a wealth of information to these two.

Julia could not help giving a sigh. "It is such a pity that he doesn't suit you. Why, he could be the solution to all your—seeing her sister's glare, she hastily amended her words—"To all your plans, that is."

"You sound exactly like my mother: 'Theodora, do you know if John is planning to call today?' 'Theodora, did you remember to thank John for his thoughtfulness?' 'Theodora, please be *kind* to John for my sake.' " Theodora sniffed. "His manners are appalling, he is concerned only about his stupid horses, and personally I do not find him attractive at all!"

"I think he's wonderful," said Julia with a little shake of the head.

"There is no purpose in our sitting and gabbling any longer," cut in Isabel severely. She picked up a paper lying on the rosewood end table. "We have today's *Bath Chronicle*. We would spend our time more profitably, examining the arrivals."

Theodora, nearly dry by now, started forward eagerly. "Oh, is there anyone new? —Suitable for our purposes, that is?"

In another moment the three heads were bent over the paper.

"Lord Afton?" questioned Julia.

"No, he's eighty if he's a day," responded Isabel.

"Sir Roger Fairford?"

"Married. I suppose his wife doesn't care for Bath."

They scanned the list with decreasing hopes.

"Why is it that there always seem to be so many more ladies arriving than gentlemen?" asked Julia.

"I am afraid it's because they outlive their husbands," remarked Theodora, as she turned from the paper hopelessly. "It's no use. I suppose I should give up now."

"Wait!" Isabel's eyes were still trained on the list. "It says that the Countess Verridge is here—"

"What good does that—?"

"—Accompanied by her nephew, Quentin Mansfield."

She looked up from the paper to see two pairs of expectant eyes. "He is unmarried, he is young, and he is very handsome . . ."

"Oh?"

She sighed, "But he also is without a fortune."

"Ah!"

A damp kid slipper tapped the carpet in irritation. "Really, Isabel! Why mention him at all, if he has no fortune?"

If Isabel had an obvious fault, it was most probably her love of the dramatic moment. She held up a finger and commanded ten full seconds of silence before speaking.

"*He* has no fortune, but the *countess* does." Seeing that she had succeeded in confusing her two auditors, she gave a little smile of triumph.

"So you mean that he will *inherit* a fortune?" Theodora asked.

"Possibly . . ."

It was Julia who ran out of patience and remarked sharply, "Stop being so mysterious, Isabel. You know that neither of us can know the answer."

Isabel smiled again, this time with all the condescension of the sophisticated nineteen-year-old toward the ingenue of seventeen. "It is very simple, really. According to what I was told in London, the countess commands vast holdings in her own name. Since she has no offspring, it is thought that these estates most probably will devolve upon—"

"—Upon her nephew!" Julia, finishing her sentence for her, looked pleased.

Theodora was frowning. "Why do you say 'most probably'?"

Isabel looked a little less smug. "Well, I was told that the countess had two sisters, each of whom produced one son. The older sister apparently disgraced herself by her marriage, though, so it is said that the countess has never met her other nephew. She *is* an eccentric old lady."

She saw the doubt in Theodora's face and hastened to reassure her. "But the countess seems entirely disposed in Mr. Mansfield's favor. And he is so attentive to her! That he accompanied her here speaks for itself."

It certainly did. For a personable young gentleman to forsake the pleasures of London for the boredom of Bath in order to accompany an infirm and elderly aunt, spoke volumes to Theodora. Then again, she could hardly assume a self-righteous attitude when her current existence depended largely upon the goodwill of the Debenhams.

"They say that his manners are particularly pleasing," continued Isabel, "and that he is an excellent dancer—"

"Enough!" pleaded Theodora. "You have convinced me. Besides, we haven't any others to consider at the moment, in any case."

"La!" exclaimed Julia. "If he is such a paragon, I am surprised that you didn't set your cap for him yourself, Isabel."

Isabel looked pained at her younger sister's ill-bred manner of speaking, and was about to comment upon it. Glancing at their visitor, she realized that her admonishments might better be saved for later. So instead, she drew herself up haughtily and remarked in an icy manner, "You of all people should know that my affections are otherwise engaged, as they have been for some time." She did not add that the daughter of even a well-breeched *cit* was quite beneath the touch of a gentleman of Mr. Mansfield's birth and expected fortune.

Happily oblivious, Julia continued on in her sportive vein. "Well, when I come out, I certainly don't intend to engage myself to the first eligible gentleman who presents himself—"

Isabel flushed with anger and cut her off. "Mr. Warwick was not the *first* gentleman who . . . and we are not engaged! We simply have an understanding until he is appointed to his post—"

"If you had bothered to *really* become engaged, then I might be allowed to come out, too. I shall probably be an old spinster by the time—"

"Ha! If you were fortunate enough to interest the heir to a baronetcy with a *very* handsome fortune of his own, you'd snap him up in a moment—"

" 'The heir to a baronetcy'—how often must we listen to that? You won't be *Lady* Warwick for another twenty years. I shall do better when I've the chance—"

"With a figure and manners like yours? Don't say another word or I may die of laughing!"

The sisters were at the most unattractive when squabbling with each other, and Theodora judged it to be time to intervene.

"Did the *Lady's Magazine* arrive yesterday as you thought it would? I told my mother that we were going to spend the morning looking at it, and I must do so before I go."

This diversion proved successful, for the two stormy faces brightened immediately.

"Indeed, it did! And you must see the new fashions!" exclaimed Julia, crossing the room to fetch the periodical. She flipped through it to find the pertinent page. "Just see this evening dress in crepe, with the vandyking about the petticoat—"

"What sort of sleeves does it have?" asked Theodora, rising to peer over Julia's shoulder.

"Spanish, and it is a new color, too—they call it 'Clarence'—"

Isabel, who could not bear to be excluded from the conversation, now rose and glided gracefully over to them, "I myself thought that the promenade costume was the more striking of the two—"

Her attention directed to it, Theodora could not help giving a little gasp.

"What is it?" asked Julia.

"I told you so," said Isabel.

"The bonnet!" exclaimed Theodora. Indeed the entire ensemble was most attractive, the prominent feature being a mantle in green. The bonnet was something quite new. The crown was in white satin, decorated with a wreath of cornflowers. The unexpected part was that the rim of the hat, also in satin, was the same shade of green as the mantle.

"How charming!" breathed Theodora. "What do they call it?"

"A Spanish hat," read Julia.

Theodora's eyes met Isabel's. Wasn't it possible that this was just the thing that might help her attract Mr. Mansfield's attention? She began stripping off her gloves determinedly.

"If you will ask a servant to bring me some paper and a pen, I will sketch it. I will speak to Mama about it when I go home."

Smiling delightedly, Julia complied by crossing the room to draw the bellpull. Isabel was more careful to guard her thoughts. It was a fine thing to have a viscount's daughter for a friend. It would be even more satisfying if she made a fortunate marriage and could give them the entree to society that they lacked. If Isabel was able to help her achieve that goal, how great must Theodora's gratitude be! More important, how great would be her sense of obligation to them. Isabel smiled to herself.

"I had forgotten to ask, my dear Theo, if you meant to attend the ball at the Upper Rooms on Monday. We should be happy to convey you there in our carriage."

Chapter Two

As it so happened, it wasn't until the next morning that Theodora was able to speak to her mother about the matter. Either the bath had taxed her strength, or it had proved less efficacious than she had hoped, for when Theodora had returned home, her mother had been confined to her room, not emerging even for dinner.

Not surprisingly, her mother did not appear at the table the next morning for breakfast. The servants, as was their custom, tiptoed around the house, for fear of disturbing her rest. Theodora, who had promised to meet her friends at the Pump Room, grew increasingly impatient. When she ventured to peep into the viscountess's room, she was relieved therefore, to find her mother reading a letter.

"Come in, my dear."

Theodora sidled in, bid her mother good morning, and closed the door behind her.

"I had a letter from Andrew yesterday," said the viscountess, indicating the paper she was reading. "It seems, that his studies are going well, and that he expects to make us proud of him."

"I'm sure he will." A lump rose in Theo's throat as she thought of her younger brother, whom the Debenhams had insisted must remain at Eton. *He* had made the adjustment to their new situation with no word of complaint. *He* had responded by becoming even more serious and diligent a scholar. Well, if her schemes succeeded, he would be one of the first to benefit.

"Did you pass an uncomfortable night, Mother?"

Lady Westmoreland smiled at her gently. "No, actually, I had the most refreshing night's sleep that I've had in quite a while—"

"Then you intend to visit the Pump Room this morning?"

"Why, yes. You will be accompanying me?" At Theo's

nod, her mother continued, "John Debenham will be so pleased, I know. Just before I went to the Bath yesterday, he called and offered to drive us both there today."

Naturally he would do his best to upset any and all of her plans. Theo hoped that her dismay did not show in her face. "H-how nice," she managed to choke out. She hoped that Debenham had not seen fit to discuss yesterday's meeting with her mother, for gentle reproaches would be inevitable. However, the viscountess merely smiled at her blandly. Theo could thank him for his discretion on this one occasion, at least. She hurried on to the topic that was dear to her heart. "Mother—about the ball at the Upper Rooms on Monday—"

"Oh, yes. I meant to mention that to you also. Mr. Debenham has offered to escort us there as well—so I hope that I may be feeling strong enough to go."

Finding that her mouth was hanging open, Theo closed it abruptly. How dare he? If he had planned it, he could hardly have devised a more effective way of thwarting her schemes. She could have shrieked aloud in frustration, but the viscountess was watching her anxiously.

"I hope that you have no objections, my dear?"

She hardly could raise any. Theo smiled grimly at her mother by way of a reply.

There was just one fortunate circumstance, Theodora mused as Debenham escorted her and the viscountess into the Pump Room later that morning. At best his manners were brusque, and often odd. When he was with her mother, though, he courteously devoted himself to the invalid. Although he did not ignore Theo, they thus were given little opportunity for squabbling between themselves.

It wasn't until he had procured a glass of water for the viscountess and seen her to a chair that he was able to address Theo. She was scanning the faces about them eagerly, hoping for a glimpse of the sisters.

Observing this, his lips curled downward. "Looking for those acquaintances of yours?" he asked.

She resented his tone, but knew better than to be drawn into an argument with her mother seated next to them. "And what if I am?" she asked, her eyes never leaving the crowd before her.

"I s'pose you'll say it's none of my affair—"

"I suppose I might!" she said, a little more heatedly, but still not looking at him.

He continued as if she hadn't interrupted him. "But you have no business associating with those so obviously beneath you—"

"*Beneath* me!" She turned to face him, glaring. "By whose standards, pray?"

"By anyone's—they are not your equals in station, in manners, in—"

She could not help but flush with anger. "If we are to judge by manners, then I daresay there are a great many people that I should no longer associate with—"

The corner of his mouth tightened, but before he could respond, Isabel and Julia entered the room, and catching their eyes, Theo smiled. As the two subsequently approached, Debenham bowed coldly to Theo. "I shall leave you to your pleasures, then. You have only to tell me when you and the viscountess are ready to leave." He strode stiffly away to another corner of the room, where the gentlemen were reading their papers and exchanging political gossip.

The two girls soon reached Theo's side, Julia irritating her by casting a lingering glance after Debenham's back. After acknowledging the viscountess, Isabel slipped her arm through Theo's. "Let us take a turn or two about the room, dear Theo."

Theodora looked down at her mother for permission. Seeing that she had been joined by an acquaintance, Theo dismissed any lingering feelings of guilt and gladly joined her friends in their promenade.

"Have you checked the book yet?" asked Isabel.

"I have been here only for a few minutes," Theo confessed.

"Perhaps he will come here today. If his aunt is ill, she surely will wish to take the waters," suggested Julia eagerly.

Their arms entwined, the three strolled over in the direction of the book that held a record of all the arrivals to Bath.

They reached it and had begun to turn over its pages, when they became aware of a stir that threatened to drown out the group of musicians who played in the recess at one end of the room. All three sets of eyes looked up at the same moment.

A lady was entering the room, wearing a tunic of white sarcenet with a ruff about the neck. Despite her age, she held herself very erect, and from her manner, it was easy to infer her social position.

The three friends hardly even saw her, though, as their attention was immediately claimed by her escort. He was a tall young man, dressed in the height of fashion, from his intricately tied cravat to his tightly clinging inexpressibles, which served to accentuate the perfection of his form. As he bent to catch a remark of the lady's, Theo was able to glimpse the faultlessly classical profile beneath the curls of dark gold, and the phrase "like a Greek god" sprang irresistibly to mind. This was the last sort of person one would expect to encounter in Bath, or indeed anywhere outside of London, and so it was hardly remarkable that the rising buzz of conversation was interrupted for a few moments by a profound silence.

Isabel was one of the first to recover. "That's him!" she hissed in Theodora's ear. "That is Mr. Mansfield . . . and the countess."

Of course. The very man they had been seeking. He was not a fairy prince, after all, no matter how much he might look like one. "I wonder if my mother knows them," whispered Theo. "I forgot to ask her."

"Oh, Isa, he's even more handsome than you said!" Julia's enthusiastic squeal was undoubtedly audible to several of the people standing about them, and it made Theodora wince. She realized that they, along with almost everyone else in the room had been staring quite openly and rudely at the arrivals for well over a minute, and she quickly changed the direction of her gaze.

"Perhaps I should go ask Mother," she said.

Her companions suffered from no such scruples. "Oh, look," added Julia, "Mr. Debenham must know them."

Glancing up, Theo found the information accurate. Debenham, ensconced in a chair with his paper and with his back to the entrance, had remained oblivious to the commotion in the room. As they made their way into the room, Mr. Mansfield had noticed him, however, and claimed his attention. A bow to the countess and a handshake with the gentleman established that they were on easy terms.

"At least you know someone who will be able to introduce you," remarked Isabel thoughtfully.

Theo could barely stifle a groan. Of all the beings on the planet, the last to whom she wished to owe an introduction was Debenham. Well, she needn't worry about it at the moment. There was a crowd gathering about the newcomers. Acquaintances, no doubt, hoping to be recognized. She looked over at her mother and saw that she had finished her last glass of water and sunk back in her chair, her weariness evident in her face.

"I had better go now."

As Theo had feared, when she asked her mother about the newcomers on the ride home, her mother responded that they were unknown to her. She surprised Theo, though, by turning to Debenham and inquiring about their identities.

He satisfied her curiosity, confirmed that it was the Hertfordshire family, and added that Mr. Mansfield was a member of his club.

"So that is how you know him. It was evident that you are more than mere acquaintances."

"Yes, he's a pleasant enough fellow—though flighty." The dark eyebrows drew together slightly. "I rendered him a service once, and he has been embarrassingly grateful to me since." Meeting the viscountess's inquiring look, he added brusquely, "It was a trifle. Stopped him one day at Tatt's when he was bidding on a carriage horse that was blind in one eye." He glanced at her and explained, "Makes 'em shy, you know. Most likely horse in the world to ditch you, more than if it were totally blind."

"It is no wonder that he is grateful to you, then. How fortunate for him that you are such an expert on horses."

"I wouldn't say expert," he returned gruffly. "I like the animals, that's all."

It always seemed to Theo that there was an almost nauseating obsequiousness in her mother's tone with Debenham. When she had confronted her, though, her mother had been struck dumb by amazement, before recovering herself enough to remark pointedly that rudeness was an even less forgivable fault than obsequiousness. It was one of the few set-tos Theodora had ever had with her gentle mother, and she regretted it bitterly. If it was hard to listen to the conversation, at least she was excused from contributing. She could more profitably turn her thoughts to Mr. Mansfield.

He was quite the handsomest man she had ever seen. It had been hard to tell from a distance, of course, but it seemed that his address was good. His air of fashion was decided. Even his claim to being a friend of Debenham's could be seen as rather a recommendation, for despite all the latter's faults, Theo knew him to be quite nice about the company he kept.

In all, Mansfield seemed almost too good to be true. Was it possible that her prayers had been answered so well? Of course, it remained to be seen whether he would be equally smitten with her. She would have to lavish extra time upon her appearance. Perhaps she might ask her mother about the new bonnet when they reached home.

During the next few days, she did manage to look her smartest, though it had necessitated conciliating Peggy. Theo had been forced to bow to her advice on more than one occasion. She could only be grateful that the servant had not seen fit to trouble her mother with the tale of what had become of the blue kid shoes. Theo herself had refurbished the bonnet with a new ribbon, but she knew it would never quite look the same.

Still, with Peggy's help, she had managed to present a reasonably fashionable appearance. If not up to London standards, she certainly was well enough for Bath.

Unhappily, as it proved, her efforts were to be for naught. Mr. Mansfield and the countess did not frequent the Pump Room the next day or the day after, though she did discover from the book that they had taken lodgings in the Royal Crescent. She promenaded there with the Simpsons between the hours of ten and noon, but did not meet her quarry.

She persuaded her mother to visit the Abbey Church on Sunday at eleven, hoping to glimpse Mr. Mansfield, but was disappointed. She supposed that she should not have been surprised since Bath boasted four other churches and at least twice as many chapels.

It was with a heavy heart that she made her preparations for the ball Monday night. She was looking her best, she knew, in her handsomest frock. Of white Persian gauze, in the Grecian form, with a square neck, it was trimmed with silver filigree and worn over a pink satin slip. It boasted Spanish slash sleeves, which were confined with silver filigree buttons and cord. Peggy had arranged her hair *a-la-Grecque,* framing her face with curls and twisting it up behind, with a bandeau in pink satin to match her gown. French kid gloves and slippers in white satin spotted with pink foil completed the ensemble. It was last year's fashion, but she knew it still was becoming to her.

She should have been cheered by the knowledge that she appeared to perfection, but it was little consolation to her. It seemed doubtful that the elusive Mr. Mansfield would be at the ball, and it was certain that she would be spending a great deal of time with Debenham.

It was not surprising that the viscountess was still dressing when Debenham arrived: it was all too indicative of the turn her luck had taken lately. She would have to go downstairs and engage him in conversation by herself. I will not lose my temper, she promised silently.

He was strolling about the drawing room when she entered, but now he paused and remarked, "A beautiful Amazon!"

It was hardly a remark designed to endear him to her. She was sensitive about her height, being quite able to look him in the eye, and towering above a good portion of the male sex as well as most of her own. She gave him a wintry smile. "Do you know, I had not fancied that I looked in the least warlike."

He drew near to her and kissed her hand before remarking gravely, "*That* is nonsense. You mean to make war on all our hearts."

"How ridiculous you are," she said uneasily, for she had never known him to make such a graceful speech before. She diverted the conversation quickly, "And I had supposed that you were planning the lecture you were going to read me about the low company I keep." It was a disgracefully rude response to his compliment, but it had the desired effect, for his brows met each other instantly.

"I *have* been sorry to see you so continually in such company."

It was her turn to flush. "Yes, I could not help but notice that your heart was immune to my wiles in the Royal Crescent the other day." She had seen his phaeton approaching as she walked there with her friends and had braced herself

for a meeting. He had done no more than acknowledge her
as his carriage flashed by. Although she had felt the snub,
her friends had seemed impervious to it, Julia merely sighing after him in her usual fashion. She told herself that it
would be worthwhile to stroll about the town in the company of even a beggar woman if it kept Debenham at bay.

He gazed at her penetratingly. "My words have no influence. Had you considered how the viscountess might feel
about your actions?"

She laughed with all the scorn she could muster. "My
mother, as difficult as it might be for you to believe, does
not seek to regulate every moment of the day for me, as
you so obviously wish—"

He was about to reply, but at that moment the viscountess appeared on the threshold. "Children?" she said
anxiously.

There was only a moment of hesitation before Debenham
crossed the room to bow over her hand and murmur a compliment upon her appearance. Lady Westmoreland smiled,
and despite her illness, it transformed her into the breath-
taking beauty she had once been.

"You are very kind, sir, but as a mother, I am aware that
my daughter outshines me and well content to have it so."

Debenham bowed slightly in Theo's direction. "Your
daughter is already familiar with my opinion," he said
harshly.

Theo managed to contain the retort that rose to her lips.

"You are looking very fine. Isn't he, Theo?"

He was attired in the usual evening dress, with a dark
blue tailcoat, white satin vest and white breeches, and white
silk stockings. His clothes fit him well enough, Theo
thought, but there was hardly anything remarkable about
his appearance. She hoped that the expression on her face
might be taken for a smile of agreement. This evening was
going to be even worse than she had imagined.

Fortune had even more torments in store for her that
evening. The Monday-night ball was always dedicated to
country-dances, and as they arrived somewhat after seven,
the dancing had already begun. Debenham saw that the
viscountess was established at the upper end of the room
upon one of the seats reserved for peeresses. Seeing that
she was comfortably ensconced among friends, he took him-

self off to the card room without even bothering to claim a dance from Theo.

Not at all displeased by his defection, Theo tried to avoid her mother's wondering eyes. Instead she turned her gaze about the room in the hopes of seeing her friends there. Both the sisters were dancing, and Theo could not manage to catch their eyes. She stood by her mother, fanning herself and trying not to listen to the flow of conversation about her. It proved impossible, as always.

"But Mama!" a young voice near to her exclaimed. "I did bow to her already. You surely would not wish me to take her up as an acquaintance!"

"Oh, dear. No, I suppose . . . It is just that Lady Westmoreland is such a lovely person. And in such difficulties! One can't help but feel for them."

"Lady Westmoreland never gives herself airs, even though *she* is a viscountess. You would think that her daughter might learn a little humility, since they are little better than beggars."

"My dear, you should not say so! And please lower your voice."

Her daughter ignored this warning. "But look at her gown. It is all pretension. You would think that the world didn't know that they are forced to rent Westleigh Abbey and live here. Personally, I think that the way the viscount lost their money is disgusting. They must have been living beyond their means for years!"

Theo was fanning herself very rapidly, her chin held high. She hoped that the color that had risen to her face might be attributable to the hot room. She knew who was speaking—Miss Bromley and her mother. Residents in the vicinity of Westleigh, they had been happy enough to accept its hospitality when her family's fortunes were more prosperous. Their attitude upon their recent arrival in Bath was markedly different.

"I know, but . . . it's not as if we were in London, after all."

"Precisely! Here in Bath, everyone is aware with whom you associate—and I don't wish to know those *cits* she has taken up. I daresay they are the best sort of acquaintances for her, after all. She may put on as many airs as she likes, and they daren't object. They may take her anywhere she needs to go, since she doesn't have a carriage of her own anymore and—oh!"

Despite herself, Theo could not help turning surreptitiously to observe what had caused this exclamation. Miss Bromley and her mother were bestowing glowing smiles on Debenham, as he made his way past.

"Oh, Mr. Debenham—what a pleasure to—"

"Will you excuse me," he replied in his usual brusque manner before stationing himself at Theo's side. For the first time in her life, she was delighted to see him. For once, she could not fault his conduct. The expression upon Miss Bromley's pretty face was one her lesser self might savor for long afterward.

"Bored with cards so soon?" asked Theo.

He shrugged. "There was hardly anyone of my acquaintance about."

That shouldn't have been too surprising, Theo thought. Bath was the home of the elderly, the infirm, and the poor. It was a wonder that Debenham spent as much time here as he did.

"You're not dancing?" he asked in some surprise.

"No one has asked me," she was forced to admit, flushing. The obvious followed, and for the half hour that they were engaged in the country-dance, she felt more in charity with him than she had ever been in her life.

This harmony was to be disrupted when he returned Theo to her mother at the finish of the dance, and Julia came rushing up to greet her. Fortunately, he did not totally ignore her friend as he might have done, but he bowed very slightly and after excusing himself, left for the card room again.

"Oh, isn't he wonderful," said Julia for the hundredth time. "He has such an elegant bow, hasn't he? And he must be a marvelous dancer!"

Theo almost betrayed herself with an unladylike snort. Despite his athleticism, Debenham rarely paid proper attention to the figures of the dance. Theo considered that her kid shoes offered inadequate protection to her toes, and attributed their preservation only to her own vigilance. There was no point in explaining it to Julia, though. Her friend would probably disbelieve her.

The opportunity for further conversation was abruptly removed as the hum of voices in the room suddenly increased in volume. Theodora looked up to see Mr. King, the master of ceremonies, making his way toward the entrance of the room, where a newly arrived couple stood. It was he!

Theodora had never seen such high shirt points or such a well-cut coat before. His cravat was an elaborate concoction. The careful arrangement of his curls must have taken some time to achieve. His tall, well-proportioned figure cast almost every other man in the room into the shade.

The countess was richly, but less modishly dressed in a gown of lilac satin, with a turban cap upon her head. In carrying tones, Julia belatedly called Theo's attention to the couple.

"I saw them," hissed Theo, hoping that everyone around them had not heard. Fortunately, Isabel, who was watching the scene develop, gestured violently at her sister to indicate that she should join her. Julia knew better than to ignore such a summons, and so withdrew, leaving Theo alone with her mother.

As Mr. King finished bowing to these important guests and greeting them, Theodora instantly realized that her luck was about to change. With a hand, he was indicating the end of the room where she stood. But of course! Where else would the countess sit? And when she took her place, how could he fail to notice Theodora, standing so close?

Fortune, having changed its mind and deciding to smile upon Theo, was to prove even more generous. When Mr. King had led the countess to her seat, he very naturally introduced her to her neighbor, Lady Westmoreland, and her daughter. The introduction to Mr. Mansfield must of course follow, and Theo's heart fluttered at his graceful bow and the dazzling smile that accompanied it. It was hardly surprising then, that it be suggested that he partner her for a dance. He accepted this charge with such alacrity that she was certain that she did not repel him, at least.

She did not know which circumstance made her the happiest: to spend a half an hour in such proximity to the handsomest man she had ever seen; or to be partnered by the most eligible man in the room. As they made their way to the floor, they had left Miss Bromley gaping in their wake, and Theo had not been entirely able to quell an unworthy feeling of smugness.

His obvious attractiveness made her a little shy, and for a few moments, she was afraid that she could not muster the words to converse with him. He had no difficulty in rising to the occasion, however, and his practiced small talk soon enabled her to respond with tolerable ease. During the course of this conversation, she learned that his aunt had been ill for the past several days, which had prevented her from leaving her house.

Theo could not help being a little surprised, but she endeavored not to reveal it. "How marvelous that she felt up to coming to the ball tonight, then. She is looking so wonderfully well, also."

"Yes, her illness is of the sort that comes and goes. *I* thought we should not be here at all tonight, but she began feeling more the thing this morning, and by this afternoon had pronounced herself to be as well as she might ever be."

"How fortunate."

The ready smile flashed, causing her heart to turn over once more. "*I* think it fortunate, myself."

Had she heard him right? The compliment was too obvious to be mistaken. She could feel a telltale blush rising to her cheeks, but he appeared not at all conscious and instead turned the conversation to more innocuous topics.

The unfortunate aspect of such a pleasant moment is that eventually it must end, and so it was with her dance. She tried not to appear dissatisfied when their dance ended, and he led another young lady onto the floor. The second most enviable position in the room was to be seated next to the countess, as she was, and she determined to make the most of it.

She had observed her mother to be close in conversation with the countess. Within a few moments of sitting down, she realized that it was Lady Verridge who was providing most of the talk, which consisted of a catalog of all the physical ailments she had suffered during her long and very full life. Theo did not know how her mother could manage to sit and listen so politely, as it seemed that the countess took a great deal of pleasure in detailing all the specifics of her ills. She also roundly abused the doctors as fools, and remarked with disdain that they could never find the cause of her trouble. She was trying a new one, here in Bath, a Dr. Parry, perhaps Lady Westmoreland had consulted him also? Receiving a negative reply, she went on to extol his successes, although she gave a great deal of credit to the Bath waters.

"—For they have always been of the greatest benefit to me—ever since I was a young girl—of course my constitution was always frail—I first visited Bath in, let me think—it was the year Beau Nash passed away, I remember. Could it have been '61 or . . . I was just a *child*, of course, at the time. I was suffering from a hysterical cholic, with wandering pains in my limbs, and seatings, and I was vomiting green bile—" she added with obvious relish.

Distasteful as Theo might have found this discussion, it yielded some fruit. Among her many conversational offerings, the countess thought to include the information that they were planning a stay of at least six weeks, in order that she might do the course of Bath waters, and that she was considering remaining here for the season. This was good news indeed. The chat had another, hidden benefit, though Theo could not be aware of it at the time. By paying strict attention, and shaking and nodding her head in all the right places, she had disposed Lady Verridge in her favor. Miss Theodora Westmoreland was discovered to be a very sensible, well-bred young lady.

Another compliment was to be learned from a most unlikely source. Despite her apparent interest in the countess's conversation, Theo was able to observe that when Debenham came out of the card room, he happened to be met by Mr. Mansfield. They spoke together for a while before Debenham nodded his farewell. Mr. Mansfield's gaze turned toward her, and she knew that one of them must have spoken of her. He smiled in her direction, but she was turning her eyes back to his aunt and managed not to intercept the look. She was dying of curiosity to know what had been said, but of course she could hardly ask Debenham.

Joining them, Debenham announced that since it was nearing eleven o'clock, when the dancing would stop, they might think of leaving. He smiled at Lady Westmoreland. "It is rather late, my lady."

Her mother returned his smile gratefully. "Yes, you are quite right. How the time did fly!"

Why hadn't Theo noticed the weariness on her mother's face before? She had been too occupied with her own schemes. Ashamed, she fell in with their plans immediately. It was as if she were to be rewarded for such good behavior.

As they passed from the room, they happened to be within bowing distance of Mr. Mansfield. As he straightened himself, Debenham remarked, "Appears you've made a conquest there."

"What do you mean?" Theo tried not to appear conscious.

"Told him I was to drive you home, and the fellow said he envied me."

It was hard to keep a smile from spreading across her face.

Chapter Three

"Oh, tell us what he said!" Julia squealed. "I am dying of curiosity."

Appealed to thusly, Theodora had no choice but to repeat Mr. Mansfield's flattering words. Julia squealed again in excitement as Theo concluded. Isabel, more restrained, merely smiled in a satisfied sort of way. The three friends had met in the Pump Room this morning, and since Mr. Mansfield was not present, had decided that their urgent need for private discussion called for a stroll about town. Obtaining their mothers' consent, they had set out at once for Milsom Street. Theo had wistfully considered the Royal Crescent as a destination, but it was much farther, after all. Also, it might seem too coincidental if she should happen to meet Mr. Mansfield there this morning.

She should have been gratified by this chance to share her thrilling news. Indeed, she had lain awake a good part of the night, savoring this happiness. It wasn't until quite a bit later that she had begun to worry.

The countess and her nephew were probably not acquainted with the Westmoreland's circumstances. Would Mr. Mansfield's interest continue upon learning that she was without a fortune? And even if it did, would the countess approve such a match? Perhaps Theo had been wrong to wear her richest gown, perhaps it might have created a false impression. Of course, she really could not regret the generosity of her clothing allowance, which the Debenhams had somehow miraculously managed out of the wreck of the estate. And it *was* true that she had needed to attract his attention immediately. There were hardly any eligible gentlemen in Bath, after all, and there were plenty of females.

"Why are you frowning, Theo?" remarked Julia lightheartedly. "I should think you would be all smiles today."

Isabel, impatient with her sister's gaucherie, gave Theo

no time to respond. "But tell us, my dear, did you ask your mother about the play tonight? We would be so happy to have both of you as our guests."

"My mother said she was quite exhausted by the assembly last night. However, she said that she would be happy for me to go." Those had not been her precise words, of course. She had said that she "could have no objection," but there was no need to dwell upon so fine a point.

It was soon settled that the sisters, accompanied by their mother, would call for Theodora in Gay Street at a quarter past six. Now the talk turned to the most agreeable topic of what they would all wear and whether Mr. Mansfield and the countess might be at the theater.

Despite her hopes, the evening was not to be one of unqualified pleasure for Theodora. It was all too evident that her mother had not been making excuses about her health, for after their visit to the Pump Room was over, she had taken to her bed for the rest of the day. Despite all her assurances to her friends, Theo could not help but feel guilty when she went to her mother's room to bid her good-bye. The latter appeared even more wasted than usual, but she complimented Theo upon her appearance and gallantly bid her enjoy herself. Theo hesitated.

"Mother, if you should wish it . . . I—I do not *have* to attend the theater. I might keep you company instead. I daresay the Simpsons would be happy to invite us for another night, since they keep a box."

Her mother smiled at her, though Theo could tell it required an effort. "No, my dear. Peggy will take good care of me. You are young and—and you should be out enjoying yourself. A young lady of eighteen should not be cooped up with an invalid when she might be out amusing herself. I am only sorry—"

"Mother!"

"No," with another smile, "I am only sorry that you should have been deprived of all that you had a right to expect—"

"Mother, I—"

"No, I know that you are too good ever to complain, but this year we should have been presenting you, and you should have had the opportunity to—"

"Mother, I don't care about that," said Theo, quite honestly, her eyes beginning to fill.

The viscountess reached out her arms, and Theo sank into them. Her mother stroked her hair softly. "I loved your father dearly, as you know," she said softly. "I married him in spite of my parents' opposition and their warnings. I have no regrets at all, except when I see what all of this has cost you."

Theo raised her head and stared her mother in the eyes. "Do not *ever* say that," she said. "Father was a darling—and he meant to do his best for us, despite what anyone else says. He . . . he was just not *practical*, that is all."

The dark eyes gazed sadly into hers. "You are right, my love. But still, I . . . well, that is why one must be so *careful* whom one marries." She smiled again now with an artificial brightness. "But I think I must be a poor sort of mother to be sending you off to the theater with red eyes and a pink nose. Go on with you now, and have a good time."

Theodora had recovered herself by the time that her friends arrived, but she still could not quite shake her feelings of guilt. Her spirits were somewhat relieved by their lively chatter during the carriage ride there. Frequent theatergoers themselves, they were able to discuss the talents of the performers in a knowledgeable way that made Theo rather envious. They had never seen tonight's offering, *A Doubtful Son*, since it was a new play, but they felt certain that it must be of interest, as Isabel could relate that it had met with great success when it had premiered in London last year. Julia added consolingly that even if the play should not please them, the farce surely would. Naturally enough, it was Isabel who had the final word.

"The play is beside the point," she whispered harshly. "We have another object in coming to the theater." Glancing at her mother, who was alighting from the carriage and satisfied that she had not heard, Isabel smiled at Theo knowingly.

Isabel was right. Mr. Mansfield might be here. She must put all her doubts and fears aside. Why, anyone of fortune might object to a practically penniless bride. Since she meant to marry money, she would have to overlook such considerations. It was not an unheard-of occurrence, after all. She must make the most of her slim opportunities. When she sidled into the box a few moments later, her head held high, it was with the determination of making every eligible man in the room fall in love with her.

As she seated herself, she was treated to a high-pitched whisper from Julia, seated just behind her. "It is he—look!"

Theo glanced up at the box opposite and encountered not Mr. Mansfield's gaze, but Debenham's. She thought she detected disapproval on his face, but he bowed to her gracefully, and she could do nothing but acknowledge it. It seemed such a mischance that he should be here tonight, though probably he had been invited by friends, just as she had.

A movement in the box next to his attracted her attention. The Countess Verridge and Mr. Mansfield were just arriving. The latter saw that his aunt was seated then, spotting Theo, gifted her with his dazzling smile before bowing.

An audible sigh escaped Julia. Her sister frowned.

"How handsome he is. Such an air of fashion" were Lady Simpson's artless comments. "An acquaintance of yours, my dear?"

"He is Mr. Quentin Mansfield, nephew of the Countess Verridge, the lady whom you see with him."

The opportunity for further conversation ended as the play began.

During the interval, Theodora quickly involved herself in conversation with her friends. It would not do to be seen staring hopefully at the countess's box. All the friends agreed on how delightful the play was. Isabel then amused herself by exercising her wit upon individuals whose dress or manner might make them an object of satire. Though her mother reprimanded her in a vague, careless sort of way, Julia giggled, which further weakened the effectiveness of Lady Simpson's homilies.

Theo, not very much entertained by this pastime, glanced out of the corner of her eyes to the boxes opposite. Debenham was gone—she wished it might be for good! Mr. Mansfield was also missing, though the countess sat placidly, surrounded by acquaintances and no doubt regaling them with a graphic account of some illness she had honored by contracting.

It was possible that Mr. Mansfield had merely gone to procure her some refreshment. Theo hardly dared to hope otherwise. A masculine figure entered their box. She turned toward the entrance with a smile, and was startled to meet Debenham's cold gray gaze.

He acknowledged her friends civilly enough, bowing courteously to Mrs. Simpson, whom he had not met before. Theo was not deceived by appearances. When he bent over her hand, she unconsciously raised her chin another notch.

Seeing that some of the Simpsons' acquaintances were beginning to fill the box, Debenham seized the opportunity to draw Theo aside.

"I would have taken you to the theater, had I known you wished it," he said.

"I would not wish to inconvenience you more than I already have."

"I do not regard *inconvenience*."

"But I do."

They stood there, glaring at each other for a moment, when he said abruptly, "Go driving with me tomorrow."

"Where?"

"It doesn't matter—Combhay, Bristol, anywhere you say."

She had never known him to talk so wildly. Combhay was a mere three miles from town. Bristol was twelve and quite out of the question.

"I must talk with you," he added urgently. "Please."

The syllable caused her to gape at him. She had never heard the word issue from his lips before.

He apparently mistook her shocked silence for assent. "I will see you at one o'clock, then." He bowed to her once more, and in turning to go, bumped into the tall, graceful figure of Mansfield, who was just entering the box.

"Mansfield—I've been meaning to talk with you. St. George means to sell his horses at last—do you know 'em? Match-bays, with deep chests and short backs. Good forward action."

There was no mistaking the enthusiasm that illuminated Mansfield's handsome features. "I say! What a spot of luck, running into you here. Do you know what he's asking for them? Oh, good evening Miss Westmoreland."

She gave him the most encouraging smile she was capable of, but in vain, as he never saw it, but returned immediately to this absorbing conversation. How dare Debenham muff her opportunity! She tried to catch Mansfield's eye, and did not succeed. She had no better luck with Debenham. They were proceeding on to diseases of the horse, from bone spavin to curbs, and how to best detect and treat them.

Needless to say, it was not a conversational topic that Theo found engrossing. It was almost a relief when the interval ended and the two filed from the box, never flagging in their exclusive discussion. It was the perfect cap to a dismal evening, which was all the more bitter considering the high hopes that Theo had cherished for it.

Had she been a placid, cheerful sort of person, Theo might have consoled herself with the thought of the happiness she would bring her mother by driving out with Debenham this afternoon. But Theo was not that sort of person, and she had slept badly, her anger with Debenham making rest difficult to obtain.

To her further irritation, Peggy, upon learning who was to be Theo's escort, had laid out her best carriage dress, of corded muslin, tied simply at the waist with a lilac ribbon. She also had extracted the lilac-trimmed chip bonnet that matched it. It became Theo wonderfully well, which displeased her even more. Peggy had done her best to see that she looked like a dowd whenever she called on the Simpsons. Gratifying Debenham's eyes was not among Theo's desires. Blackening them was a more distinct possibility.

Naturally, it would take too long to press another gown. Theo bottled the invective she felt like hurling at the servant. It would be better employed against Debenham.

The weather was similarly uncooperative. It would have been an excellent opportunity for rain, and yet the skies, though not cloudless, did not threaten that eventuality.

She did feel rather like a traitor when she saw the happiness that registered on her mother's face.

"How *lovely* you look, my dear."

"Thank you," she returned unenthusiastically.

"Where do you and Debenham mean to drive?"

"He didn't say." After a second or two of silence, she was forced to respond to the inquiry on her mother's face. "He mentioned Combhay and Bristol."

"Oh, then he was jesting with you."

"It didn't seem so at the time." An idea occurred to Theo. She turned to her mother with a ray of hope in her eyes. "If you think it improper, you may forbid my going—"

"I see no impropriety in it. His stepmother was your aunt, after all. And you will have a groom with you. No, I am sure that his mentioning Bristol was only a joke." She looked at her daughter's face doubtfully. "I wish that he wouldn't tease you so, but then it always is so with young men who are in . . ."

She seemed to lose the thread of what she was saying, and though Theo waited, she did not finish the sentence. Instead, she wished her daughter a pleasant drive, and Theo took leave of her mournfully.

Debenham was waiting for her when she went downstairs. He was attired suitably in a black tailcoat, buckskin breeches, and top boots. Julia might have sighed over him, but Theo could not help comparing his quiet mode of dress unfavorably with that of the dashing Mansfield.

He wished her good afternoon, but said nothing else. His eyes took in her appearance, but he made no comment upon it. Though always brusque, he was rarely silent. One of his usual backhanded compliments would have given her an excellent opening for venting some of her spleen.

Instead, having no inclination herself for making *pleasant* conversation, she held her tongue as he handed her into the phaeton, explaining that he intended Combhay for their destination. They set off without another word.

His continued silence did not surprise Theo overmuch, as he was concentrating on maneuvering through the traffic in town. Though she knew it was unworthy of her, she could not help a certain feeling of satisfaction as he directed his highbred horses and fashionable equipage down the street. Debenham at least was a notable whip, and his passage must always attract attention. It was very difficult to keep from being smug when she saw that one of those bonnets that turned to observe them as they drove by, rested above Miss Bromley's disconcerted face.

She was almost in charity with Debenham by the time they reached the outskirts of town, but she recalled herself to her duty sternly. His transgressions had been many, and she must keep that in mind. By renewed effort, she had managed to work herself into a fresh fit of anger by the time they reached the canal.

She must have looked surprised when Debenham turned his horses from the main road, for he explained, "Thought we might visit the caisson. Knew you hadn't seen it yet."

Although she had heard mention of the hydrostatical lock, she had no real interest in it. She had no real objections either, except for a faint resentment at being so little consulted. Still, he would have to provide a better opportunity for her to make an attack.

They reached the machine after traveling a few hundred yards, and despite herself, she could not help but be impressed. It was a huge thing, resting in a cistern over seventy feet long and eight feet high. Curiosity temporarily overcame her anger, and as Debenham handed her down from the carriage, she asked, "What is it supposed to do?"

If he was amused by her ignorance, he did not show it. He replied, "It was meant to convey boats from the higher level—up there d'you see—to the lower, about sixty feet, I'd judge."

"Do you mean it is not used?"

"It was never successful. They built it some thirteen years ago, but the cistern there, in which the lock operates, was badly constructed and would not hold the water well enough for it to operate."

She was slipping again. They were actually having a pleasant conversation. She recalled to mind all the wrongs he had committed and fell silent once more.

She waited for her opening, and it seemed for a time that she should have to wait in vain. They walked together about the area for perhaps ten minutes without speaking. When she thought she could scarce contain herself any longer, Debenham finally spoke.

"I brought you here for a reason. There is something I have to tell you, and I need to do so in private."

She bit her lip, restraining herself for a few seconds longer.

"Because Lady Westmoreland's health is so poor, I thought I had better talk to you directly instead of speaking to her—"

About what? And what was this sudden need for privacy?

"I know that you are concerned about your future—considering your situation, it's understandable. I wish I could offer you the same sort of position you once enjoyed, but I'm afraid that I can't. Still, the arrangements that I am making are—"

Good heavens! Surely he didn't mean to declare himself *here*, her mother's health notwithstanding. Well, she meant to nip this in the bud. "Stop it. Stop it this instant!"

He looked up at her, startled. "What?"

"Stop making all these 'arrangements' for my future, and my present, and every minute of the day." She was warming up to her topic now. "Did it ever occur to you that I am capable of taking care of my own affairs? Of seeing that my mother gets to the Pump Room myself? Of walking to a friend's house all on my own? I do not need a watchdog!" She was being unforgivably, abominably rude. But how satisfying it was.

He was taken entirely by surprise. The black eyebrows had drawn together. "I did not intend—"

"Had you thought how uncomfortable it must be for me, to have the world see that you are living in my pocket, particularly when I have offered you no encouragement? Did it ever occur to you that I might like to visit places and do things in society other than yours?"

Her arrows had all found their marks. He flushed with anger. She was waiting for an equally acid retort, but instead he pressed his lips firmly together. After a brief struggle with himself, he said, "I suppose it would be too much to expect gratitude for any efforts I may have made. Well, you may be happy at last. I meant to tell you that I shall be spending a few weeks in London. You will not be troubled further by my society. You will have an opportunity for proving yourself as capable as you wish."

The pleasure she was taking in this victory suddenly evaporated. She could not let him guess that, though. "Good."

They glared at each other for another minute, then he said abruptly. "We might as well go, then."

The carriage ride back was also made in silence, except for Debenham's commands to his horses and his groom. It was a much more uncomfortable one than before. Theo held her chin high, but there were spots of color on her cheeks. She could not let him guess her shame. After all, despite his aggravating bluntness, he had never shown her anything but kindness, really, when one thought about it. It was as her mother had said, also, he was not actually tied to them by blood. Her father's sister had been his stepmother, that was all. He and his father had been more kind to them than any of their blood relations had been.

Her mother! There was another lowering thought. Debenham had been so consistently good to Lady Westmoreland. He was so solicitous of her, so concerned for her health. Her mother would faint if she ever knew what Theo had said to him. And how could Theo explain that she had driven him from their door forever?

When they returned to Gay Street, he silently handed her down from the phaeton. She fled inside, unable to look him in the face. Neither could she bear an interview with her mother just yet. Encountering Peggy on the stairs, she said that she meant to lie down immediately, for she had a sick headache. She accepted Peggy's offer to help her out of her things, but she declined any further offices. Though the headache was becoming real by now, she would not have her head rubbed or have lemon rind applied to her temples. She might as well suffer. She certainly deserved it.

To her relief, her mother did not question her closely the next morning about her ride. She was able to prevaricate and tell her that they had enjoyed a pleasant drive. She also informed her mother that business had carried Debenham to London for a few weeks. At least his absence had an explanation for the moment.

Visiting with her friends in the Pump Room later that day, she could not bring herself to confide what had happened, instead just mentioning to them that Debenham was out of town. It was Isabel who found the silver lining for her.

"This will leave the field clear for Mr. Mansfield," she announced with some satisfaction. "You must convince your mother to let you accompany us to the Lower Rooms Friday, for I feel certain that he will be there. Come, let us add our persuasions to yours."

It was certain that her mother would have some objections, but she was eventually overruled by the importunities of the three girls. She said nothing while in their company, but Theo could tell that she had some reservations about the scheme. It wasn't until they had returned to Gay Street that the viscountess voiced them.

They were seated around the table, eating a spot of nuncheon. Theo, who possessed a healthy appetite, was enjoying the remains of a calf's feet pie. Her mother dined upon white bread and buttermilk, as her physician had prescribed. Theo grimaced as she watched her mother sip from the glass.

"I don't know how you bear that."

Her mother put the glass down with an expression of

distaste. "I am not sure sometimes, myself." More cheerfully, she added, "But it is well worth it, if it helps my health to improve. There are much worse remedies that might be prescribed."

Her eyes became serious. "By the by, there is one matter I meant to speak of to you, Theo. About your friends the Simpsons, and the assembly on Friday—"

Theo leapt to her own defense. "Oh, I am looking forward to that so, Mother. You said that I might go with them—please do not say that I may not."

The viscountess shook her head. "No, I had already said that you may go." She sighed. "What concerns me, my dear, is the sort of obligation under which you are placing yourself."

Theo frowned. "But they said it would be no trouble. They were going to be attending the assembly anyway—"

"My dear, it pains me to have to say this . . . but had you considered that in accepting their hospitality—a visit to the theater here, and an assembly there—that it is something which you cannot reciprocate? We have no carriage in which to take them for a ride. We have no theater box which we might invite them to share—"

Angered, Theo lashed out at her mother. "It is all arrogance, isn't it? You object to them because their father is engaged in trade—"

Her mother's brow wrinkled as she began painfully, "I own that they are not the friends that I would have chosen for you, my love, however—"

"If it were the Bromleys that had invited me, you would be happy to have me go—"

"The Bromleys are a different matter—the obligation is all on their side. Still, I would not like to see you make yourself *their* dependent either."

Theo was not listening. She jumped up from the table, without offering any excuse. "You and Debenham share the same opinion, don't you? You have never worried about my placing myself under an obligation to him!"

"Debenham is related to us by marriage, if not blood, so the relationship is entirely dissimilar. Besides which—"

"Besides which you mean for me to marry him, don't you? Admit it, Mother. That is what you have intended all along."

"My dear!"

"You needn't attempt to deny it. I've known it ever since Father died—"

Haltingly, Lady Westmoreland began, "It is only natural for a mother, particularly in my circumstances, to concern herself with her daughter's future. If you suggest that I ever meant you to do something you disliked, however—"

The rage of helplessness, frustration, and shame combined rose within Theo to a boiling pitch. "Don't bother, Mother. I understand. You might as well know now that it will not work. I am not going to marry Debenham, no matter how much you might wish it. *I* have a plan for my own future, no matter how much that might surprise you." She took a deep breath. "I am going to make a *brilliant* match, Mother. And as long as my friends, the Simpsons, care enough to help me, I will accept their invitations whenever I may."

With a flourish of her skirt, she swept from the room. The drama of this exit was spoiled somewhat as she bumped into Peggy, entering. The latter took one look at the viscountess before rushing over to her. "My lady!"

Despite her anger and her sense of guilt, Theo could not help glancing back. Her mother's face was white, and she had sunk back in her chair. Peggy was chafing her hands. "My lady!"

Dismayed, Theo turned and came back into the room. "Mother?"

The viscountess did not respond. Peggy looked up to direct a burning glance at Theo. "What have you done?" she asked harshly.

"Mother!"

"Miss Theodora, I—"

"Oh, be quiet, Peggy, and see if you cannot help me get Mother to her bed. Then let us send Patrick for the doctor.

Chapter Four

Time seemed to creep until the doctor finally arrived. Although the viscountess regained consciousness, Peggy would not allow her to speak, fearing that she might again be overcome. Her breathing was so laborious that it might have proved an unnecessary precaution, in any case. It was evident that Lady Westmoreland was extremely anxious to communicate with her daughter, so to her dismay, Theo found herself banished from the sickroom.

Unwilling to spend her time pacing in the small hallway, she returned to her own room where she relieved her feelings by a flood of tears. What seemed like hours later, there came a tap on the door.

"Come in," she said in a choked voice.

Peggy stepped into the room. "The doctor would like to see you, Miss Theo."

Taking her handkerchief, she dried her eyes as best she could. They would still be red and swollen, and her nose would still be pink, but she could not change that. Raising her chin a little, she stood. "I am coming."

Trailed by Peggy, she walked down to the drawing room, where she discovered the doctor waiting for her. His face was tired and his expression grave, but he smiled at her as she entered. "Good afternoon, Miss Westmoreland."

She walked forward, extending her hand to him. "Dr. Mapleton. What can you tell me? Is she—"

He bowed over it before replying. "Your mother is resting quite comfortably for the moment."

Her eyes almost brimmed over, but with an effort, Theo kept the tears from escaping. "Thank you. It is such a relief—won't you be seated?"

She took a chair and he followed suit. He studied his hands for a moment before beginning.

"First of all, I was most surprised to discover Lady Westmoreland in an agitation of nerves, which was not relieved until I cupped her. My lady made known to me that you had some sort of disagreement. She wished me to assure you that it did not precipitate her attack. I wish I could do so."

Theo gasped, but he did not take notice of it. He looked Theo in the eyes. "You are a grown woman, Miss Westmoreland, and you have the right to know the truth. You probably already know that your mother's illness is a grave one. It is most important that she have no undue excitement—it places her weakened system under too great a strain. She needs quiet and rest more than anything. The waters can be of little benefit without that."

Theo had regained mastery of herself now. "Is there anything else we should do?"

He considered the question for a moment. "Just see that she keeps to her diet, and avoids exertion." He inclined his head toward Peggy, still standing in the corner of the room. "You are fortunate to have an excellent nurse here in Mrs. Chambers, and I know that I may trust her to see that my recommendations are carried out." He paused. "Lady Westmoreland informed me that the baths are fatiguing her. They seemed to be of benefit for the pain and the swelling, however, so I told my lady that she must be the judge of what is best."

He rose from his chair and bowed his farewell.

"Wait! I did not ask—are there any other remedies we might try—any other treatment you would prescribe?"

He hesitated before replying. "There are those of my colleagues who believe that great benefit may be obtained from electrifying. I myself do not believe that it would prove a remedy in this particular case, but if you wish—"

"No, no. Thank you." It was really a frightening idea. So little was known about electricity, after all.

He smiled once more at her. "With the proper care and rest, I think that your mother may be here with us for a good many years yet. We are all in God's hands, after all."

There was one more question left to ask. She regarded the doctor with uncharacteristic timidity. "M-may I go see her?" Her voice was humble.

He glanced involuntarily at Peggy, still in the same place. Theo was able to read her opinion quite easily on her face.

"I left my lady *resting*," she remarked, a reprimand in her voice.

Theo pressed her lips together to keep them from trembling. She could feel her eyes begin to fill once more. The doctor regarded her, understanding in his eyes.

"I think that you may see your mother, as long as you take care not to disturb her. If she is sleeping, of course you will not waken her."

"Of course." She rose, dashing away a tear with the back of her hand. "Thank you for coming."

"Do not hesitate to call me whenever I may be of assistance," he said formally, then bowed and left.

She turned in the direction of her mother's bedroom, but Peggy was standing beside the drawing room door, scowling fiercely.

"I am going to see her."

"You heard what the doctor said about exciting her, Miss Theo."

"I am not going to—" She was forced to wipe another tear away. "I just want to *see* her, that's all, Peggy." Without another word, she brushed past the maidservant and into the hall.

All was quiet. She crossed to her mother's room and scratched gently on the door. No sound came from within. She opened it quietly. Her mother was asleep. Theo tiptoed over to her bedside.

The viscountess was propped up on her pillows, her breathing laborious. The paleness of her face was accentuated by her prematurely white hair. Her countenance still bore the lines of pain and weariness, which sleep should erase. Theo reached out a hand to stroke her hair, but drew it back. It was better not to waken her. "Sleep well, Mother," she said softly, then turned and left the room as quietly as she had come.

She no longer bothered to repress her tears as she went hurrying up the stairs to her bed. There was no confidant to whom she might pour out her guilt and misery. There was no shoulder on which she might rest her face and weep. There were no comforting arms to go about her, no hands to pat her gently and reassuringly. She exhausted herself with crying before finally falling into a nightmare-troubled sleep.

*   *   *

She was awakened the next morning by a soft tapping on her door. She opened her eyes to see daylight filtering through the curtains. "Come in," she called.

Peggy entered, bearing a steaming tray loaded with eggs, bacon, muffins, and jam. Theo's eyes opened wide in surprise. Peggy put down the tray gruffly, commenting, "Thought you'd be hungry this morning, since you didn't have anything to eat last night."

"So I had not. I had forgot." She saw the apology in the gesture and smiled at the old servant. "Thank you so much. I *am* hungry."

Peggy would have left the room, but Theo detained her. "Is . . . is my mother awake this morning yet?"

"That she is and feeling much more the thing, as she says." There was gruff pleasure in Peggy's voice. She nodded to Theo and left the room. The latter sent up a little prayer of gratitude, then applied herself to her breakfast.

As soon as she was dressed, she went downstairs to her mother's room. Upon entering, she was pleased to see that the viscountess had not been exaggerating when she spoke to Peggy. She did look much better. Her breathing seemed easier, and there was some color in her face.

Conscious of their last, unpleasant scene, Theo had some color in her face also. But she smiled shyly at her mother and asked her how she did.

Her mother responded by holding out her arms, and Theo found herself rushing into them and sobbing. When at last she was able to find the breath, she looked up at her mother.

"I-I am so sorry about everything, Mother. I was up half the night, reproaching myself with—"

Her mother stroked her hair. "Now, now, my dear. I knew how upset you would be. This attack simply was not your fault. And you do not know how I regretted speaking to you—"

"You were only trying to help me." At a signal from her mother, Theo crossed the floor and extracted two handkerchiefs from the painted chest of drawers. Helping herself to one, she handed the other to her mother. "And you are quite right. I have been accepting their hospitality far too often—"

"Please, my dear."

"No, all those things I said—unforgivable!"

"No, they are not." The viscountess had actually raised her voice a little, which surprised Theo so much that she could only stare at her. "They are not unforgivable. I hope that my words are also not unforgivable. If you will agree, I think that we may both forget what was said in the heat of the moment."

"But Mother," said Theo, her eyes streaming afresh, "You said *nothing* to me. It was all me. I was the one who—"

"Hush." She patted the counterpane invitingly, and Theo sat obediently beside her. "My dear, you have been so good all this time—and your life is so difficult. You have had to give up everything you loved at eighteen, the very way of life to which you were accustomed, to come and live in very modest circumstances, with only an invalid to bear you company—"

"But—"

"And you have not complained. I have never heard you bemoan the fact that you were forced to give up everything to which your birth should entitle you—"

"Please, Mother, don't go on," choked Theo.

"I do not mean to distress you, my dear." She patted her daughter's hand. "I only wanted to tell you that you should not blame yourself for being angry. You have been so good and so patient for so long that some reaction was—"

"*Please*—"

Lady Westmoreland shook her head slightly. "If you do not wish me to, I will say no more about it. If you agree, we will both forget that we ever had a disagreement. Yes?"

Theo nodded tearfully.

"Very well, then," said the viscountess brightly. "Tell me, what do you plan to wear to the ball tonight?"

"The ball . . . ? Oh, no . . . I could not go."

"Nonsense. You already accepted the invitation."

"I will send round a note . . ."

Her mother gripped Theo's hand tightly. "My dear, one of the characteristics I have found most admirable about you during our misfortunes is that while you always did what was needful, you never made a martyr of yourself. *That* is the way to self-pity."

"But I could not go, Mother, knowing that—"

"I will be fine. Peggy will be here, and you can see that

I am feeling much better. So, let us discuss it. Which gown will you wear?''

It was not as if she had so many, thought Theo later as she readied herself for the ball. A girl born into humbler circumstances might have been awed by the notion of one person possessing four ball gowns, but having anticipated greater things, Theo could take no joy in it. She was consoled somewhat by the knowledge that they were all handsome and fairly new, her Uncle, Sir Francis, having insisted upon her being adequately gowned when they removed to Bath.

She had chosen her most modest gown, a white frock of French cambric, with a square neck and short, plain sleeves. The gown was tastefully if not lavishly decorated with white embroidery worked in a pattern of flowers and leaves, which ran in a stripe down the front from neck to hem. Fortunately the weather was warm enough to permit the donning of her blue twilled-silk spencer, which complemented the dress perfectly. Simple white kid shoes and gloves completed the ensemble. Her only other ornaments were the white beads that she wore in her hair.

Theodora was still chastened, but she was eighteen, after all. Her spirits could not fail to be lifted by the knowledge that she presented a very charming picture, indeed. If she did succeed in snaring Mr. Mansfield's heart, then her mother would no longer need to fret over her. Theo would also be able to see that her mother was more comfortably circumstanced. For a moment or two, Theo lost herself in pleasant dreams of her future.

She was brought to herself when Peggy entered and announced sharply that the Simpsons had arrived. From the expression upon her face, it was easy to infer that Peggy disapproved of this outing, also. Theo chose to disregard her sour looks.

As she went downstairs, it occurred to her that this might well be the last ball she would attend for a good while. Clearly it would not be wise to continue to accept the Simpsons' invitations. She was forced to acknowledge that her mother was right. Of course, Debenham might still escort her to a ball, but he was no longer in Bath. She had an uncomfortable suspicion that when and if he returned, he would no longer seek her company so eagerly as before.

That was just what she wanted, she told herself. If she meant to fix her interest with Mr. Mansfield, the less interference, the better.

She found the two sisters in divergent moods. Isabel was very gay and sparkling, Julia a little sullen. The reason for Isabel's high spirits was soon explained. Isabel's intended, Mr. Warwick, had come to Bath for an extended visit. Within a few moments, the reason for Julia's quietness was also apparent. Isabel chatted gaily about the various outings she and Mr. Warwick would take, the shopping his visit would necessitate, and commented gleefully that she might never have to sit out a dance this evening or any other. Theo could not help but wonder if Isabel were more fond of Mr. Warwick or of the opportunity to gloat.

They arrived at the Lower Rooms at precisely seven o'clock, when the doors opened, for Lady Simpson, always fatigued by standing, deemed it of the utmost importance to procure a good seat. Mr. Warwick was waiting for them, and Isabel's attention was immediately claimed by a tall, quiet, thin young man, with spectacles and a serious expression. As introductions were made, Theo tried to conceal her surprise. She had expected that it would take a rather dashing young blade to attract the vivacious Isabel. The latter, however, appeared smugly content, and quickly deserted the other two girls in order to take a turn about the rooms with her intended. With the dancing yet an hour away, Theo and Julia were left to talk with each other, as Lady Simpson had plunged into deep conversation with an acquaintance. Julia, at least, did not lack for a topic.

"Oh, she makes me so angry! I am so tired of hearing Isabel carry on as she has—" The words fairly exploded from her.

"Well, I am certain that she must be glad to see Mr. Warwick. After all, they have been separated for some time, have they not?" Theo tried to soothe her.

"For two months only. *She* acts as if it's been two years. And I am so tired of her talking about him and about 'their plans.' "

"Of course, since I am not in her position, it is hard for me to say—but it is natural that she should be . . . preoccupied. He is her intended, after all."

"Her intended!" Julia snorted contemptuously. "If they would bother to actually become engaged, then I wouldn't mind so much. Mother would take me to London this year, and *I* could have a chance to go to the parties and meet eligible gentlemen, too. Mother says that I should be content to be here in Bath, but it is just not the same!"

Theo, who was quite in sympathy with this opinion, remained silent.

Julia's lower lip protruded ominously. "I'll probably be an old hag by the time they permit me to come out. And then she'll say that it's my own fault that I can't attract a gentleman's notice."

This flight of fancy was too much for Theo. A chuckle escaped her. "Oh, Julia—"

The lip inched out a little farther. "You think it's humorous, don't you?"

Theo shook her head, although she could not keep from smiling. "No, no. It's just that I can't imagine you as a hag." Seeing that she had not mollified her companion, she added. "Besides, your mother has said she will bring you out next year, without fail, hasn't she?"

Julia nodded sheepishly. She paused for a moment, then added, "I'm sorry, Theo. It's just that she irritates me so with those airs. You would think that no one else ever attracted a gentleman's eye."

Theo started to murmur a response, but Julia cut her off. "Well, look at you! You'll be dancing with the handsomest gentleman in the room tonight, and I don't see you carrying on about it."

Theo was put to the blush. She suddenly wished Isabel were still about to dampen her sister's heat. "Really, Julia, you should lower your voice. And besides, Mr. Mansfield is not my intended."

Unabashed, Julia responded, "But he will be. And *that* will take the wind out of Isabel's sail." She turned a confidential look on Theo. "And I mean to help you, too, however I may. Your match will put Isabel's in the shade."

"Miss Westmoreland." There could be no mistaking that pleasant baritone. She turned, and her reaction was the same as usual. Her heart skipped a beat as she stared at that handsome countenance. That tall, elegant figure was dressed to perfection. He smiled at her, and she could feel her cheeks turn pink. Drat it! How she hoped that Julia's carrying tones had not reached his ears!

"I hope that I might have the honor of a dance with you this evening."

Theo smiled and responded appropriately, but all the time she was praying that Julia was not casting any arch glances in her direction. She needn't have worried. When she introduced her friend, she saw that Julia, overcome by Mansfield's magnificence, could do no more than blush and giggle. It was clear that Theo's luck was in this evening.

The assembly was to surpass Theo's most sanguine expectations. Not only did she stand up with Mr. Mansfield twice, enjoying the envious stares of less fortunate damsels, but they also sat together for tea, which gave them their first real opportunity for conversation. Due to Mr. Mansfield's practiced manners, Theo found there was no end to trivialities that might be discussed. It wasn't until the topic had strayed to horses, though, that real progress was made.

They were discussing the differences between country and town life when Theo confessed that what she missed most of all was her daily ride. He looked shocked.

"Do you mean to say that you have given up riding entirely?"

Aware that she had come perilously close to complaint, Theo shook her head slightly. "I simply haven't had the opportunity since coming to Bath, that is all."

A look of resolution appeared upon his face. "Well, I can certainly remedy that. Do you know of the riding school—the one in Montpelier Row, that is?"

Indeed, Theo was familiar with this establishment, as well as Ryles in Monmouth Street. She had even gone so far as to make inquiries about the fees. But since she could not afford the lordly sum of three guineas a month, and indeed did not wish to squander even the five shillings, threepence for a single lesson, she had not frequented either of these premises. Mendaciously, she shook her head.

"I would be honored if you would accompany me there. I am quite an habitué of theirs."

Seeing her golden opportunity hovering so near, Theo lost her head. "When?" she breathed.

Fortunately, he did not appear to take offense at this unbecoming lack of reticence. "Why, tomorrow, if you wish it. I'll be happy to collect you." His eye lit upon Julia, seated quite close to them. "And if your friends wish to join us, I should be delighted," he offered magnanimously.

He was rewarded for this invitation with more blushes and giggles from Julia.

And so it was arranged that he should call for Theo at ten the next morning. After some consultation, the Simpsons decided that they also would join them, under Mr. Warwick's escort, of course. It would form an unexceptionable party.

It was the fulfillment of all of Theo's hopes. There was no one handsomer than Mr. Mansfield, no one better dressed, no one with more graceful manners. Debenham could certainly benefit from his tutelage. And Mr. Mansfield, though his aunt was a countess, did not consider Theo's friends to be beneath his notice. How Theo would love to point this out to Debenham, though, of course, as she recalled immediately, it was much better that he was in London.

She confided her happiness to her mother, and if the latter did not respond with quite the degree of enthusiasm Theo anticipated, it was no doubt due to her continued weakness. The viscountess was much improved, however, so Theo could feel no qualms about leaving her in the hands of the servants the next morning.

Peering from her window down to the street below the next morning, Theo was conscious of a pleasant fluttering inside her when she saw her handsome escort drive up. After a suitable wait, she joined him downstairs. Mr. Mansfield was apologetic about his equipage. He considered his gig, drawn by only one horse, to be a shabby conveyance, but confided that the countess had promised to buy him a proper turnout as soon as he found one that satisfied him. It was an uncomfortable reminder of his dependency, but Theo shrugged off the thought. She must concentrate her energies upon winning Mansfield's affections. It was useless to worry about the countess until then.

The riding itself was pure pleasure. Theo knew that she was not beautiful, or clever, and she had very few ladylike accomplishments of which to boast, but she was acknowledged by all to be a superior horsewoman. It was with difficulty that she persuaded the proprietor of the establishment to let her ride one of the more spirited animals there. Once mounted, her handling of the skittish horse provoked his admiration, and he was heard to confess that he thought he hadn't much to teach Miss Westmoreland.

It was otherwise with Mansfield, who, though elegant as ever, was astride what Theo saw was a rather sluggish bay mare. But when she advised him to ask for another mount, he replied gently that he was well used to the horse and had, in fact, become particularly attached to it. She was much struck by this evidence of the sweetness of his nature. Debenham, if presented with such an animal, would probably have withered the proprietor with a few choice remarks. Opportunity for further discussion ended when their instructor called, "Better lengthen your rein a bit, Mr. Mansfield, and then she'll stop tossing her head like that."

Isabel and Mr. Warwick also had selected quiet mounts. Isabel seemed to be managing hers with ease, but her intended appeared nervous about the whole process. Julia, a self-confessed coward when it came to horseflesh, was content merely to observe them all.

As satisfactory as this outing was, it possessed one disadvantage that Theo had not foreseen. The opportunity for conversation naturally was limited by their circumstances. She did not know how she could fix her interest with Mansfield when she was hardly given a chance to speak with him.

The carriage ride home was a short one, but as they drove along Russell Street, Theo was able to enjoy the sight of pretty Miss Bromley fairly gnashing her teeth with envy as they drove by. Theo acknowledged her with only the merest hint of a smile.

Mr. Mansfield missed this exchange, being preoccupied with problems of his own. He had told Theo that he had promised to accompany the countess to the Pump Room at midday, and that he dared not be late. While she could sympathize with his problem, her heart sank within her as they approached Gay Street without any mention made regarding when they might meet again. The thought crossed her mind that she might visit the Pump Room herself, but she dismissed it as unworthy.

When they made their good-byes, she thanked him in the prettiest way possible, but apparently was not able to make an impression upon him. He took his leave of her most gracefully, but was not totally unable to conceal his wish to be off that instant. She was conscious of a feeling of chagrin mingled with something approaching vexation as she entered her home. It was ignoble of her to be irritated with him, of course. Why, it was his thoughtfulness that made him so appealing, after all. Not everyone would have such a regard for the welfare of an elderly aunt—even one upon whom they were financially dependent. The last thought was jarringly unpleasant, and Theo turned her mind from it. It was foolish beyond belief to look a gift horse in the mouth.

Chapter Five

The elderly, bewigged gentleman drew a deep breath and, leaning back, clasped his hands together reflectively. Though his conservative black suit with its old-fashioned knee breeches proclaimed him a man sadly out of touch with the times, the intelligence in his still sparkling black eyes suggested otherwise.

"Well, sir, will you help me?" his visitor demanded baldly.

The gentleman sighed and, not to be hurried, leaned forward on the massive mahogany desk. "Had you considered consulting the proper authorities?"

Debenham gave a quick shake of the head. "As far as the courts are concerned, it's settled. Don't wish to bring in Bow Street, in case I should be wrong. Also—nothing alarms a fox as much as having a pack of hounds baying behind him. Shouldn't wish him to go to ground, as it were."

Mr. Thomas gave an appreciative smile. "Had you considered that there might be some danger involved?"

"M'father means to go to Bath to look after the ladies."

"I meant to yourself, though of course there is the possibility—"

"I can take care of myself," said Debenham curtly.

The black eyes regarded him assessingly, as if measuring the inches of hard muscle that lay beneath that well-cut tailcoat. They at last met Debenham's own gaze and held it, as if determining the sort of person who dwelt inside. Debenham did not flinch under this scrutiny or indeed even seem to resent it, but after about a minute, his patience gave way. "Well?" he demanded.

"I feel sure that you can" was the other's decision. "You say that Sir Francis is going to Bath. I take it that he knows of this scheme."

"Of course. He advised me to consult our man of business, and Moffett told me to come to you. He said that you were up to every rig in town—that there was little in the City that escaped your notice."

Although he was inwardly gratified, Thomas's countenance, schooled by habit, revealed nothing. "I am certain that the ladies must be grateful to you for wishing to make such efforts in their behalf."

For some reason, this remark seemed to amuse Debenham. One corner of his mouth curled upward sardonically. "Grateful is hardly the word." He gazed levelly at Thomas. "Fact is, I don't mean for the ladies to know what I'm doing until something's been accomplished, one way or the other."

"Well, you must know best," remarked the banker enigmatically. He apparently had come to a decision, for he added, "I will do what I can for you, though if things should become rough, I hope you will be sensible and call in the Runners."

It was Debenham's turn to reveal nothing.

Thomas sighed. "Youth must always be impetuous. Let me ring for Sanders. He may be able to tell you more than I."

It is a rare day when fortune does not offer a compounded mixture of good and bad, though not necessarily in equal amounts. Thus, Theodora, though chagrined because she believed herself to be at a standstill with Mansfield, was also given her dose of happiness with the news that her mother was feeling much more the thing.

In fact, the viscountess was so much improved that she declared herself well enough to attend services at the Abbey Church the next morning. She did prudently yield to everyone's advice and decide that she and Theo should take chairs there, the distance being great for one who was, after all, an invalid. It proved a prudent course of action in any case, for the skies had become gray and threatened rain.

Accordingly, just before the hour of eleven, they alighted at the abbey. Theo was gratified to hear the peal of ten bells, used to announce the arrival of any visitor of rank. It was satisfying to know that in Bath, they were still entitled to all the observances, despite the meanness of their present situation.

Most visitors to the abbey found themselves compelled to admire what a guidebook termed "one of the noblest monuments of ecclesiastical Gothic architecture in the kingdom." The beauty of the abbey and its noble proportions excited admiration and awe in most persons. The more thoughtful among the newly arrived were rendered solemn by the sheer number of monuments to the dead. The pillars, the walls, and the floor were literally covered with inscriptions to the memory of those travelers who had not found the waters sufficient for their cure.

Happily, Theodora's preoccupation rendered her proof against such a sobering train of thought. Though she might have taken her place in the pew with studied indifference to her surroundings, once seated she soon began peeping about from under the edge of her bonnet, in order to see who else was there. It seemed that again she was doomed to disappointment. Aside from Mrs. Bromley, who had acknowledged them with an inclination of the head, her daughter apparently being too lost in prayer to do so, there were no others of their acquaintance there. The almost constant hope that she might encounter Mr. Mansfield died in Theo's breast. With a sigh, she opened her prayer book. The service would begin shortly.

Again, the peal of ten bells rang out. She hoped her looks did not betray her agitation. She heard footsteps echoing up the aisle and glanced in their direction. It was Mr. Mansfield and the countess. The latter acknowledged them very civilly, while Mansfield smiled meaningfully and swept them a bow. Theo's heart doubled its pace. Perhaps she need not give up all hope just yet.

A more dutiful person than Theo would have abandoned her thoughts of Mansfield, and turned her attention to the service as it began. Though she did make all the proper responses, there was a dreamy smile on her face, which implied that her mind was elsewhere. In reality, she was indulging in the most pleasant speculations.

As time was to prove, reality showed itself to be equal to even the most ambitious of her dreams. After the end of the service, it was only natural that the countess and Mr. Mansfield should fall into conversation with the viscountess and her daughter. Lady Verridge had soon claimed all the viscountess's attention, leaving Theo free to speak with Mansfield.

With his customary good manners, he complimented Theo on her appearance, and thanked her for accompanying him to the riding school the previous day. He apologized for departing in such haste, adding that the countess tended to fret herself unnecessarily about his safety, if he was late. Theo was murmuring that she quite understood when he suddenly made up for his omissions of the day before by asking if she would like to go driving with him on the morrow. It was the chance for which she had been waiting, the chance to actually converse with him in some detail. Glancing at her mother, she realized that there would be objections. His gaze followed hers, and he seemed to read her thoughts, for he asked if she would not care to invite her friends, the Simpsons, and make a party of it. She accepted, gladly.

"You meant that you took chairs here today? Well, my dear Lady Westmoreland, you and your daughter simply must accompany us in my carriage. It is far too damp to be standing out here waiting for a chair, particularly for persons in frail health such as ourselves. I do not trust these chairmen anyway—they are swindlers, and robbers, and so terribly careless! Well, one need say no more than that they are Irish, after all. I refuse to take a chair, myself. It is settled. I am sure that your daughter agrees with me," she added, turning her gaze on Theo.

The viscountess, who had been about to refuse this offer, took a look at Theo's pleading eyes and reluctantly accepted.

It was bliss. After the carriage arrived, Mansfield handed Lady Verridge and the viscountess in the carriage before turning to Theo. Theo felt magnanimous enough to nod graciously at Miss Bromley and her mother, water dripping from their bonnets as they waited for their chairs.

The topic of conversation on the way home could not be said to be wide-ranging. As usual, the countess dominated it, choosing to discuss her elderly female companion, who had been thoughtless enough to fall ill.

"And though the doctors say that they do not know what is wrong, I have no doubt that it is something contagious, and that I shall most likely contract it myself. It is most inconvenient having to do without her services, though I will say that she was not giving perfect satisfaction as it was, since she was not getting about so well as formerly."

The viscountess murmured something suitable. Mansfield gravely added, "This companion is an impecunious cousin of my aunt's late husband. She has been most charitable in offering her this position."

"Oh, as to that it is no great matter. I hardly regard such a thing myself, although—"

Theo was no longer attending to Lady Verridge's remarks, being preoccupied with her nephew. What commendable loyalty he showed. Anyone might take the countess for a self-centered bore, but he was determined to show her in a more favorable light. She could not help but glance admiringly at him. When her eyes met his, she met such a look of warmth there that she had to lower hers again in confusion. Her heart was beating rapidly, and her cheeks grew pink. What a delightful sensation!

As they approached Gay Street, Theo realized that for the first time, the countess would surely be made aware of their circumstances. It was not that their house was impoverished, but it was small, and certainly a great deal less grand than the countess's quarters in the Crescent. Happily, Lady Verridge did not appear at all conscious, but upon their arrival, interrupted her own monologue long enough to bid them farewell and to express a wish that they might call upon her in her own lodgings.

"I hope that you do not mind, Theo," said her mother quietly after they had departed, "but I am afraid that I was feeling rather too weak to invite them in today."

Theo's conscience struck its blow. Her mother was looking paler, and this was her first venture out since the attack. "No, of course not, Mother. How could you think so?" As she helped the viscountess to a chair, she added shyly, "Mr. Mansfield has asked me to go driving with him tomorrow. As long as the Simpsons go also, I hope that you have no objections."

An almost imperceptible line creased the area between her mother's fine brows, but she replied evenly. "No, of course not. I hope that the weather may improve."

This thought had also crossed Theo's mind, but she dismissed it, firmly resolved to thrust away all such pessimistic thoughts. After their nuncheon, the viscountess announced her intention of resting, while Theo resolved to set out immediately for Laura Place, to ask the Simpsons about the drive. Her mother mentioned that she might send a servant with a note instead, the weather being so dirty. Theo overrode this objection, as well as her mother's suggestion that she take a chair.

"It is hardly sprinkling now. I shall dress warmly and take Molly with me. Please, Mother, may I go? Do not say that I cannot."

It was uncertain whether Lady Westmoreland suddenly thought the better of Theo's scheme, or whether, in her exhaustion she simply lacked the energy to oppose it. In any case, Theo received the requested permission. She went upstairs to change into a walking dress, while, unbeknownst to her, her mother went upstairs to pen an anxious letter. Within the hour, Theo set out, obediently clad in the despised merino pelisse and her sturdy, but far from fashionable boots. Considerations of fashion were beneath her today.

She had the good fortune to find both of the sisters in. They greeted her with delight, and begged to hear of the latest developments. "—For he was so handsome, riding about yesterday. I'm sure I don't know how you stayed on the horse, Theo. I should have swooned and fallen off every time he came near to me," commented Julia.

The entire afternoon had to be recounted in detail, as well as the surprising developments of this morning. Both the girls exclaimed in delight at the news of the proposed outing. Isabel was quick to assure Theo of her availability. "Mr. Warwick drove to town in his gig, and I am certain that he would be pleased to drive me out tomorrow with you."

Julia's face lost a little of its exuberance. "What about me? Aren't I going, too?"

Isabel gave her a calm smile of superiority. "His gig only seats two, although you would be in the way in any case, Julia."

Her eyes turned hopefully upon Theo, who berated herself for not having thought of this complication before. "I'm sorry, Julia. We would take you if we could, but his can only carry two, also."

"Think, Julia! This is Theo's first chance to have private conversation with Mr. Mansfield. The last thing she wishes is to have *you* along on the ride!" added Isabel cruelly.

Julia's face reddened. "We might take our family's carriage, and I could ride with you then, Isa. It has plenty of room for all of us."

"It wouldn't be at all the same. Dear, although you are too young to understand, Theo wishes to be alone with Mr. Mansfield—"

"I didn't mean Theo, I meant you!"

"—Just as I wish to be alone with my fiancé—"

"He's not your fiancé!"

Isabel bestowed her haughtiest look upon her sister. "Of course, if you had some beau of your *own*, we should be happy if he drove you out along with us, but since you have not . . ."

Tears welled in Julia's eyes. "You're a selfish beast, Isa!" She turned her reddened orbs upon Theo. "I expect it of her, Theo, but not of you! You have so many beaux already. I thought you were my friend." She sniffed audibly, and Theo stretched out a remorseful hand to her. Julia shook her head, as the tears began to flow.

"No, I suppose where *gentlemen* are involved, friendship must always be forgotten. I hope you are both pleased with yourselves!" A half-stifled sob escaped her, and she fled the room precipitately.

"Really, Isabel," said Theo, exasperated, "Did you have to be so unkind?"

Isabel shrugged. "It is her own fault. She has the foulest temper—but really that's neither here nor there. She'll recover soon enough, believe me. So, tell me, what did he say once you were in the carriage together?"

Although the next day dawned gray and menacing, as if in answer to Theo's prayers, the skies began to clear and by eleven o'clock the sun was shining. By the time Mansfield arrived, at half-past one, it had turned into a beautiful day. After they had exchanged the usual greetings, Theo could not help confessing her previous anxiety to him.

"—For I should have been so disappointed if we had to postpone this outing."

"So should I," he agreed, but there was a meaningful note in that pleasant baritone that made Theo's heart pound.

Again he apologized for his equipage, Theo responding quite sincerely that she was perfectly happy in it. Indeed, it seemed fortunate that he was driving a gig with only one horse. He must be as smitten with her as she was with him, for he had trouble keeping just the one animal on the road. She could not be cross with him, for whenever she looked up, she encountered his eyes on her. It was the most flattering sensation imaginable!

They drove to Laura Place, as she had arranged, in order to meet Isabel and her beau there. In contrast to Mansfield's elegant figure with its well-cut tailcoat, tight-fitting buckskin breeches, and shining top boots, Mr. Warwick was clad soberly and plainly in black, with old-fashioned knee breeches, a quite modest cravat, and shirt points that scarcely reached his chin. Moreover, he wore the same serious expression that Theo was beginning to believe was habitual with him, and he continued to maintain his stoic silence. Obviously, he regarded driving, and riding, and even dancing as matters that should not be taken lightly. More than ever it amazed her that he should have been the one to have attracted Isabel. Julia, who obviously still was miffed, did not put in an appearance.

After a little discussion, to which Warwick listened earnestly but did not contribute, it was settled that they would drive to the top of Lansdown Hill, which promised a view of both of the cities of Bath and Bristol. The sun was out, the air was fresh and cool, the horse was docile. Theo could not have asked for a better opportunity.

Conversation between her and her escort flourished. It was not difficult to discover what Mr. Mansfield's hobby-horses were. With only the mildest encouragement, he happily expounded upon his plans for the acquisition of not a pair, but a team of 'prime 'uns.' For his carriage, he would not be content with a shabby old gig like this one, but intended to get a first-rate turnout. Clearly he meant to cut a dash. He mentioned that Debenham had promised to keep an eye out for such an equipage while he was in London. Unfortunately, his admiration for Debenham caused him to expound upon this nonpareil among whips and how he could drive to an inch. He recounted Debenham's famous exploit of driving through a gate just wide enough to admit his carriage some twenty-two times in succession.

"—Which equaled Sir John Lade's record, and not once did his wheels ever graze it. You know, he's a member of the B.D.C.—and though their numbers are strictly limited,

I wonder if—of course, I suppose it's no good thinking about it until I have a proper set of prads and a—"

Theo, who was heartily bored by this topic, diverted the conversation. "How do you find Bath? I understand that you spend a great deal of time in London. I suppose Bath must seem dull by comparison."

He gave the warm smile that made her heart race again. "I suppose I might have said so at one time, but certainly not now."

What a wonderful thing love was. She savored the pleasant fluttering sensation for several moments in silence. He startled her by asking abruptly. "Do you like music?"

Judging that the correct reply would be affirmative, Theo responded appropriately.

"It has always been one of my interests. I belong to the Harmonic Society. We meet at the White Hart one week and at the Lower Rooms the next. We try to obtain the best performers that we can, Mr. Ashe being one of the most notable, and so we are entertained with catches and glees and duets."

Theo, who had no real liking for music, fixed a smile upon her face and murmured that it sounded most enjoyable.

"My aunt, of course, is equally fond of music, and usually attends with me. I wonder if you and your mother would care to accompany us to the concert on Wednesday?"

Theo smiled and replied that if her mother was willing, they would be pleased to attend. She hoped that the viscountess would not consider that she was placing herself under too great an obligation again, but surely matters might be seen differently when one was in love. She expressed a hope that his aunt might not tire of their society.

"Oh, no," he replied, "for your mother is a great favorite with her, and she has remarked more than once what a pretty and well-behaved young lady you are, not at all like the flighty young misses one is inclined to meet with nowadays."

Such praise could not help but encourage her. If the countess's approval was necessary for this match, it seemed that at least she had made a good start toward securing it. Of course, she was being premature. She and Mr. Mansfield hardly knew each other yet, though if his searing glances were any indication, she had cause to be optimistic.

Lansdown Hill was notable not only for the beauty of the

view, but for the number of sheep which grazed upon it. When they reached it, Theo gladly alighted from the carriage with Mansfield's help. Isabel, who was city bred, did not care to be in such proximity to what she termed "noisy, smelly creatures" and so remained in Warwick's carriage.

They were fortunate in having such a fine day for the outing, for they could see the Bristol Channel quite clearly, and part of Wales and Gloucestershire. The breeze was blowing briskly, and Theo, who had opted for a shawl instead of the drab pelisse, drew it more tightly about her. Mansfield was immediately concerned.

"You are chilled. Should we return?"

"No. It is . . . it is delightful." She pinkened self-consciously as she spoke, but meeting his eyes, saw an understanding smile in them. It was an exhilarating feeling, and Theo could not remember ever being happier.

The drive home was filled with many more such moments. By the time Mansfield set her down in Gay Street, she felt as if she might have floated into the house. Her mother noticed her dreamy expression, but did not comment upon it. To Theo's great relief, she consented to accompany the countess and Mansfield to the concert Wednesday, although as Theo had predicted, she worried about the obligation.

"—Still we might ask them to dine here with us very privately—I daresay she has no greater desire to attend a party than I do, so the relationship need not be entirely one-sided, I suppose."

She was rewarded with an enthusiastic hug from Theo, who granted her the title of "the best of mothers," before leaving for her own room and pleasant daydreams. With a little frown on her face, Lady Westmoreland watched her depart.

The happiest part was knowing that she would not actually have to wait to meet Mansfield until Wednesday. It had been arranged between the two that they might encounter each other in the Pump Room every day just before noon. A conference with Isabel could not be delayed. The latter made many flattering observations, and concluded with her belief that Mansfield was every bit as taken with Theo as she was with him. Isabel confidently prophesied an early engagement, over Theo's protests.

That night Theo dreamt that she was the mistress of a

great estate, one which looked suspiciously like Westleigh Abbey. She was bedecked in jewels and wearing a modish gown of gold silk. There was an assembly in progress, and the ballroom was filled with distinguished personages. She nodded graciously to them as her partner prepared to lead her to the floor to open the dancing. The orchestra struck the first note and still smiling, she turned to curtsy to her partner. As she straightened herself, she raised her eyes to encounter Debenham's face at its most sardonic. She woke up, her heart pounding, filled with fury. How dare he intrude himself upon her dreams! What right did he have to take Mansfield's place there?

It took her some time to calm down. She told herself that it was only natural that she should have dreamt about him. All the bliss that she was experiencing with Mansfield was making her feel more and more guilty about Debenham, though she did her best to thrust it from her mind. After all, he had been a good friend to her and her family. It was a pity, but her romance would undoubtedly hurt him. If only he could find happiness on his own, with someone who was more suited to his . . . to his temperament. All sorts of ladies evidently found him appealing, after all, though Theo personally could not fathom why. There was Julia, for instance. Yes, Theo must consider what was to be done with Debenham upon his return. She could afford to be charitable to him.

The object of her pity would doubtless have been quite surprised by it. Theo's romantic pastimes were far from his mind right now. At the moment, he was seated on a bench in a dark, smoky, and unpleasantly fragrant coffeehouse, doing his best to persuade his nervous accomplice to leave.

"There's no reason for you to remain. You've told me what I need to know already."

The `accomplice, a thin, high-strung man, attired quite conservatively and modestly, looked about him in an agitated manner. "Oh, no. It would never do. I can't imagine what Mr. Thomas would have to say to me if I were to leave you here alone. There's no telling what could happen to you here—" He looked at the company about him in evident distaste.

"I think he'd agree that I'm well able to take care of myself and less likely to attract attention without you here," said Debenham impatiently. A blowsy woman, whose appearance proclaimed her profession had been eyeing him fixedly, if slightly drunkenly, for a few minutes. She now made her way unsteadily across the room to lean heavily upon Debenham, displaying her attractions, such as they were, in an obvious fashion.

His companion, Mr. Sanders, though he could not make out her words, correctly judged them to be obscene in nature. He was startled by Debenham's response, which was to thrust the woman from him, and with a quick turn at the waist to elbow a small, slight fellow standing unobtrusively beside him and send the latter flying across the room. Debenham's lips curled back from his teeth in a sneer. "Tell your buzman to keep his fambles off my cly, unless he feels in the mood for a little turnup."

The pickpocket, needing no further warning, scurried from the room rapidly. The woman, seemingly not at all offended by this rough treatment, approached Debenham again.

"So, it's a flash swell, is it? You're out, though, deary. I've never seen that dirty little prig before, so help me." Seeing the implacability of his expression, she turned to Sanders. "Your friend here looks in need of a spree with a dimber mort like me—"

The clerk recoiled from her, with such an expression of horror upon his face that Debenham, in spite of himself, could not prevent an unpleasant laugh. Seeing her answer, she shrugged philosophically and retreated, remarking to one of her sisterhood that the cove in the corner was cagged.

If Debenham had been able to raise those bristling black brows, he would have done so now. "Well, have you had enough of lushey bunters or are you just waiting for the chance to kick up a dust on your own?"

"Good heavens, Mr. Debenham. Did I understand you to say that the fellow was trying to pick your pocket—and that he was in league with that . . . that creature over there? I am certain that I have made a mistake by bringing you here. Let us go."

He started to rise, but his wrist was clasped in a grasp of iron. Sanders might never have heard of Gentleman Jackson or Thomas Cribb, but even to him it was obvious that sparring must be one of Mr. Debenham's hobbies.

"Go if you wish, but I intend to remain. I don't intend to let the tag, rag, and bobtail keep me from my quarry. Lud, I've been in worse company than this before."

Mr. Sanders stared at him for a moment, before sinking slowly down on the bench again. With commendable determination, he said, "If you intend to stay, then so do I, Mr. Debenham. You need me to help spot the fellow." He let out a despairing sigh. "—That is, if he actually comes.

"Please yourself," replied Debenham indifferently. He signaled the proprietor of the establishment. "Care for a muffin?" he asked his companion. Sanders took a look at the pathetic remains of a human specimen who was toasting the victuals before the fire and shook his head, shuddering delicately. The corner of Debenham's mouth curled up with something that might have been amusement. "A flash of lightning for you, then, or do you actually want coffee?" He looked at Sanders and gave a sigh. "Try to look inconspicuous if you can."

The latter looked utterly bewildered at these instructions. Debenham considered explaining himself, but abandoned the effort as a lost cause. There were a few surprised glances when Debenham called for coffee instead of gin, the more traditional beverage in a coffeehouse, but the word had already spread. It was better to leave that "ugly customer" in the corner alone.

As their cups of coffee were served, Debenham took upon himself the task of gently pumping the proprietor. Again, their conversation was largely unintelligible to poor Sanders, but he pricked up his ears at the words "Bow Street." Debenham shook his head emphatically, and some coins were slipped into the proprietor's hand.

As soon as the latter had left, Sanders leaned forward earnestly. "I wish you *would* call in the Runners."

"I know what I'm about. Hush—" His eyes were trained on a party of people now entering the shop. "Is that him?"

The proprietor was making various signals at them. Sanders focused upon a heavyset gentleman just coming in the door. "Yes."

"Good, he's already well fuzzed. Wait here. I don't want him to recognize you."

In a moment, Debenham was across the coffeehouse and beside the heavy man. "Mr. Hawke, isn't it? Won't you come and have a cup of cheer with my friend and me?"

The bloodshot eyes blinked blearily at him. "I'm sorry, but—"

"We *insist* that you join us," said Debenham in a low, meaningful tone. Hawke twitched suddenly as a small metal cylinder came into contact with the clothes covering the flesh about his ribs. "Eh?"

His exclamation was not noticed above the raucous din supplied by the other customers. "Don't say anything else," warned Debenham. His face suddenly relaxed into a cold smile that was even more frightening than his scowl. "It will be to your advantage to talk to us, I promise you."

He linked his arm in Hawke's as if they were the oldest of friends, and called for another cup of coffee. He seated him on the bench opposite Sanders. Hawke squinted at Sanders for several seconds before responding. "I know *you*, don't I? It's . . . you work for—"

"Ssh!" Sanders shook his head in an agitated way.

"It's not for you to ask the questions," Debenham said mildly. "We want to know about your former place of employment, and a particular client of his—"

"I don't know—"

"The Viscount Westmoreland."

"—Anything about it," Hawke finished sullenly.

"Don't you?" asked Debenham. He thanked the proprietor as another cup of coffee was delivered. "You'd better drink this," he ordered Hawke. "It might help your memory."

He did as he was told, and it was clear that the beverage had a sobering effect. He drained off the cup, but volunteered nothing.

"Remember anything now?" asked Debenham.

He shook his head and was wiping his lips with the back of a hand, when he suddenly felt the metal cylinder in his stomach. He put down his hand and stared into Debenham's eyes with bravado. "You wouldn't kill a man in a public place like this. The Watch would be on you in a minute, and there'd be witnesses."

"Reliable ones, too," commented Debenham sardonically, casting his eyes upon the dirty, ragged, and for the most part drunken mob about them. "You can't be certain, can you? Of course, you're right. It might be better to kill you out behind the shop."

Hawke might have been shaken, but he did not show it. "You won't learn anything from me that way."

"You're right." Debenham extracted a purse of coins from his pocket, and showed them discreetly to Hawke. "It's yours if you tell us what we need to know."

"I don't need your money," said Hawke defiantly. With a quick gesture, Debenham reached out and snatched the handkerchief that had been wrapped about the thick neck, revealing only naked skin. There was no shirt beneath the coat, which had been buttoned up tightly as high as possible.

"Gammoning the draper?" asked Debenham coolly. "I'd say you could use a bit of the ready."

Resentfully, Hawke snatched back the handkerchief and rearranged it untidily about his neck. "I'm an honest man."

"But your master wasn't. Was that why you were dismissed?"

Hawke shot him a suspicious glance. "If you don't mind my asking," he began with elaborate sarcasm, "just what's *your* interest in this—and Thomas's?"

"Ssh!" hissed Sanders uncomfortably.

"It's my concern entirely," replied Debenham equably. "My father was the executor of the estate—and neither he nor I enjoy being gulled. The viscountess is still alive, but ill, and she has a young son and a daughter. Oliphant swindled them out of their inheritance, and I mean to make things right."

"Sssh!" This time it was Hawke doing the hushing. "Not so loud, if you please."

The polite tone was new to their discussion. Hawke glanced from one face to the other, anxiously. "You don't understand. He'd kill me just for sitting here with you like this. I wouldn't even have to say a word."

"Seems it's to your advantage to talk to us, then," commented Debenham dryly.

Hawke snorted. "Easy for you to say. I've a wife and children to consider—"

"—Which is undoubtedly why you are here tonight."

It was left to Mr. Sanders to provide the voice of reason. "You need not be implicated in any way. The gentleman here is taking all the risk upon himself and should he prove successful, Oliphant will end in prison, where he belongs. All we need from you is information—"

Debenham interrupted. "It was enough to make anyone damned suspicious. First, on behalf of his wealthiest clients, he invests in a company that promptly goes under, and he is forced to declare bankruptcy himself. He is acquitted of all wrongdoing, yet within a year, he's taken a new name, purchased a fine, large house, and hired a staff to go with it, bought two new carriages, and—"

"He was always a little too clever for his own good. Not quite clever enough to cover his own tracks, though I suppose he thought no one would bother to try and find him," interjected Hawke.

Debenham met his gaze squarely. "Name your price. He won't present a danger to you after we've finished with him, we can promise you that. All we need to know is how the thing was done."

Hawke gave a sigh of capitulation. "I'm putting my life in your hands. What's more, you haven't a hope of proving anything in a court of law. The only reason I know anything is because I happened to see a letter, which he burned later . . ."

"Well?" asked Debenham impatiently.

"The money first."

It was handed over and quietly counted. Perspiration beading on his forehead, Hawke looked up at his benefactor. "The same again if you can help us," responded Debenham.

Hawke glanced about him, then leaned forward. "It was the neatest rig you've heard of, gentlemen. They've had such success with building these canals nowadays that it was thought that this company would meet with the same. A friend of his was one of the directors, and was able to tell him in advance that the company would soon go bankrupt. Between them, they managed to doctor the books to show he'd invested all that money in the company. When it failed, he could not be blamed, except for poor judgment." He glanced about, the reddened whites of his eyes showing prominently, then lowered his voice even further. "That money was never invested anywhere. He and his friend pocketed it themselves, probably in accounts under false names. The letter I happened to see was from his friend, who was accusing him of taking an unfair portion of the profits. Damned little he could do about it," he added.

"Honor among thieves," mused Debenham. "What was the partner's name?"

"I don't know." He met the unbelieving stare, and without thinking, removed the handkerchief from his neck and wiped his forehead with it. "I swear to you, I don't know. There was no signature and no address."

Debenham gave Hawke a penetrating look. Several seconds of silence passed before he spoke, coldly, "Where shall I send the rest of your money?"

"I'll be here tomorrow and the next and every night until you return."

"Very well. Don't make your master's mistake. Spend it a little more slowly." With these words, Debenham rose and, with a nod to Sanders, began to make his way out of the coffeehouse. There were one or two interested stares, but no one was willing to risk the same treatment the pickpocket had received, so they were allowed to depart in peace.

Once outside, Sanders could contain himself no longer. "Mr. Debenham," he hissed, "you should not have rewarded that unscrupulous person so generously. I noticed that you did not inquire how a clerk came to be reading his master's letters. I shall be surprised if anything that he has told us is at all true."

"I imagine he was reading it with an eye to blackmailing Oliphant himself. A pity he didn't manage to keep the letter. It would have been quite useful. I think he's given us an accurate account, however. A man like that has no difficulty in lying. Telling the truth is what makes him nervous, and I'd swear he was ready to hop out of his skin by the time we left. Trust Westmoreland to become mixed up with thieving scoundrels like these. I've no doubt that some friend recommended Oliphant highly—"

"With all due respect, the late viscount was a most trusting man, but Oliphant did enjoy the patronage of several noble houses. He presented a most creditable appearance, and I myself did not suspect that—" He sighed and did not complete the sentence. "In any case, I suppose that this . . . this scapegallows is right. There is no more that we can do."

"I wouldn't be too certain of that."

Chapter Six

Theo knew that she was looking her best this evening, and the awareness lent her a certain complacency, a feeling to which she had been a stranger for many months. She had chosen one of her most becoming evening dresses of India muslin worked with gilt spangles. Special attention was given to the floral embroidery about the hem, the low, square-cut neckline, and the short sleeves. A separate train fell away from her shoulders and lent her an air of added distinction. Her hair was dressed in the fashionable antique Roman mode, being confined in the back in two light knots. White kid gloves and shoes finished her ensemble. She looked tall, elegant, and regal, and she knew it.

It was so very satisfying, after all. Although she had already been on two outings with Mansfield, there were hardly any witnesses. It was true that their dances together had set some tongues wagging. There had been others who had noticed the time he devoted to her in the Pump Room. Her presence here at the concert could only mean one thing, however. He was singling her out, for all of Bath to see. Society here was limited and gossip flourished. By tomorrow, everyone would know. She gave Mansfield a serene smile, aware that she was dashing the hopes of less fortunate girls all about her. He leaned toward her.

"I think you will be pleased with tonight's program."

Her mother was nobly bearing the burden of the countess's company. Theo was relieved to hear that the topic of conversation was music, rather than Lady Verridge's latest disease. Mrs. Billington was mentioned and Catalini, Miss Comer, and Rauzzini. The countess obviously felt that modern singers could not rival those she had heard in her youth. If music was a hobbyhorse of Mansfield's, it was apparent that the countess also rode it with a vengeance. Theo turned her attention to a more pleasant topic—the charming compliments Mansfield was uttering.

It was probable that the singer performed well that evening, at least if one was to judge by the warmth of his reception. Since she had no interest in music herself, Theo spent the evening lost in a happy daydream, interrupted only by surreptitious glances at Mansfield's rapt face beside her. What a thrill it was every time he happened to intercept one of those glances and exchange a smile with Theo. A month ago, her outlook had held nothing but gloom. It was almost inappropriate that her prospect should have changed to one of unshadowed bliss within such a short time. What a fortunate young lady she was. It seemed there were no obstacles before her now.

It was possible that in her moment of triumph, Theo overestimated the matter and that not every eye in the room was fascinated by the picture that she and Mansfield presented. In any case, however, there was at least one pair of eyes that were surveying her with appreciative interest. Keen and gray, resting beneath bristling black brows, they spent most of this part of the concert observing the byplay between her and her escort rather than the plump gentleman perspiring in front of the orchestra. They noticed the whispers during the intervals, the glances and the smiles.

This observant, dark gentleman remained in place on his bench until the first part of the program was over. Rising, he clapped his hat on his head and left the room quickly, while the rest of the audience was still busy applauding the performers and trying to decide who should be elected to go in quest of tea.

After breakfasting the next morning, Theo returned upstairs to dress with particular care. It had taken a great deal of persuasion, but Peggy had obliged her today. Theo had decided upon her new walking dress of white muslin, with the bishop sleeves tied up with the green ribbon, which perfectly matched her new Spanish bonnet. It was a pity that she couldn't afford the green mantle to match. Still, she looked rather striking, she had to admit.

In her conversation with Mansfield last night, he had happened to mention rather purposefully that he meant to return some of the countess's books to the library this morning. Although it was a task that might have been left to a servant, Theo did not remark upon it. It seemed more than coincidental that he happened to patronize Duffield's library in Milsom Street, just a street away from her home. It apparently did not strike him as peculiar that Theo also had some urgent business to transact there. She mentioned, rather boldly, that she thought she would be there around half-past ten o'clock the next morning and, taking his cue, he replied that was just about the same time he meant to go and that perhaps he would see her there.

It was dangerously close to an assignation, which Theo knew her mother would frown upon, so she had dispatched a note to Isabel early this morning, begging her to meet Theo there. She had misgivings as to whether Julia would wish to oblige her in this way.

It was only ten o'clock now, but Theo had decided it would be just as well to be prompt. Mansfield undoubtedly would have to leave early to escort the countess to the Pump Room. Theo made her way downstairs and was surprised to hear masculine tones coming from the drawing room. Surely it was early for her mother to be receiving company? The voices stopped abruptly as she neared it.

As she crossed to the doorway, she encountered a pair of deepset, piercing gray eyes under black brows, and she could not prevent a gasp. After blinking her eyes, this vision swam into focus and she saw that this gentleman's dark curls were shot through with silver, which oddly became that leathered face. The lips parted in a smile, revealing even, white teeth.

"Sir Francis!"

"How are you, my girl?" He rose and, crossing the room, took her proffered hand, as well as giving her a buss on the cheek. He stepped back a pace to admire her. "You look neat as ninepence, my dear. What a fetching bonnet! Where are you bound? Off to slay the hearts of all the young bucks, I daresay. Bath has probably been ringing with the sighs of unfortunate young gentlemen since you arrived."

His words made her blush. "Really, Sir Francis—"

"*Uncle*, please—"

"Really, Uncle, I—"

Her mother interrupted gently. "We are both so very grateful for your generosity. The clothing allowance you made for Theodora has enabled her to—"

"Pshaw." A modest man, Sir Francis disliked having his

praises sung. "I am a selfish fellow, you know. Even an old man like me enjoys seeing a beauty like this dressed to the nines—"

The two ladies had to protest this self-deprecation immediately. Sir Francis, just past fifty, was still a remarkably attractive gentleman. His eyes twinkled in response to their comments, and he smiled even more broadly.

"Well, just think what she'll do for my credit if she consents to stroll about the town with me. Although I suppose I'll have to bring my pistols to warn away those jealous young hotheads."

Theo was feeling guilty already. It was true that Sir Francis had paid for all of the wardrobe that *she* was using to ensnare Mansfield's heart. Now she must refuse his invitation in order to rendezvous with Mansfield. "Uncle—" she began reluctantly.

"How good it is to see you, my dear. I expect you to catch me up on all the latest *on-dits*. My graceless son never can spare the time to share the news of the town with his elderly father, you know."

"I was just going out now to meet some friends at Duffield's—"

"Then I will escort you. I meant to have a look at the papers today, in any case."

There was little Theo could do when her objections were crushed with such charm. It was always hard to believe that Debenham was his father's son, for despite their physical resemblance, their personalities were most dissimilar.

He turned to Lady Westmoreland, and bowed over her hand gracefully. "I will return later, and then we may talk at some length," he said.

"Oh, Sir Francis, I—"

"You are not to worry any further," he told her in a low voice, which did not quite carry to Theo's ears. He picked up his hat and walking stick from the nearby chair on which they rested, before turning to Theo. "Now, my girl, we're off. I shall have to depend upon my cane to defend myself from interlopers."

They were soon out the door, and he placed his hat carefully on his head, tilting it at a rakish angle, before tucking Theo's arm firmly in his own.

"When did you arrive in Bath, Uncle?" asked Theo, having abandoned all hopes of losing him.

"Just yesterday evening. That son of mine had the nerve to write me from London, and tell me he'd run off and left you without an escort. I've no doubt that you'd prefer not to be seen with a relict like me, but—"

"Oh, don't be so ludicrous. But you needn't have come. My mother and I can manage by ourselves." The words were almost the same as what she had told Debenham at their last meeting, and she blushed with a sudden consciousness. Sir Francis shot a swift glance at her, but otherwise appeared to take no notice of her confusion.

"I had asked your mother's doctor to notify me if anything went wrong. If anything should go amiss, you would be my responsibility, you know, my dear. He wrote and mentioned the attack to me, though he added that she seems to be recovering from it."

Theo let out a sigh. "I have been so worried—"

"Yes, I know, and the responsibility is too great for a young lady, alone as you are. Aside from our connection, your father was one of my dearest friends. I should feel disloyal to his memory if I did not lend you my support." He patted the hand that he held. "There are times when each of us must rely on our friends."

Theo was close to tears. "You are so good—"

"No, it's a selfish pleasure. I've told you that. But tell me, what do you make of these Bath quizzes? Have you ever seen such an odd-looking gown in your life?" His voice had dropped to a conspiratorial whisper as they passed a bewigged lady, wearing a sack gown, which she had attempted to modernize by the simple expedient of raising the waistline. Unfortunately, this had made the gown quite short, and so passersby were afforded a fine view of knobby ankles. "I think we should charge her fivepence for staring at us so, don't you think?"

Theo tried to smother a giggle, but with this and other such drolleries he kept her well entertained all the way to Milsom Street. When they arrived at the library, she was relieved to see that Mansfield was not yet there. Sir Francis excused himself and joined the gentlemen perusing the papers, while Theo pretended to take an interest in the books.

She was a little inconvenienced by the presence of an eager young clerk, who, more than a little smitten, persisted in inquiring what books she was seeking, forcing her to fabricate.

"It was—do you know, I just cannot remember the title. It will come to me, I know, if I just think about it a little . . ."

"Do you know the author's name?"

"No, I'm afraid that I cannot remember that either, though it was most highly recommended."

"Oh, well then, I am *certain* that I can help you. Is it a new book?"

"Rather new . . . well, perhaps not all that new. If I just look at the titles upon the shelf there—"

"Well, if you can just give me a hint as to what it was about . . ."

Desperately, she screwed up her forehead in a frown of concentration. "It was about a lady—"

"Good, good. Well, that narrows it down—"

Blast him. Would the idiot never leave her alone? And where was Isabel, anyway?

"Can you remember anything else about it?"

She mumbled something negative.

"Miss Westmoreland!"

Turning, she saw that Mansfield was at her elbow, a loverlike expression upon his face. The fat was in the fire now.

"Good morning, Mr. Mansfield," she said formally, then gestured frantically at a book. "That's the one there."

The clerk was more than a little irritated by the appearance of a handsome and adoring young swain, whose presence he felt was superfluous. "*The Lady of the Lake*? You should have told me at the first that it was a poem," he responded gruffly.

"I have these books to return," said Mansfield, stepping forward to place them on the counter, "and my aunt would like to order some others."

"You'll have to wait your turn," said the clerk rudely. He departed to get a ladder so that he could reach the desired volume.

"How happy I am to see you today," said Mansfield in a low, feeling voice. "It seems an age since last night—"

There was no time to warn him. Sir Francis suddenly materialized beside her. "Ah, Theo—run into one of your acquaintance, I see. How do you do? Permit me to introduce myself. I am Sir Francis Debenham, and it is always a pleasure to meet one of my niece's *friends*."

It had every appearance of being an assignation, and Theo knew it. Drat Isabel! Where was she?

Mansfield's countenance brightened. "Sir Francis *Debenham*, did you say? I am very pleased to meet you, sir. My name is Quentin Mansfield, and your son John is a particular friend of mine."

Sir Francis looked a little surprised. "Indeed? How very interesting—"

They were interrupted by the clerk, who having obtained the volume, thrust it without preamble at Theo. "There you are."

Sir Francis took the book from her trembling hand. "My dear Theo! Though I have known you all these years, I had no idea that you enjoyed poetry. What unsuspected depths you have!"

Mansfield was not one to let a little interruption deter him. "My aunt, Lady Verridge and I, have taken a house in the Royal Crescent. I hope that you might call upon us there if you wish—"

Sir Francis was not able to make a reply, for another voice pierced their ears at that moment.

"Oh, Theo! *Dearest* Theo!" Isabel had arrived, with Mr. Warwick and Julia close behind. Again introductions had to be made, which went as Theo might have predicted. Isabel was arch, Mr. Warwick was silent, and Julia giggled. Sir Francis seemed bent on charming them all.

"These are the *friends* that I told you I was to meet," said Theo, not without a touch of defiance.

"Indeed," commented Sir Francis, but he added quickly, "I think we had better allow these good people to transact their business here."

Quite a crowd had gathered behind them, and there were several angry stares, as well as comments about persons who didn't know enough to wait their turn. Abashed, Theo withdrew with her friends, leaving Mansfield to make his requests for the countess.

Sir Francis was full of pretty compliments for the girls, which encouraged both Julia and Isabel to treat him with great familiarity, quite embarrassing Theo. Warwick looked on in gloomy silence. In turn, the girls felt free to rally Theo about her handsome beau, and to assure Sir Francis that she and Mansfield were fast becoming the talk of the town. Theo felt ready to sink through the floor. Sir Francis, for his part, took it in good grace, flirting with the girls outrageously all the while. When they took their leave of

one another, one would have thought from his words that
Sir Francis would languish in despair until the moment he
saw their faces again.

Mansfield insisted upon coming up to make his farewells
also. At least Theo had nothing to blush for in his manners.
He clearly would have liked to offer them a ride in his
carriage, but since he was driving his gig, there was room
for only one other, making it an impossibility. If there were
one thing Theo might have faulted him for, it was his enthusiasm. She had long ago tired of hearing all John Debenham's virtues cataloged. Her head was beginning to pound
by the time he finally departed, and they were left to go on
their way.

"What a *polite* fellow," commented Sir Francis mildly.

The adjective seemed inadequate to Theo, but wearily,
she let it pass. "Yes," she said dully.

"And those friends of yours. Lovely girls. Charming. But
that beau of hers—what was his name?—does he ever say
a word or not?"

Despite herself, Theo had to smile and confess that the
matter remained a mystery to her also. Another thought
struck her, and she looked at her companion questioningly.
"Your *son* does not find them charming. He thinks they are
vulgar *cits*, and it offends his sense of niceness that I should
associate with them," she reported, accusation in her tone.

Sir Francis smiled, unoffended. "Did he say so? You'll
forgive me for saying so I know, but I can't think how I
came to sire such a stiff-rumped fellow. I've known two-
year-old children with better manners. Come to think of it,
he had better manners when he was two," he added, much
struck.

Theo had to laugh.

Sir Francis turned to her, his eyes twinkling again. "So,
he's been lording it over you, has he? Expecting you to
dance to his tune, no doubt. What a young clodpoll it is."

Theo's conscience had been troubling her, and now she
felt that she had to make a confession. "I am afraid that
we had an argument before he left for London. I told him
that we did not desire all of his interference. He was quite
in a rage, I think."

To her utter surprise, Sir Francis, instead of being taken
aback, began to chuckle, softly at first, and then gradually

louder, until his face became quite red. He had to stop and pull a handkerchief out of his pocket and wipe his eyes.

"I imagine that he *was* in a rage. Young idiot! It will do him a world of good, too."

His words were unfathomable to Theo, but at least she had the satisfaction of knowing that his father did not blame *her* for the quarrel. If only her mother would feel the same! But there was no sense in wishing for the impossible. Even though she disliked his son, Theo could have no difficulty in being cordial to Sir Francis.

Very much in charity with him, she made her way back to Gay Street. Sir Francis inquired after her mother, but they had delayed too long. She was already at the Pump Room.

"Perhaps I shall meet her there. Do you care to accompany me?"

She shook her head, fatigued. Not even the promise of meeting Mansfield there was enough of an inducement. She bid him farewell and went dragging upstairs to recover from the nervous strain that had been imposed upon her this morning.

Sir Francis went on his way, whistling a merry tune in what his son would have undoubtedly condemned as a vulgar manner.

From that day on, Sir Francis devoted himself to the ladies just as he had promised. His carriage appeared promptly every day to take the viscountess to the Pump Room. His escort was offered for whichever play, concert, or assembly that Theo had a particular desire to visit. Oddly enough, her desire to visit them had dropped off sharply with Sir Francis's arrival.

It was not that she didn't enjoy his company. It was hard to imagine anyone who would not enjoy Sir Francis's company. It just seemed so unfortunate that he had to appear at the exact moment when her relationship with Mansfield had become an accepted thing. Not that Sir Francis himself seemed to resent that. He looked upon the young couple with a fond eye. In fact, if Theo hadn't known better, she would almost have said that he was thrusting her at Mansfield. Mansfield himself was equally fond of Sir Francis. In fact, when she really thought about it, there appeared to be no reason for her to feel such dissatisfaction. Only one cloud shadowed her horizon. John Debenham.

She felt guilty about all that she owed him, despite his father's protests to the contrary; and when Debenham returned to Bath and found her on the verge of being engaged to his friend, she could only suppose that he would be deeply hurt. After all, he had practically declared himself before he left. Poor John. What a terrible blow it would be. There was the problem of her mother, too. Despite all Lady Westmoreland's protests, Theo knew that her mother still secretly wished that she would marry John someday.

It was while she was musing on this situation one morning that the great idea materialized. Julia had come to pay a call. She was very penitent about her previous rudeness, and determined to make it all up to Theo. At the moment, she was sighing over Mansfield, whom she had seen coming out of a chemist's in Milsom Street.

"Such a handsome gentleman and such an air as he has." She looked over at Theo with grave blue eyes. "You are so very fortunate, you know, dear Theo. He is perfection, and he is only *one* of your beaux." She had to give another sigh at the thought of Debenham. "I admit that I was jealous as a cat, but you must see that I had good reason." She looked at her friend with some diffidence. "I don't suppose you know if Mr. Debenham means to return to town soon?"

"No. I should think his father would know if anyone did, but there has been no word, apparently." She sighed for a different cause. "I don't know what I shall do when he returns. If only he had something to occupy him . . ."

Julia blinked rather rapidly. "You must admit it's not fair, Theo. Why, I would give anything in the world just to have Mr. Debenham take any notice of me or perhaps ask me to dance." Her expression became dreamy. "He's just so marvelous. I just know that we would be well suited." Her mouth drooped petulantly. "But I hardly have even secured an introduction to him. And of course, he won't look at anyone else while *you're* around." She gave Theo a sideways glance. "It's just not fair that you should have *both* the handsomest and most eligible gentlemen in Bath as suitors—"

Theo was heartily sick of hearing John Debenham's praises sung from this fresh quarter. *Handsome* indeed!

"And Mr. Debenham is so—"

"I know," said Theo in some irritation. "He's so wonderful. He's so perfect. He's everything a gentleman should be. Well, as far as I am concerned, if you want him so badly, you can have him!"

The words were scarcely out of her mouth before Julia pounced upon them. Her eyes opened wide in delight, she said, "*Really* Theo? Do you *mean* it?"

Oh, my word, what had she done?

"Are you serious—or were you just teasing me?"

The last part of the sentence had a rather plaintive note to it. Julia regarded her with expectation. "Let me think," said Theo.

It was true that she was herself uninterested in having Debenham as a suitor. Moreover, if he truly became enamored of someone else, her mother would finally have to abandon her hopes, thus paving the way for Mansfield. If Debenham was busy with Julia, surely it would distract some of Sir Francis's attention away from herself also. She and Mansfield would finally be allowed uninterrupted time.

"If you could just contrive for us to be thrown together for a little while, that would be all I would ask," added Julia pleadingly.

Of course the main obstacle was Debenham himself. He regarded Julia and her sister as vulgar *cits*, or so he had said. Of course, Julia *was* pretty, Theo admitted, as she regarded her friend narrowly. She was more conventionally lovely than Theo herself was, if less distingué. If the few novels Theo had read could be believed, many romances had even less auspicious beginnings. Sir Francis, for instance, seemed to have no objection to the girls.

"I know that my hopes may be for naught," continued Julia, "but if you would just be willing to make the attempt—"

What could it hurt, anyway? The worst that could happen would be that Julia's feelings might be injured, and she certainly seemed willing enough to take that risk.

"I'll do it," announced Theo suddenly.

Julia leaned forward, her eyes sparkling with excitement. "Oh, *dearest* Theo, will you really? Oh, I can just imagine how Isa's nose will be put out of joint. Mr. Warwick is the heir to a baronetcy, also, of course, but it is a new-made title, unlike Mr. Debenham's, and there can be no comparison between their fortunes!"

Theo was a little taken aback at the sheer ambition revealed in these artless words. "I thought you said that you thought Mr. Debenham himself was wonderful."

Julia looked at her, surprised. "Of course he is." She stared at her friend, trying to fathom her meaning. "I mean, after all, it would be foolish beyond measure to pay no attention to a gentleman's station in life if you mean to have him for a suitor. *You* did yourself."

Her words made Theo blush. How right Julia was. She herself had been no less mercenary in her pursuit of Mansfield. It made Theo a little uneasy when she considered it. Of course, she might comfort herself with the thought that it had all worked out for the best. Mansfield was smitten with her, and she . . . well, she had never met a more charming, handsome, or obliging gentleman in her life. Perhaps Debenham and Julia would be equally fortunate, although . . . She dismissed these doubts. There was no saying that this scheme would work in any case.

"You're not changing your mind, are you?" inquired Julia doubtfully.

"Of course not," Theo reassured her.

"Good! Then let us plan what is to be done."

How irritating Julia could be. "There is one small obstacle," Theo told her dryly. "Nothing can be done until Mr. Debenham returns from London."

Chapter Seven

As it so happened, succeeding events were to drive the Debenham problem far from Theo's mind. Among all the amusements of Bath, there was one that Theo had not yet been able to sample. As much as she wished for it, she had never been privileged to attend one of the fancy-dress balls. In London, masquerades might be considered rather *passé*, but in Bath, where time had essentially stopped, two fancy-dress balls took place each week.

For Theo, aside from the cost of the tickets, there was the expense of a costume to be considered. It could not be judged other than an extravagance. After listening to Julia and Isabel's raptures, she had once approached her mother timidly about it, but Lady Westmoreland had merely shaken her head at the idea. Not without sympathy, the viscountess had remarked that it was far too costly and had added that she was somewhat dubious about Theo's attending a *public* masquerade in any case.

Theo had borne this disappointment with fortitude, and had turned her mind to other things. In fact, the matter had not troubled her terribly greatly. It had been recalled to her mind forcibly when she learned that Mansfield was to escort the countess to one of the balls at the Upper Rooms on Thursday, Lady Verridge having a particular fondness for masquerades. Theo knew it was no use applying to her mother again.

It was therefore, a most pleasant surprise when Sir Francis coincidentally announced that he meant to attend the same ball, and asked the ladies to accompany him. The question of expense was raised and dealt with summarily. Slightly dazed, the ladies were left with the impression that his heart would break if he were not allowed to escort them and that money was of no consequence whatsoever, considering that it might easily prevent such a tragedy.

Theo was delighted by the result of his high-handedness. Noticing her mother's sparkling eyes and the new color in her cheeks, she had to conclude that the viscountess also was happy at the prospect. Sir Francis's coming had done her a world of good. The doctor himself had said that this sort of distraction, if not indulged in to excess, might do more for her than all the medicines in the world. Theo was certain that Sir Francis's solicitude had been of great benefit to Lady Westmoreland. She hardly could step outside without his carriage appearing. His coachman had standing orders to convey her to the Pump Room every day, as well as to church on Sundays. In addition, she was to let him know whenever she had an errand or a call to make. The only time Theo had seen Sir Francis really angry was when her mother had dismissed the carriage after arriving at the Pump Room, preferring to walk back home rather than make it wait. Sir Francis had been furious, particularly since the day was a damp one. He had told her that even if she did not wish to consider her own health, she might at least consider the plight of her daughter and her son, and what it would mean to them to be orphaned at their ages. He was equally irate with his coachman for disobeying his own orders at the viscountess's insistence, and had it not been for Lady Westmoreland's intervention, the fellow might have lost his position. Having never seen this side of Sir Francis before, Theo was taken aback, the more so as Sir Francis in a rage reminded her forcibly of his son.

Today, however, though still autocratic, he possessed all that charm that his son lacked. Theo found herself agreeing readily to take charge of procuring costumes for her mother and herself, with the bill to be directed to Sir Francis. Her mother had raised her objections regarding the possible vulgarity of the occasion. Sir Francis had smiled and answered that Bath had the advantage of being smaller than London and thus more restricted. A public ball here was akin to a private one in town. If Lady Westmoreland saw anything about which to object upon their arrival, he would be happy to whisk her and her daughter back home. There were no options left other than acquiescence and smiles.

Accordingly, in obedience to his directives, Theo had set out this morning to the costumiers, in order to procure suitable rainment for her and her mother. Although she knew it doubtless would be more expensive to hire, Lady Westmoreland could not resist asking for a Vandyke costume, for such had she been wearing the night that she met the late viscount. Theo had no such sentimental considerations and had decided upon a pink silk domino and mask. Both less striking and more concealing than a historical costume, it might allow her a certain degree of anonymity and thus permit her the chance to confer in private with Mansfield.

As long as she was in the shopping district, she had taken this opportunity to stop and buy some of the new brocaded ribbon she had been admiring. She had made her purchase, handed the parcel to the maid, and just stepped out into Bond Street when she almost collided with Mansfield. He smiled at her in the way that made her heart race before sweeping her an elegant bow. The little maid behind her stood dazzled.

As it transpired, he had been discharging an errand for his aunt, returning an unsatisfactory bonnet to the milliner's. He was on his way back to the Crescent now. Was Theodora also headed home and might he escort her? It was the moment for which she had been waiting.

She acquiesced in what she hoped was a pleasant rather than an eager manner, and they began the walk up Bond Street, talking all the while, the maid trailing behind them. They continued up Milsom Street, turned on George Street, and passed Edgar's Buildings with hardly any awareness of their surroundings. They were almost to Gay Street when Mansfield exclaimed, "This is utterly delightful. Might I ask that we prolong our walk?"

This sentiment was so much in tune with Theo's own that she agreed quickly and took the rather bold step of dismissing her maid, on the pretext that the latter needed to return the diminutive parcel to the house for her. Molly, having little experience of the duties of a true abigail, and somewhat more in the field of love, sympathetically abandoned the two to their stroll. Theo knew her mother would not be pleased, but such chances did not present themselves often.

They made their way to the relative seclusion of the gravel walk, and were amply rewarded for there were few others in it. They could talk to their hearts' content.

Their relationship had progressed both rapidly and well these past several weeks: all that had been missing was this opportunity for private conversation. Mansfield's tone now, while still gentlemanlike, was decidedly amorous, and Theo could not keep her hopes from rising.

She was the loveliest, the most estimable lady he had ever met. He found it hard to be apart from her and the current situation was intolerable, where they were only permitted together under someone's watchful eye. There was so much that he wanted to tell her, that he *had* to tell her. He had done his best to exercise restraint, but he could not any longer. He hoped that she would not be taken aback by his importunity, but he was willing to swear that although they had known each other only a short time, his feelings would remain constant. She was perfection itself, and he knew that he should not hope that she would return his affections, but—

"Ah, children, how are you today?"

Theo had never been less glad to see Sir Francis. What unfortunate timing! Absorbed by Mansfield's conversation, she had not even noticed the crunch of his footsteps approaching from behind. She turned and saw that he was smiling at them. She abruptly realized that this again must look like an assignation and flushed guiltily. Mansfield greeted Sir Francis politely, but with somewhat less effusiveness than previously.

With the greatest suavity, Sir Francis managed to detach Theo from her handsome escort, and before she knew it, her arm was tucked firmly in his and they were taking their leave of Mansfield. She was expecting and dreading a lecture, but to her surprise it never materialized, Sir Francis seemingly being content to discuss the more innocuous topic of the masquerade and how she had fared with her costume hunt. Keeping Julia's charge in mind, she asked if his son meant to return soon, but he replied frankly that he did not know. He understood that business was keeping him much occupied in London, but John was the poorest of correspondents.

"Another of his defects, my dear. I imagine that he'll turn up when I least expect him and when it is most inconvenient to my plans, for that is his usual method. A careless fellow, my John and I say so even though I am his father."

There was little Theo could say by way of response, so heartily did she endorse this opinion.

She was afraid that upon their return to Gay Street, he would step inside to apprise her mother of her transgressions. Instead, after seeing her in, he simply swept her a bow and remarked that it had been a pleasure to have been her escort. She was greatly relieved, but surprisingly, she felt more guilty than she had before.

She trudged up to her room, considering the matter. It was inauspicious that Sir Francis had appeared when he did. She could have sworn that Mansfield had been on the verge of making a declaration in form. It was a pity, too, that Mansfield couldn't have come to the point sooner—not, of course, that she wished any of those beautiful compliments unsaid.

Theo was not the type to let her spirits remain oppressed. After all, the proposal had merely been delayed. Perhaps Mansfield might call upon her later today or tomorrow to continue the conversation that had been interrupted. From this premise, it was not too hard to imagine her own acceptance and the bald green stares of envy the announcement of their engagement would inspire.

She could easily picture to herself the large wedding they would have and the beautiful satin gown she would wear. How Mansfield would delight in spending his wealth on her, pleasing her with one acquisition after another. They would have a large and comfortable establishment of their own, of course, with a generous suite of rooms for her mother, who naturally would have a substantial retinue of obedient servants to wait upon her. Westleigh Abbey would be restored to her brother somehow, though her dreams were deliberately vague in this respect. During the Season, she and Mansfield would be found in London, along with the rest of the *haut ton*. The countess would give her blessing to the match and . . . Theo's dreams abruptly ceased.

The countess was the problem. Of course, she had been most complimentary of Theo. She seemed to have a flattering desire for Theo's company. Lady Westmoreland attributed it to loneliness, since the countess's companion was still bedridden, and seemed likely to remain that way. Theo thought the explanation insufficient. The countess appeared to seek Theo out whenever possible. She certainly had exhibited nothing but complaisance at the sight of Theo dancing with Mansfield or being escorted by him here and there. She had not been along for most of their outings, it was true, but surely she was aware of them. Mansfield's nature was too frank for him to conceal anything of this kind. The thought comforted her. Why, his character was quite transparent! He would never declare himself without the countess's permission. He probably meant to call upon Theo formally, but happening to meet her, had been overcome by his emotions. Yes, she could certainly expect him in the next day or two. She smiled to herself in a self-satisfied way.

To her surprise, he did not come that day. She rose early the next morning and took special pains with her appearance, choosing a round dress of white India muslin, edged with lace about the high collar and fastened with silk buttons from neck to toe. It was in the very latest mode, and Theo knew she looked the picture of elegance in it.

It was therefore most disappointing when the morning passed without a visit from Mansfield. Her mother joined her, and though she noticed Theo's habiliment, she did not remark upon it. Instead, she asked if her daughter wished to accompany her to the Pump Room today. Normally, Theo would have accepted readily, for it often presented her only chance of having conversation with Mansfield, even though there was no privacy. Today she felt torn.

Should she go to the Pump Room in hopes of seeing Mansfield and thus possibly miss his visit here? Was it likely that he should decline to escort the countess today, though he had always gone whenever she felt up to it? It seemed improbable, and yet, Theo must admit that their business together far outweighed in importance a visit to the Pump Room. If he had the countess's approval, as she was sure he had, that lady would doubtless understand his defection for one day. In fact, knowing her routine as well as he did, he might realize that it would be his one opportunity to see her by himself, before speaking to her mother. That settled it. She could not risk disappointing him. She manufactured an elaborate yawn.

"I'm afraid that I stayed up rather late reading last night. I think I will just stay home and rest today."

Her mother looked a little skeptical, but made no comment, accepting her daughter's defection with good grace. Sir Francis arrived in his carriage, and as the viscountess departed, Theo could hear her laughing at some sally he had made. It was good to know that she was that happy.

Soon she would be even happier, Theo hoped, with her daughter's future settled, as well as her own.

It was hideously boring sitting in the drawing room by oneself. Full of desperation, Theo finally resorted to needlework, a task that she despised. She stretched the muslin in the tambour frame before it, and with a needle, jabbed at the fabric with unseeing eyes. She was working on a cap, a project that had involved many months of sheer avoidance. Peggy, checking on her young charge, was hard put to avoid exclaiming aloud in surprise when she saw Theo sewing. An hour or so later, the viscountess returned, and to do her credit, also did not mention how startled she was to see her daughter so engaged. It was as Theo had begun to suspect. Mansfield had accompanied his aunt to the Pump Room today.

She might have berated herself for this lost opportunity, but it could hardly matter, after all. He was merely fulfilling his obligations before he called upon her. Nothing could be more natural. The afternoon wore on, and yet she sat stitching away, more or less patiently, until the light began to fail. Would he never come?

The answer, she discovered sadly, was yes. He did not appear that day. She tried to conceal her disappointment. There were probably a hundred good reasons why he had not come. She had no idea of his schedule, after all. The masquerade ball was fast approaching, and the countess might easily have a hundred errands for him.

She considered the matter in a practical light. What had almost been a declaration had been surprised out of him, after all. Upon reflection, she must conclude that he had not *planned* to speak to her. Probably there were matters he must settle, business he must attend to, before he could make a formal proposal. She herself was not greatly conversant with such matters, but it seemed obvious that her mother or Sir Francis would wish for some kind of accounting from him before they permitted the engagement, and that the process might involve some time and trouble. She remembered the urgency in his voice and felt reassured. There was no need for her to worry.

At the same time, it would be less than wise to remove herself entirely from his presence. She would seek him out at the Pump Room and wherever else she could in order to stoke the fires of their affections. A few setbacks were inevitable. If she wished for another moment alone, there was always the masquerade.

In the next few days, she was successful in her quest for Mansfield. She met him at the Pump Room daily and at church. Though his eyes burned into hers speakingly, he obviously could not declare himself in public. It was the most frustrating situation she had ever experienced in her life. She was even denied the solace of Isabel and Julia's confidence, for she did not feel that she could talk to them as matters stood. She would be happy to inform them when things were settled, but for now she avoided all occasions for serious conversation.

It wasn't until the day before the ball that Theo managed to snatch a moment when the countess and her mother were otherwise occupied and whisper in Mansfield's ear.

"We should talk."

"How I have wished to! You cannot imagine—"

Her mother had turned her head and was looking back at her with a smile. "Ssh. Not here. At the masquerade. I will be wearing a pink domino."

He nodded in quick understanding. "I shall look for you, then."

She was able to tell her mother with perfect truth that they had just been discussing the fancy-dress ball.

It seemed to Theo that an interminable amount of time was required for the passage of the next day and a half. Her mother eschewed the Pump Room on the day of the masquerade, deeming it wisest to save up her strength for that evening. Theo could hardly excuse herself to go without the invalid. She would have to content herself with seeing Mansfield this evening.

She had chosen to wear the silver-trimmed Grecian frock that she had worn the day she had met Mansfield, not so much for sentimental reasons as because it was her finest. The pink satin slip beneath it would compliment her domino nicely, also.

Peggy had dressed her hair in a becoming new fashion, caught up with a silver net that left just a few ringlets on the left side of Theo's neck. When Theo put on her domino and mask, she had to admit to herself that she had never presented a more sophisticated or intriguing picture, despite

Peggy's deprecatory sniff and her muttered remark concerning "fine feathers."

It was the viscountess, though, that took her breath away. Dressed in pale pink satin from head to toe, she looked as if she had stepped out of a painting. The full skirt and fitted waist might seem incongruous beside modern fashions, but they were undeniably becoming. The gauzy sleeves, trimmed with lace and pink ribbon, gave her an ethereal cast, which was heightened by her pallor. The little fullbrimmed hat, caught up at one side with an ostrich feather lent her a rather dashing aspect.

"Mother!" Theo exclaimed. "How wonderful you look!"

Lady Westmoreland smiled rather self-consciously. "I was wearing just such a costume the night I met your father. I hope I do not present too odd an appearance."

Theo was murmuring to the contrary when her mother remembered herself and exclaimed, "But I have not even said how charmingly you look, my dear. That shade of pink becomes you so." She took her daughter by the hands and stepped back a pace to admire her. "Your very first masquerade! I can well remember how excited I was when I attended mine." She let out a little sigh. "How proud your father would be if he could only see what a lovely young lady you have become." A shadow crossed her face as she spoke.

"Mother—"

She squeezed her daughter's hand and released it. "No, we are only to think happy thoughts tonight. Is that Sir Francis I hear downstairs? Perhaps we had better go to greet him."

If Theo had been impressed by the picture her mother presented, it was clear that Sir Francis was even more so. Forgetting his immaculate polish for a moment, he exclaimed "My word!" then bowing deeply to her, added, "My lady!"

He was looking quite smart himself in a blue satin Vandyke costume, with a slashed doublet and breeches, falling lace collar, and a dramatic hat, boasting three ostrich feathers. He took Lady Westmoreland's hand and kissed it.

"You look precisely as you did when I first met you, at the first ball you and Harry gave at Westleigh."

She smiled, though she said severely, "You are shameless—and you have not even admired my daughter yet, though she is more deserving of your compliments."

His eyes crinkled around the corners as he turned to Theo. "You are wrong if you believe that I have not admired this beautiful young lady. I *did* fail to do so aloud, but will promptly rectify my omission."

Five minutes later, both ladies, by now laughing at the outlandishness of his flattery, were begging him to desist. "For," as Lady Westmoreland observed, "we are hopeful of arriving at the ball before it is over."

He obediently desisted and led them both, still in high spirits, to his carriage.

When Theo arrived, she was able to see that Isabel and Julia had not exaggerated about the delights in store for her. It was the most beautiful and picturesque spectacle she had ever witnessed. Various historical figures from Mary, Queen of Scots to Henry the Eight traversed the ballroom floor, shimmering in satin and lace and jewels, real and paste. Here was a Shepherd, there a wood nymph, conversing with a Chinese mandarin and a lady in Turkish costume. The elderly, the embonpoint, and the ill all were made glamorous by their costumes in Theo's sight. Defects were concealed or at least glossed over. It was little wonder that this outmoded form of entertainment had survived on in Bath.

And there were dominoes in every color: purple, pink, blue, and red, with black predominating. Admiring the effect, Theo thought that perhaps she had been wrong not to select a black one. It was so very striking, though the shade was not one that would become her. She could be satisfied with one thing, though. She had selected the best costume in which to assure anonymity.

She had been so impressed by the scene before her that she had forgotten to look for Mansfield and the countess. Lady Verridge was not already at the peeresses' seats. A quick scan of the room did not reveal the two to Theo's eyes. How thoughtless she had been in not thinking to ask what his costume would be. It might prove almost impossible to find him in this crowd.

Just as she was beginning to despair, she saw them enter the room, his height giving them away. They were attired somewhat incongruously as Harlequin and Columbine. He looked handsome even in motley, and it made her heart race faster just to see him. She abruptly remembered what this night might mean, and for a moment it was hard to keep from rushing over to his side.

It was clear that he was looking for her, too, and once again she could be grateful for the peeresses' benches. As he led the countess over, he spotted her, and she was rewarded by the broad smile that spread under his mask. What an evening this would be.

It was well after seven o'clock already, and the dancing had already begun. No one was surprised when Mansfield claimed her hand for a dance. When he led her to the floor, she whispered, "Let us dance for a few minutes, then we may withdraw quietly, so as not to attract attention."

He nodded his comprehension, and they took their place in the set.

Though they were somewhat obscured by the crowd, Theo kept her attention trained on the area where Lady Westmoreland sat. Satisfied at last that her mother was well occupied in conversation with Sir Francis, she gave Mansfield a meaningful nod. He crossed to her, took her arm, and they made their way from the floor together.

It is usually difficult to obtain privacy in a crowded, public place, but to ingenious youth there must always be a solution. No sooner had they located an isolated part of the building, than Mansfield seized her hand and kissed it passionately.

"You can't imagine the torment I have been enduring these past several days," he said huskily.

"I know," replied Theo softly, "for I have suffered also."

"What an angel you are!" he said, kissing her hand once more. "It has been agony to see you and yet not to speak to you."

Theo waited patiently for him to come to the point.

"When I think of Sir Francis's intervention while we were in the gravel walk—ah, I was never less happy to see any man."

"He may still interrupt us here," she reminded him. "I dare not linger too long."

He still retained her hand in one of his. With the other he removed his mask, and then hers. "I must see you to speak to you. Miss Westmoreland—"

"Yes—?"

"This is not the time or the place I would have chosen,

but I must ask you—that is I should be honored, although I know I am undeserving—"

"Yes—?"

"That is—" He actually was close to trembling. His face was flushed, and he was having difficulty speaking, "That is—I find that I cannot exist without you. I should be honored if you would consent to give me your hand in marriage—"

It was a time for maidenly protests and denials, but Theo ignored convention. "Oh, yes!"

They stared for a moment at each other, not quite sure what to do next, then he bent his head swiftly to her and kissed her. She had never been kissed before, and it was not quite as exciting as she had hoped. Perhaps it was an experience that one was able to enjoy better with practice.

He was ready to fold her in his arms and kiss her again, but Theo held him back. She spoke with maidenly diffidence, "I suppose, that is, I think we should go back and speak to my mother first."

He looked startled. "Yes, yes, actually, though, you see . . ."

"What is it?"

"Well, if the truth be told . . ."

This hesitation was beginning to drive Theo wild. "*Tell* me," she demanded.

He dropped his eyes. "It's only for a little while . . . I simply wish for the countess to become accustomed to the idea gradually."

"You mean you did not speak to her first?" asked Theo in shock.

He still could not quite meet her eyes. "No, well, you see, this all came upon me so suddenly—"

"In that case, I retract my answer," said Theo, her cheeks flaming pink.

He looked up now, genuinely panicked, and took hold of one of her hands as she was about to sweep angrily from the room. "My *dearest*! No, please do not say that. I understand how it must seem to you—"

"It seems to me that you have taken me for a lightskirt," said Theo wrathfully.

"No, no, my dear. It is for such a little while only. As I said, we have known each other such a short time that I imagine my aunt would hesitate—but after she has come to know you and to appreciate all your excellent qualities as I do, she cannot fail to give her consent."

Theo regarded him ominously. A secret engagement! It was the most shocking thing in the world, hardly better than an elopement. She looked into those pleading blue eyes and her heart softened. Would it be so very terrible to do this thing for a short time? After all, it was what she had been hoping for all along, to be married to him. If they were engaged, there would be no fear that some more beautiful young lady might come along and steal him away.

"*Please,* dearest. I promise you that it shall only be for a little while—I give you my word of honor."

It was insufferable and yet . . .

"I cannot live without you. Please say you will be mine."

The words were intoxicating. "Yes," she heard herself saying softly and then closed her eyes for another kiss. It was not disagreeable, precisely, but it was certainly not the sensation for which she had been hoping.

"Harumph."

They jumped apart guiltily to see a man in a black domino regarding them, his arms folded across his chest. "Good evening," he said unpleasantly.

"Debenham!" Theo exclaimed.

Chapter Eight

"How flattering that you should recognize my voice after all these weeks," he remarked, picking a bit of lint from one fold of the domino in a casual manner.

The color had risen to Mansfield's face. "This is not what it seems to—"

"You do not owe me an explanation. Come, Theo. Your mother has been wondering where you are."

He held out a hand. Theo felt like telling him what she thought of him, but in this instance she was on rather soft ground. How long had he been standing there? She prayed he had not overheard Mansfield's last words. She pressed her lips firmly together, and cheeks aflame, placed her hand in Debenham's.

He regarded her appreciatively, but he said, "You'd better replace your mask. Those blushes will give you away."

Mortified, she did as he asked. Mansfield was about to follow them, but Debenham held up a hand to keep him back.

"I should wait before returning. Less likely to occasion remark."

As Debenham tucked her arm in his and led her away toward the ballroom, Theo, burning with a combination of anger mixed with shame, could not entirely contain herself. "Insufferable—" She choked.

"It's not the time or place for a quarrel. Needn't worry I'll tell your mother, either. A shock is the last thing she needs."

His words were true, but oddly, it made Theo resent him even more. Just how much did he know? "You are the most despicable, interfering—"

They had reached the ballroom door and now he opened it. "Try to look pleasant, won't you?"

Aware of a few interested stares, Theo fixed what she

hoped was a smile upon her face, though her fingers dug cruelly into his arm.

"Foul-tempered vixen," he murmured, inclining his head low to her as if paying her the most delightful of compliments.

"Foul-tempered," indeed! He was one to talk. Still, she relaxed her fingers slightly and remained silent as he bore her into the room.

As they made their way, the dance ended and the master of ceremonies, Mr. King, announced that the time for unmasking had come. Debenham pulled off his own mask carelessly, while Theo followed his example. In the general hubbub that followed, they were able to make their way unobtrusively to the viscountess's side.

"She's better now, my lady," he said, bowing to her mother.

"Oh, Theo!" Her mother's eyes were anxious. "I never dreamt that *you* would take ill. It *is* dreadfully hot on the floor, though. Sir Francis persuaded me to take a turn with him, and I am afraid that I simply lost track of you. Do you feel like returning home? We may call for the carriage if you wish."

She did feel like going home, though not for illness's sake, but two things prevented her. One was the sparkle in her mother's eyes. Lady Westmoreland was truly enjoying herself for the first time since the viscount's death, Theo could tell. It would be wrong to cut her happiness short.

The other reason was the vision that had materialized at her elbow. Dressed as a shepherdess, in yellow satin from head to toe, Julia was at her most becoming, the tightly cinched waist emphasizing her generous curves. "Good evening, Theo." She cast her eyes hopefully at Debenham and colored prettily.

He made the minimum response politeness dictated, as Theo completed the introductions, though at least he did not leave. The music was beginning again. He looked at Theo. "Care to dance?"

Julia's eyes opened very wide. Now was her opportunity. "I am still feeling a little faint," Theo replied, "but it is possible that Miss Julia Simpson does not yet have a partner for this dance."

It was done as gracefully as she could manage. If Debenham did not follow her suggestion, Julia could save face by asserting that she had already promised it to someone else. To Theo's surprise, Debenham did not hesitate.

"Miss Simpson, would you care to dance?"

His invitation was accepted with alacrity, and putting her hand in his, he led her swiftly to the floor.

Really, Theo thought, watching them, anyone looking on might think that he had asked Julia to dance *first*. She was so preoccupied that she hardly noticed Mansfield's return to his aunt's side, nor the brief conversation that followed.

She recalled herself suddenly. This was going exactly according to *her* plan, after all. If Debenham did develop an interest in Julia, although Theo could not help but feel that event unlikely, the viscountess might at last give up her hopes. And of course, it would leave Theo free to spend time with Mansfield. The thought was not an entirely blissful one, but she shrugged off her doubts. The events of the night had happened too precipitately. She would need time to think them over. It was odd the way Debenham was smiling at Julia. He had never smiled that way at *her* before.

She had the entire night to think about Mansfield and her future. As she lay tossing in bed, it would seem to her one minute that she had been terribly wrong in agreeing to a secret engagement. The next moment, she would remember the melting look in his eyes and think that perhaps it was not such an *inexcusable* thing, after all. They were in love and they meant to marry. What could be more logical? Moreover, this match would bring her the wealth and position she had been seeking, for her and for her family. Bath was not full of young, handsome eligible gentlemen, after all. Her opportunities were limited. As long as he was willing to enter into an engagement, there was no point in delaying. If she set him free, was it so entirely unlikely that some pretty, scheming, ambitious miss should manage to divert his affections away from Theo? And he had promised that it would be for a short while, after all.

If only they'd had the opportunity to really talk, after the decision had been made. She thought of Debenham and her blood boiled. What a high-handed, interfering . . . But it did no good to continue with that train of ideas. She must speak to Mansfield alone. He would be able to soothe her worries on many points, she felt certain. Perhaps by "a short time" he meant just a day or two. Yes, she must certainly confer with him and discover what his plans were.

She rose the next morning with an aching head, but determined to visit the Pump Room and draw Mansfield aside. In contrast to Theo's malaise, Lady Westmoreland looked better than she had in weeks. Instead of being pale, languid, and drawn, there was a new glow in her eyes and color in her cheeks. Theo could not help remarking it.

"Oh, yes, thank you. I am feeling ever so much better today. I actually slept without interruption last night, for the first time in months—I suppose all the exertion of last night fatigued me sufficiently to do so," she said, dropping her eyes. She glanced up at Theo. "You don't look well, though, my dear. Are you still suffering ill effects from that fainting spell last night?"

"I have a touch of the headache," Theo acknowledged.

"My goodness, then you should certainly return to bed. You need not accompany me to the Pump Room, as Sir Francis has already promised to be my escort."

Theo blinked a little with pain, but she forced herself to speak. "No, I mean to go with you today."

"You *are* ill. No, I will not allow you to sacrifice your own health in this way. I will give Peggy orders to rub your forehead with a little Hungary water. You will be surprised how much better you feel. With that, and rest, and a little broth perhaps, I am sure that you will soon be feeling more the thing."

"No, Mother, I am going."

"I'm sorry, my dear, but we can take no chances with your health. I will call Peggy now—"

Seeing her plans vanish so rapidly into thin air, Theo, desperate, tried a new tack. "That's why I mean to go to the Pump Room. I feel sure that the waters will cure my headache."

"Cure your headache?" asked the viscountess doubtfully. "I never have heard of such a thing."

Theo improvised hurriedly, "Why, Lady Verridge mentioned it to me just the other day. It seems that when she was a young girl, she often suffered from the most dreadful headache and—"

It was an inspired direction for her argument. Lady Westmoreland had been heartily bored by the countess's recitations of all her various ailments, and had no desire to hear them recounted again in third person. Neither did she have cause to doubt Theo's story. By now, she was certain that there did not exist an ailment from which the countess had *not* suffered. "That's fine, my dear," she said, cutting her off. She frowned a little. "Are you sure that you wish to drink the waters yourself, though?"

Theo had reason to blush. She had often expressed herself upon the subject of the Bath waters, in no uncertain terms. She had tasted a glass, thought it quite unpleasant, and never sampled it again, exclaiming that she did not know how her mother managed to get it down. To suddenly wish to drink it was a most abrupt reversal.

She tried to smile and winced. "My head aches so that I would be willing to try anything which might be of benefit."

Her mother regarded her narrowly for a moment, and was apparently convinced. "Very well. If the waters have no effect, perhaps you may try the other remedies."

Theo gratefully agreed that she would.

The little incident should have served to warn her that the day was an inauspicious one, but Theo was too preoccupied to worry. It came as a shock, then, when Sir Francis arrived to escort them with his son at his side. Her mother had not seen fit to warn her that John would be accompanying them.

He was perfectly polite, but she felt that his eyes bored holes through her. He undoubtedly blamed *her* for everything that occurred. How like him! Of course, he could not guess about her secret engagement. He certainly would not have remained silent if he had known. She forced herself to be coldly pleasant, for the sake of her mother and Sir Francis, who were looking on. Oh, well. If he meant to reproach her, he could hardly do so with these two present.

Sir Francis and her mother had a delightful conversation on the way to the Pump Room in contrast to the marked silence she and Debenham preserved. Upon their arrival, Sir Francis, in his gentlemanly way, went through the crowd and procured the glasses of water, only raising his eyebrows slightly when he heard that Theo was to drink, also. Debenham looked at her curiously, but made no remark.

Drat it! Mansfield and the countess were nowhere to be seen. She took the glass from Sir Francis's proffered hand and smiled weakly. She was aware of three sets of curious eyes upon her. She tilted the glass toward her lips. My word, the smell of it was foul. She took a sip gingerly and choked upon it.

Her mother was drinking hers gracefully. "One doesn't mind the taste so much when one becomes accustomed," she told Theo.

The last thing Theo wished was to take another swallow of the water. All her protestations would ring hollow if she refused it, however. She bravely raised it to her lips and drank.

"That's the easiest way," her mother encouraged. "To swallow it all down at once."

Having finished, Theo could not wait to hand the glass back to Sir Francis, who was regarding her quizzically. If anything, the water was making her feel worse than before. Her head was pounding, and she was decidedly queasy.

"Shall I procure your second glass for you, then?"

She was hit by a wave of panic. Her mother did drink three glasses faithfully at every visit to the Pump Room, making six a day in all. Theo was certain that she could not get even one more glass down. Her fears were alleviated when her mother interposed, "Oh no, of course not. The physicians advise beginning the treatment with only one glass of water, in order to let the system become accustomed to its effects. Although," she added, regarding Theo doubtfully, "I am not certain that one glass will produce any effect at all."

It was producing an effect; it was making her sick. Theo thought it best not to mention it. "I am feeling better," she lied. "I don't think that I need to drink another glass."

Debenham turned away, though she had seen the corner of his mouth rise in a suspicious manner.

At last, here were Mansfield and the countess. He looked as handsome as ever, and she couldn't help feeling some pride. My fiancé, she thought, and soon the whole world will know it. She even had it in her heart to pity Miss Bromley, who was staring openmouthed at Mansfield in a most unbecoming way.

As soon as they spotted Theo's party, Mansfield and the countess made their way across the room. While Mansfield went to procure her glass of water, the countess took Theo's arm and engaged her in conversation. It was of the usual sort: her battles with flux and rheum, with piles and pleurisy, and the strong suspicion that an aching in her toe might be due to a latent case of gangrene. It was not Theo's favorite subject matter, but the way in which she had been singled out gave her hope. Perhaps Mansfield had confided in the countess.

Despite this optimism, she was glad to see Mansfield return with the glass of water. Her headache was not improved by listening to the account of the countess's ills, and her queasiness was growing. She was almost relieved when Debenham drew her aside, for Mansfield's attention was entirely taken up by the countess at the moment.

"Thank you," she whispered to him, as he took her arm and began to stroll about the room with her.

"—Intend to listen to that for the rest of your life?" he said in a low, angry voice, but having failed to catch the first part of the sentence, she could not imagine what he was discussing and merely regarded him in some confusion. He obviously did not expect an answer, for now he said more kindly, "You were looking peaked. Thought I'd rescue you."

Her gratification at these words evaporated as he regarded her keenly, and added, "In fact, you don't look the thing at all. You've lost weight, haven't you? It don't become you. All this hurry-burry don't agree with you."

Under normal circumstances, Theo had a hard time dealing with Debenham's tactlessness. With her current stressful situation, with a throbbing headache, and with a stomach that threatened revolt, it took everything she could give not to scream at him and begin tearing her hair out.

He seemed to sense that something was amiss. "Don't suppose you'd care to go for a drive with me," he said in a surly manner, "even if I needed to tell you—"

Thank heavens! Mansfield had managed to free himself from the countess, who was happily boring one of their acquaintances with sickroom news. Now he interrupted them. "Good morning."

"Morning," said Debenham curtly.

"I didn't have a real opportunity of speaking to you last night—"

Theo held her breath. Was he going to tell *Debenham*?

"About whether you had the chance for a look-in at Tatt's. I mean to set up my carriage soon, you know—"

Whatever Debenham felt toward her, it was apparent that

he did not bear Mansfield any ill will. "You're still settled on a team? You wouldn't rather purchase a pair and become used to driving two first?"

Mansfield's eyes brightened with excitement. "Of course not!" He glanced back at the countess and lowered his voice. "My aunt . . . well, she is an excellent lady, of course, but a little whimsical sometimes. *Now* she is happy to buy me a phaeton and four. I cannot say what her feelings on the matter will be in a few months, or even a few weeks."

Debenham's teeth flashed whitely as he smiled. So he had one attraction, Theo admitted. "It runs in the family, then? Very well. I did not mean to tell you unless you were determined, but as I mentioned to you before, St. George means to sell his horses at last. Poor fellow! Unless he lays his hands on plenty of the needful, he'll end up in the Fleet."

"As bad as that? Where should I write him?"

Surely this room was warmer than usual. Theo was feeling worse and rose.

"Don't need to. He's coming to Bristol next week. Told him to stop in Bath, and I might have a buyer for him."

"How can I thank you?"

Debenham smiled ruefully. "Try to avoid breaking your neck with them."

Theo was fighting the pain and the nausea with all her will, but she didn't think she could take much more. To her relief, Julia and her sister entered the room. The former smiled shyly at Debenham, and he promptly deserted them. Theo was feeling too ill to wonder at it.

"Mr. Mansfield—"

"Quentin, please, my dear."

"Quentin, I must talk to you—"

"I know." He had lowered his voice and was glancing about them nervously. It was certain, then, that he had *not* told the countess. It seemed as if he would rather not discuss the topic, but Theo was too ill to care.

"We must meet."

"It will be difficult."

Of course, it would be difficult. What a ridiculous thing to say! She put a hand to her forehead. Her illness was taking its toll. She must not let it exasperate her.

"I think I could contrive to slip out to the abbey tomorrow and then rid myself of my maid. We should have privacy there, and it will be most unexceptionable."

He stared at her admiringly. "Of course! How clever you are!" He frowned suddenly. "But I think my aunt might remark it if I told her where I was going."

Theo was truly feeling faint by now. Did she have to do all the thinking? "Then tell her you are going somewhere else." She had to get out of this overheated room. "Ten o'clock tomorrow. Please excuse me."

She darted away from him, barely hearing his assent. Her stomach was twisting itself about angrily. She rushed down the stairs and outside, and within a few minutes treated passersby to the spectacle of a young lady being sick. Fortunately in Bath, it was too common an occurrence to occasion more than a remark or two, though most of the invalids were less young, less attractive, and less well dressed.

The relief was great, but her head was still pounding mercilessly. She leaned on the stone wall, ignoring disdainful looks and remarks. A hand caught her elbow. She tried to shake it off, half turning to see who it was. Debenham.

What a sight she must be. She recoiled from him, but he did not appear to notice. He extracted a handkerchief and held it out to her. She wiped her face gratefully. "I am sorry, I—"

"I'm taking you home," he said firmly, and signalled to the coachman, who, miraculously was within sight.

"No, I—"

"It's all right." He spoke with surprising gentleness. "Don't worry."

In this instance, she was glad to be overpowered. She might have taken a chair, but didn't think she could have borne the motion. Walking was out of the question, as was a return to the Pump Room.

She allowed him to help her sagging frame into the carriage, and she settled back into the comfortable squabs with a sigh. For once she was grateful that he was laconic. She didn't feel like making conversation.

She glanced at him under her lashes. How like him it was to be kind when one least expected it. One could never understand him. She sighed again.

"Feeling a little better?"

She put a hand to her forehead. "Yes, it is just that my head—"

"You've been worrying too much. It will be all right."

She could almost believe him when he spoke in that sincere tone of voice. Of course, he didn't really know all of her troubles.

The short trip took an eternity. She closed her eyes and tried to bear it as best she could. Debenham took her hand and pressed it, reassuringly. For once, contact with him did not bother her.

When they arrived at Gay Street, he helped her down from the carriage, and over her slight protests, swept her up in his arms. She was rather a handful for him, she knew, but he did not seem to mind it. Peggy appeared, with a militant look in her eye. "What is—"

"Your mistress is ill. I will carry her upstairs," he informed her, as he proceeded to do so. Peggy offered no more resistance, but instead followed meekly behind, surprising Theo.

He laid her almost tenderly in her bed, and turned to Peggy. "She has a severe headache, and her stomach is upset. I think what she needs most is rest. Will you be able to see to her yourself or should I send for the apothecary?"

Peggy muttered gruffly that she was well able to take care of her young mistress. She began removing her slippers and her gloves. Theo was aware of lips brushing her hand and of a man's tread leaving the room. Peggy efficiently stripped her of the soiled gown and loosened her corset. She then drew the curtains, and Theo sank into unconsciousness as a roughened, but cool hand began to gently massage her forehead.

She must have slept until evening, for when she awoke, it was nearly dark outside. Her head was no longer troubling her, and she felt free to think matters over calmly. Perhaps it had been wrong to engage herself secretly, but marriage to Mansfield had been her goal all along. She would just have to make it clear to him tomorrow that she did not intend to delay informing their families. He was the most pleasant man she had ever known, and she suspected that it was his nature to avoid difficulties if he could. He probably just needed some gentle urging, to see how this entanglement reflected upon *her*. Debenham had been right. The last thing she needed to do was worry. Why, she had been making herself ill with it!

Thus directed, her thoughts turned to Debenham. How was it that he had happened outside at just the right moment? She had been quite preoccupied of course, but it had seemed to her that his entire attention had been taken up with Julia. She had seen the latter smiling and blushing at whatever compliments Debenham had thought to utter. Compliments! Could the leopard change his spots?

It was a puzzling question, but, after all, it was one that did not concern her. His momentary kindness to her was typical of him, as was his boorish, detestable behavior the rest of the time. Debenham was not without his virtues; it was just that they seemed insignificant in comparison to his flaws. Having thought the matter over to her satisfaction, she put on a dressing gown and began to make her way downstairs.

She encountered Peggy on the stairs, who regarded her with a look of surprise. "Are you feeling better, then, Miss Theo?"

"Yes, I am, Peggy."

"Don't you think you had better lie down again and rest longer? The cook's boiled a hen so I could bring you a cup of broth, and perhaps you would care for a crust to dip in it, too."

The concern in Peggy's voice was genuine. It was quite a novelty for Theo. She smiled at the servant again and said, "Thank you, no. I am feeling almost myself again. I will have the broth downstairs, and I might eat a morsel of chicken, too."

Peggy's face cleared. "In that case, Miss Theo, your mother would like to see you. She's been worried half out of her head about you. If you like, I'll bring a tray to her room for you."

Theo thanked her and proceeded downstairs to her mother's chamber.

Her mother was not reclining in bed, as usual, but instead was seated at her satinwood escritoire, writing a letter. Seeing Theo, she laid down her pen with a glad cry, and rose. "Oh, you are better. I am so glad! I was just writing a letter to your brother. He means to join us at the end of the term."

"I am sorry if I caused you any worry."

"Oh, my darling girl." The viscountess had crossed the room to take Theo's hand and gaze deeply at her daughter, as if to take in every detail of her face. "I should be the one to apologize. I had no idea that you were feeling so ill. I would have brought you home myself. Let us sit down, though, and talk. I can ring for Peggy to bring you some broth, if you wish it."

Theo murmured that it was on the way, as they took their seats in the little satinwood chairs, with French cushions in blue.

"I hope that your headache is quite gone, now. How I wish I had known! I really should have made you stay at home to rest."

"It is gone, and you could not have convinced me."

"And the water's making you sick! They are so mild, I was surprised—"

"I think it was the headache that made me sick."

"Well, I am most sorry," said her mother patting her hand lovingly. "I can be glad that Debenham was there, in any case."

Perhaps her curiosity might be relieved. "I myself was surprised to see him there—"

"Yes, well he said he had happened outside for a breath of fresh air and spotted you. It was most fortunate after all. As soon as he had taken you home, he returned with the carriage and told us what had occurred. Sir Francis was inclined to be irritated with him for absconding with it, but of course after he learned the cause—"

Well, she supposed it was probable, though she still didn't know why he had left Julia so quickly.

"He is the most amusing man."

Theo did not have to guess to whom her mother was referring. Seeing that the viscountess was prepared to talk, Theo settled back to listen. It was wonderful to see her mother so animated.

Lady Westmoreland's concern about her daughter extended beyond that evening. When Theo rose the next morning and prepared to dress, Peggy, instead of obeying her order to press her mull gown, went downstairs to report to her mother instead. The viscountess actually came up the stairs to confront her in her own chamber.

Theo protested that she had an urgent errand to run. Her mother countered that the maid might easily run it for her. She added that if Theo wished to prevent a recurrence of her headache, she should remain at home and recover her energies today. Theo stated that what she wished for most was a brisk walk in the fresh air. She was sure it would be of the utmost benefit to her. The argument continued on in this vein for some time until the viscountess tired and was finally obliged to yield to her daughter's determination, though she added that she could not quite like it.

Unfortunately, the time expended made Theo fear that she would be late for her rendezvous. Peggy dressed her more slowly than usual, complaining all the while, and siding with the viscountess in the matter of excursions. Theo felt like begging her to hurry, but she was afraid to arouse her suspicions. Once outside, she did not scruple to tell the maid Molly to step briskly along, and set off at a fast pace herself.

Every carriage that approached from the back awakened fear in her heart. It might be Debenham. Every masculine voice behind her made her quicken her steps, until Molly was obliged to protest. It was past ten o'clock, and Theo prayed that Mansfield was still waiting for her.

They reached the abbey in safety, Theo almost disbelieving that she had not been intercepted this time. She dismissed the maid, telling her to fetch a parcel from the shoemakers, Sir Francis having insisted that Theo have a pair of smart new boots.

When the maid protested that she did not wish to leave her, Theo replied repressively that she wished to pray and required privacy for doing so. Ignoring the girl's shocked look of unbelief, she added that Molly might easily return here afterward and meet her, so that she would again have an escort.

It was now well past ten, and Theo's heart was in her throat as she stepped into the gloomy magnificence of the abbey. After taking a few moments for her eyes to adjust, she saw that there were visitors here as usual, but she did not notice a tall, blond gentleman among them. Trying to be unobtrusive, she skirted the pews, looking for a familiar face. She listened to the voices, but Mansfield's was not forthcoming. Surely he wouldn't have given up so soon? To her relief, at least Debenham also was absent, although she had not really expected to encounter him here.

It seemed her plans were for naught. Perhaps it was just her nerves, but it seemed to her that people were beginning to stare at her curiously and make remarks. Surely a young lady should not be here unescorted. She chose a pew at the back and sat. Suddenly prayer did not seem like such a bad idea. She sank to her knees and closed her eyes.

As if in answer to her pleas, she felt a tap upon her shoulder. There stood Mansfield, his face shadowed by the pillar beside them.

"Here you are, at last!"

"I came as soon as I could. My aunt had errands for me to run."

A face a few pews in front of them turned around to glare at them. Theo rose, he took her arm, and they began to stroll casually about the abbey. She hoped they looked like visitors.

"They said you were ill the other day. I hope that you are well now."

She murmured an assent.

"My aunt thought it might well be the onslaught of influenza. I hope it is not a . . . communicable disease?"

It struck her that he was holding her rather gingerly. Perhaps she was imagining it, but it seemed to her that he relaxed as she returned a negative reply. She must not be so severe. Many persons were afraid of contagion, and in the household he lived in, well, it was little wonder that he should be nervous about it. But none of this was getting nearer the topic at hand.

"Quentin—you know that I cannot bear this sort of arrangement for long. Even the notion of having to meet surreptitiously as we are today, disgusts me."

"You were the one who suggested it."

She sighed. "Yes, because we have had no opportunity to talk. I cannot continue this way indefinitely."

He turned to her, his eyes anxious. "But things are going so splendidly. I told you that my aunt had taken a fancy to you. She was quite upset to hear about your illness. In fact, she said that she had been planning to invite you and your mother to the public breakfast in Sydney Gardens on Monday."

The melting blue eyes were weakening Theo's resistance.

"I am sure that if you are together only a time or two more that she will love you just as I do, and then we need have no fear of telling her. As I said the other day, it is just that she is such a whimsical person. If we tell her before she knows you well, she might take you in dislike—"

He did not need to explain the consequences to her.

"—Which would be fatal to our chances. Besides which, she is going to purchase a phaeton and four for me as you know and—"

"Quentin," said Theo, furious, "do not tell me that your carriage means more to you than I do!"

He appeared shocked and hurt. "Of course not! Why the very thought . . . naturally, there can be no comparison. But had you thought, my dear, that the carriage will be *ours* after our marriage? Wouldn't you rather ride in a phaeton and four than in a shabby gig with only one horse in front of it?"

What he said made sense. The picture he painted was an attractive one.

Chapter Nine

The expected invitation had materialized after services on Sunday. Though her mother again hesitated, conscious that they were placing themselves under an obligation, she at last had been forced to yield to the importunity in Theo's eyes. Again Theo had been aware of being singled out among the young ladies present. Miss Bromley had stared after her enviously as she walked along the aisle on the countess's arm. Theo could not quite contain her hope. Surely such distinguishing attentions could only mean one thing. Lady Verridge herself had selected Theo as being the young lady most worthy to receive her nephew's hand in marriage.

Given this fact, it was hard for Theo to understand why Mansfield did not choose to share the good news with his aunt. Yet, when the Verridge carriage, with its lozenges on the sides, arrived at Gay Street Monday morning, it was obvious from the manner of the occupants that the countess still did not know.

Theo had dressed with particular care today, again choosing the walking dress with the bishop sleeves and the new Spanish hat that accompanied it. Lady Verridge commented favorably upon her appearance, but without the archness that would have indicated that she was in on the secret. Theo tried to master her irritation with Mansfield. At all cost, she must be as pleasant as possible. She must make a good impression upon Lady Verridge. Theo opened her eyes wide and murmured to indicate her attentiveness as the latter began describing her latest symptoms of pains about the pit of the stomach, as well as the inevitable digestive disorders that accompanied them. The countess concluded with evident satisfaction that she thought she was succumbing to the first onslaught of the hysteric cholic, to which she had often been subject. It obviously pleased her that she had succeeded in mystifying her physician.

"For he recommended that I take quicksilver daily for a month in my water—which would cure a nervous cholic—but I told him that it would do no good for an hysteric cholic. Thirty or forty drops of Balsam of Peru upon fine sugar, if taken twice or thrice a day would have more good effect upon me than all the quicksilver in the world, and so I told him." She gave a pleasurable sigh. "He is considering giving me a course of electrifying treatments. I understand that one is given fifty to one hundred small shocks each time. I suppose it cannot hurt to try, since every other remedy has had no effect upon my illness."

Though her mother's expression indicated polite interest, Theo could read the thoughts it concealed. Wasn't it just possible that they would be treated to accounts of pustules and phlegm over breakfast?

By way of relief, she averted her eyes and turned hers to Mansfield's. They were as ardent as ever, and as she met them, he gave her a little smile. She imagined that she could read his thoughts also. It was as if he were telling her not to be misled by his aunt's eccentricities, that underneath she was a most worthy person, that she and Theo would come to value and esteem one another. His gloved hand was only inches from her own. How she would have liked for him to take her hand in hers and hold it. Unconsciously, she gave a little sigh. The countess glanced at her sharply, and Theo pretended interest once more.

Her determination to win the countess's regard was obviously meeting with some success, for when they arrived at breakfast, Lady Verridge tucked her arm in Theo's and said, "Let this pretty young lady sit down beside me. You may share her with me, Quentin, and Lady Westmoreland may sit on my other side."

The season still being in its early stages, the breakfast was not crowded, and they were able to secure their places upon the bench with ease. Theo had the impression that the countess was quietly studying her.

"Oh, how pleasant it is to have these fresh young faces about me. I am sure, Lady Westmoreland, that you realize how fortunate you are to have such a lovely young lady to bear you company."

The viscountess murmured an assent.

"Since it does not appear that my companion will ever recover enough to take up her duties again, I find myself in the awkward position of having to replace her. So difficult when one is far from home!"

The viscountess murmured that she was certain that Lady Verridge must have other relatives happy to take on the position.

"Yes, I do, but to tell you the truth, I am tired of having elderly people to wait upon me. I think I will try to find someone young and with more stamina this time—"

Theo hardly heard her words, for at this moment her eyes were attracted by a party just entering the room. It consisted of Sir Francis and his son, which was hardly surprising. What did make Theo open her eyes wide in astonishment was that they appeared to be escorting Miss Julia Simpson, with every evidence of complaisance. Julia was looking particularly fine this morning, Theo could see. But what made her gasp with indignation was that perched upon Julia's head was a white satin Spanish hat with a green rim, ornamented with cornflowers. In short, she wore a hat identical to Theo's own. What added insult to injury was that Julia, unbarred by pecuniary restrictions, had also been able to afford the green silk mantle that finished the ensemble.

If Theo's greeting was perfunctory when they approached, none of the party seemed to notice it. Sir Francis found a place just opposite to the viscountess, while Debenham helped Julia to a place beside him in the most solicitous way possible, before seating himself. He had removed the mantle before she sat, and Theo could see that Julia was wearing a new and exquisite dress of French cambric, heavily embroidered about the bodice and hem. The falling collar framed her seraphic features perfectly. Theo had to admit that she looked marvelous, and wondered if the color in her cheeks was due to rouge.

There were the usual sorts of greetings and banter exchanged. The best thing to have done would have been to have ignored Julia's pretensions, but Theo could not help remarking in a high, irritated voice, "How *lovely* you are looking this morning, my *dear*. What a pretty bonnet you have on, too. Just like mine, is it not?"

Julia did not appear at all conscious, replying brazenly, "How nice of you to notice. Yes, they are remarkably similar, aren't they? But do you know, I prefer mine just a trifle. I found a new milliner on Bond Street—French, as you may guess—and I think her work far outshines everyone else's."

It was not a remark calculated to conciliate Theo, nor did it. Unfortunately, further trials awaited her.

To begin with, although she might be honored by being seated near the countess, it was as she had foreseen. Graphic accounts of past illnesses were given, with the result that Theo had very little appetite for the cakes and rolls the establishment offered. It seemed as if every time she was about to take a bite, the countess would mention her experience of the bloody flux or something equally unappetizing, and Theo would put the roll back down, untasted. At least her mother was not suffering, for Sir Francis had taken it upon himself to monopolize her attention.

She might have expected some consolation from being seated by Mansfield, but he provided no conversational relief. In fact, his entire attention seemed to be concentrated upon attacking the rolls and cakes with all the energy he had. He reminded her not so much of the proverbial horse as of a young, healthy, and particularly vigorous horse, which has been deprived of its fodder for several days. The rolls and cakes were disappearing at a prodigious rate. She could not tell whether he allowed himself time to breathe between mouthfuls. The butter knife seemed to be everywhere. Once, she only narrowly avoided being stabbed. It occurred to her, forcibly, that she had never seen her intended eat before. Was this his usual manner of dealing with comestibles?

Her unspoken question was answered by the countess, who had noticed the direction of her gaze and now smiled upon her nephew fondly. "What a joy it is to be young! Such a wonderful appetite he has. I do love to watch him eat, also, my dear. My family were always prodigious eaters." She noticed the untasted roll on Theo's plate and frowned. "But you must have some breakfast also, to keep up your strength. You never know what will be required of you."

As Theo obediently lifted her roll and prepared to take a bite, the countess's mood shifted to a reminiscent one. "I remember when I was a girl, I could eat a tremendous amount of food. There was the time I ate three roasted chickens all by myself. Of course, I ended by succumbing to a cholic with great shooting pains, and the doctor decided to purge me. He gave me a spoonful or two of Daffy's elixir, but the chickens surprised us by coming right back up instead, although I do think he was wrong in maintaining that they had been the cause of my illness. Dr. West, I think it was. We did not use his services long."

Theo had put her roll back on her plate.

She toyed with it absentmindedly for a moment, then looked up to see Debenham's eyes upon her. Had he heard the entire exchange? She looked away, and her gaze fell upon Mansfield who was masticating obliviously and with great content. She dropped her eyes, very nearly blushed, and looked up at Debenham again, but his eyes were on Julia now.

This was perhaps the worst part of the entire breakfast, to be treated to the sight of Debenham and Julia with their heads close together. Theo was certain that Debenham was not being nearly as witty as Julia indicated. If she had to listen to one more fit of giggles, to one more exclamation of "Oh, Mr. Debenham!" she thought she would go mad.

She was relieved when they finished their meal and Debenham suggested to Julia that they take a stroll about the gardens, and amuse themselves among the serpentine walks, the Merlin swings, and the grottoes.

"I should like to see the labyrinths," squealed Julia enthusiastically. Theo was not surprised by this choice of destination.

Debenham courteously asked his father if he cared to join them, but Sir Francis waved away this offer with a languid hand. "I leave this sort of exercise to the young, and do not fear that my presence will be missed at all. Meanwhile, I shall be most happy in the company of these two delightful ladies." The countess smiled vividly at him. She was no less susceptible to his charm than anyone else.

Theo was busy counting her blessings. At least she wouldn't have to listen to any more of Julia's giggling this morning. Perhaps she and Mansfield could contrive to slip out later and have a private conversation of their own, that is, if he were finished eating by then. She dared to glance at him again, and saw thankfully that he evidently had finished the repast, for he was wiping his lips with fastidious care.

She was a little taken aback when Debenham turned to Mansfield and asked if he and Theo also cared to take a stroll. She was disconcerted even more by his acceptance. The last thing in the world that she wished to do was to take a walk about Sydney Gardens with Debenham and Julia. She shot Mansfield an anguished glance, but he had already risen and was holding his hand out to her politely.

There was nothing to do but to put a good face upon it. She rose, and with his assistance made her way from the bench, although a stout lady who was sitting on the other end of it scowled at them dreadfully as they made their way with difficulty past her.

Once outside, it was clear what her fiancé's motives had been in agreeing to this promenade. He had his new equipage very much upon his mind.

"I say, Debenham. Have you had any word yet from St. George about when he'll be in town? I shouldn't wish to waste any time in speaking to him about his horses and his carriage."

"I expect him tomorrow afternoon. Your mind's made up, then."

"Yes, quite."

They fell into a discussion of curb chains, and pole chains, and splinter bars, and various other incomprehensible things that bored Theo half to death. It was inevitable that she and Julia should find themselves walking along together as the gentlemen obliviously rode off on their favorite hobbyhorse.

There was a certain stiffness at first, but then Julia took her arm and said cajolingly, "Oh, Theo! Don't be angry with me. I thought your bonnet was so smart, I had to have one, too—a lot of ladies have them by now."

It was really impossible to remain angry with Julia, but Theo tried, "They are all not *exact* duplicates of mine. How awful, too Julia, to say you thought yours was prettier."

"I couldn't resist teasing you a little. Besides, you always look so . . . so . . . I don't know how to say it, but you know, your clothes always look more elegant than anyone else's. Something about the way you hold your head, I think. Come, Theo, I couldn't bear it if you were *really* angry with me. Say you're not."

Theo could hold out no longer. "Very well, I am not."

Julia giggled and drew her arm closer into Theo's. "I just

had to tell you. I left Isa at home, mad as fire. Mr. Warwick has a cold and is forced to stay in bed, so she has no escort. I lorded it over her this morning, since I had a beau coming to take me out, and she had none. And John has a far older title, is much handsomer, and a good deal richer than Mr. Warwick. She can't stand it!"

Theo winced. She was shocked to hear Julia refer to him by his Christian name. Why she herself had never called him "John" in her life. She also disliked the casual tone Julia used, as if he were some sort of prize she had won at a fair. It seemed terribly cold-blooded, and she hoped that Debenham had an inkling that . . . She stopped herself suddenly in mid-thought. Worrying over Debenham! Why that was the most ridiculous turn she had taken in her life. It would serve him right if Julia did break his heart. Somehow, though, she hoped Julia wouldn't.

Her run of bad luck was not yet out this morning. In between admiring the vistas and the waterfalls, and losing themselves momentarily in the labyrinth, the gentlemen decided that, upon purchase, the new equipage should be tried out on a real expedition. Before Theo knew what was happening, it had been agreed that they would all drive out Thursday morning to see Farley-Castle, which Julia had apparently been hungering to see. It was odd how Mansfield's fear of upsetting his aunt's schedule disappeared when the topic of his carriage arose. She was forced to remind him that Lady Verridge would be waiting for them. He consulted his pocket watch, remarked that he had no idea it was getting so late, and they began back to the breakfast room.

At last they were rid of Julia and Debenham. Theo sighed with relief, an emotion that was to be short-lived. For now Miss Bromley approached them, on the arm of a young lady Theo knew only slightly. Theo had not seen her antagonist at breakfast, but Miss Bromley apparently had been there, for she now asked whether they were returning to the breakfast room. When they assented, she invited herself to join them, and Theo unwillingly found her arm drawn into the other's.

"It is too narrow, we cannot walk so many abreast," Theo protested.

"Well, your beau may escort my friend then," said Miss

Bromley casually. "I wish to talk to you, dear Theo. We've hardly had a chance to chat since you've arrived in Bath."

And whose fault is that? thought Theo, but she left the sentence unuttered.

"Your beau is so very handsome," commented Miss Bromley, parting her pretty but slightly pointed teeth in a smile. "But then, I always thought Mr. Debenham the most attractive gentleman here. It looks as if that younger Simpson girl has stolen him away from you, though."

Theo stiffened. "Mr. Debenham never was my beau, and I do not appreciate your speaking as if he were."

Miss Bromley shrugged. "Well, if that's what you want everyone to believe, no one shall ever hear otherwise from *my* lips. You're keeping a good face upon it, my dear. How much has Debenham got, though? Twenty thousand pounds a year anyway, I should say. What a pity he slipped through your fingers!"

Theo withdrew her arm from Miss Bromley's. "You are insulting!"

The other opened her eyes in mock disbelief. "I am *so* sorry. I certainly did not intend to be." She attempted to take Theo's arm again. Though the latter had no wish for her to do so, to wrestle with Miss Bromley could only create a scene. Theo submitted reluctantly.

"All this talk has almost driven it out of my head. Mother and I intend to give a little party—not really a ball, though there will be dancing. I do hope you and the viscountess can come, provided she's well enough. We shall be sending out the invitations soon."

They had reached their destination, and Theo parted from her tormentor with admirable restraint. She could not help venting an exclamation as soon as Miss Bromley was out of earshot. Mansfield turned to her, surprised. "Whatever is the matter, my dear?" he asked in his gentle way.

"I simply can't stand that . . . that person!"

He gazed after Miss Bromley's retreating figure puzzledly. "She seemed nice enough to me," he commented. Then added before she could elaborate, "But here, my aunt and Lady Westmoreland are looking for us."

"Your letter, sir." Debenham took the letter from the silver salver. Nodding a dismissal to the liveried servant, he broke it open and perused it eagerly. Sir Francis, seemingly preoccupied with his newspaper turned a page and shook it ostentatiously, before settling down to read again.

An exclamation burst from his son's lips. Sir Francis dropped the paper and peered over it. "Good news?" he inquired.

"We have him, at last. I think we do, anyway. Sanders has said that his inquiries have met with success. He thinks he has the address of the partner in this affair. Had to go through the entire list of directors to try to find one who might be linked to Oliphant."

"Do you mean to return to London now?"

Debenham shrugged. "He advises me to wait until things are more certain. I'll give him a week or two."

"I trust you are making all this worth his while. You still are opposed to calling in Bow Street?"

Debenham shook his head. "Yes, I am. If he got wind they were on his trail, he'd vanish. And even if they found him, he wouldn't conk. It was his scheme, and he was in it just as much as Oliphant. He was just unlucky enough not to benefit."

"If by not 'conking' you mean that he would be unlikely to talk, I can see the force of your argument, although I wish you would refrain from using such low expressions around your aged parent." He had abandoned all pretense of looking at the paper now and gazed directly at his son. "If you imagine that you are going to see this pursuit to its end all on your own, you are mistaken, however."

Debenham began to protest, but Sir Francis cut him off. "Understand me. I was the executor for the estate as well as Harry's best friend, and those ladies are *my* responsibility. Like it or not, you will need my aid."

Seeing that he had silenced his son, he picked up the paper again. "And you might well consider that I was up to every rig in town long before you were breeched. I'm as leery a cove as there is, I am." He smiled with pleasure.

"But sir—" Debenham again was moved to words.

"I also need to know before we get close to our quarry. The ladies will be all right here in Bath as long as one or the other of us is here to keep our eyes upon them. I am concerned about the boy, however. I have asked his Head Master to keep an eye on him for now. He will require additional protection if the game becomes dangerous, though."

"Yes, sir."

Sir Francis studied his son keenly. "There is that one other little matter."

Debenham made no reply, but waited recalcitrantly.

Sir Francis pretended to interest himself in his paper once more. "I am only a doddering old man, of course, but I would advise you to tread carefully. It's not that I don't appreciate your strategy—it's just that I've seen this sort of thing misfire more than once."

"Sir?" Debenham pretended incomprehension.

Sir Francis, who by now clearly was absorbed by the news of the Regent's plans for a grand fete, apparently was not attending.

By now Theo had no real expectation that Mansfield would inform the countess before the purchase of the carriage was made final. Therefore, although she passed the next several days with no delightful surprises, there were no crushing disappointments to be borne, either.

The countess continued to set Theo apart by her attentions, and the latter thought it unlikely that there could ever be a more propitious time to inform her. Theo had said all she could to Mansfield on the subject, however. Now she must submit to his superior knowledge of his aunt's peculiarities.

His looks were as ardent as ever, but his preoccupation with the subject of his carriage made his company less appealing than formerly. In any case, Theo did not arrange for any more rendezvous with him. Her conscience was already paining her in that regard, and it was obvious that an assignation would accomplish nothing. With luck, no one would ever know about this period of secrecy.

There was Debenham, but if he had known, he surely would have said something to her by now. Of course, he had other matters on his mind at the moment. He had spent Tuesday morning at the Pump Room in the company of Miss Julia Simpson. Although Theo had not been privileged to attend the dress ball at the Upper Rooms on Monday night, Miss Bromley had and was kind enough to inform her that Debenham had danced twice in a row with Julia and remained by her side for most of the rest of the evening. Theo had also happened into the two coming out of a shop in Milsom Street together, and once she had seen them flash by in Debenham's green and gold phaeton. A curious feeling had pricked at her. It was not really envy, for soon she would be riding in a phaeton with the hand-somest man in Bath. She supposed that despite all their branglings, she did not really wish for harm to come to Debenham. It surprised her a little that he apparently en-joyed Julia's company so well, but given that he did, she hoped that Julia did not disappoint him. She was a flighty creature, after all. Should an eligible peer present himself for example, it was only too probable that Julia would aban-don Debenham without a backward glance. Theo almost wished that such a person might happen along, if only that Debenham might see Julia for what she was before it was too late.

The thought surprised her as soon as it appeared. Julia was not such a terrible person. She was Theo's friend, and if she was a little flighty, well, she certainly might improve with maturity. Theo should be much obliged to her for tak-ing Debenham off her own hands, although Mansfield's courtship had certainly not gone as Theo had planned.

It had been suggested that Isabel and Warwick accom-pany them on their excursion to Farley-Castle, but these two had been forced to bow out, as Julia gleefully informed Theo Wednesday morning at the Pump Room. "—For, as you know, Mr. Warwick only has a gig with one horse, so they should be left far, far, behind us. John was most polite and suggested that he take his father's barouche, so that they might ride with us, which I confess I would rather he hadn't done, considering the way Isabel has treated me— but luckily, she was too proud to accept such an offer and said instead that they had made other plans. Other plans! I know she has been dying to see Farley-Castle for a month— ever since our aunt went there and gave us such a good report of it. Neither of us has ever been inside a real cas-tle," she added ingenuously.

While Theo could understand Julia's desire to revenge herself on her sister, she found her gloating distasteful. There was little she could do, however. It was true that a one-horse gig had little chance of keeping up with a team of horses. She turned the subject instead to what Julia meant to wear on their expedition, a topic that the latter entered into enthusiastically. She had gone on at some length about her new carriage dress of blue lustring, as well as her smart new bonnet of chip with *three* ostrich feathers dyed a shade of blue to match her gown. Only after a few minutes did she tactlessly inquire which dress Theo meant to wear.

"Oh, I suppose my corded muslin," said Theo carelessly, as if she also had a number of gowns to choose from. In fact, she only had two carriage dresses. It occurred to her that the last time she had worn this one was on her drive with Debenham. She refrained from mentioning it, and was glad when she turned her eyes to see Debenham hovering near them.

"Oh, Mr. Debenham!" squealed Julia. Theo was grateful, at least, that she did not choose to shout his first name aloud. "You must not monopolize me so. What will everyone say?"

He bowed to them both, glancing briefly at Theo before letting his eyes come to rest on Julia. "I have never cared what anyone might say—"

Which was true enough, Theo had to admit.

"Come, take a turn about the room with me, Miss Julia."

With a giggle and a flutter of her gloved fingers at her friend, Julia allowed herself to be led away. It was true that opposites must attract, thought Theo, for she would never have imagined that Debenham would be courting a girl of whom he spoke so slightingly just weeks earlier. She sighed without knowing it, and turned to look at Mansfield. It appeared that he was boring some young gentleman of his acquaintance with details of his new equipage. Theo had no desire to make a third in that conversation, nor to join the countess, who appeared to be pouring an account of all her sufferings into Sir Francis's sympathetic ear. But perhaps she was misreading the situation, for her mother, on Sir Francis's other side, appeared to be very much amused, and at his next remark, both ladies broke into pleased laughter, and the countess rapped him playfully with her fan. Theo wondered bleakly why his son could not have inherited at least a trace of the father's charm. Of course, Julia seemed to have a different opinion of him. Those shrill giggles, clearly audible across the room, were making Theo ill. Well, at least she wouldn't have to listen to them on the carriage ride.

*   *   *

When Thursday morning arrived, Theo was prepared to overlook all these minor irritations and to allow herself to wholly enjoy the expedition. It was true that their relationship had lost some of its sheen, but she was to have almost the entire day alone with Mansfield, and she meant to make the most of the opportunity. She was looking her best in the corded muslin dress with the lilac ribbon about it. They were fortunate in their weather, for the day promised to be a lovely one. She had asked Cook to pack a lunch so that they might have the pleasure of dining alfresco. Mansfield was certain to be in a good mood, with his new carriage and horses to flaunt. She must not allow anything to mar this bliss. In fact, in a few months, or perhaps even weeks, they might be husband and wife, setting off on a similar expedition. She tried to make the picture attractive and failed. Of course, she hadn't seen the carriage yet. She must be prepared to admire it when he arrived.

It was not difficult for her, for the claret-colored phaeton, picked out in black, was a dashing vehicle, and privately she thought it more noticeable even than Debenham's. Though Mansfield remarked courteously on her appearance, she could tell that his thoughts were full of his new equipage, and he certainly did not disdain any of her compliments upon it. He was looking handsomer than ever, with that glow of excitement in his eyes, and Theo could feel her breath coming a little faster than before.

Debenham, who was to meet them there, was a trifle late, but they passed the time so pleasantly, that a full five minutes elapsed before Mansfield remarked that it would not do to keep the horses standing about. Theo had secretly worried about what her mother might think about this expedition, not only to see her with Mansfield, but also to see Julia with Debenham. Of course, she must have noticed them at the Pump Room, too, but whatever the viscountess might have felt upon the subject, she kept to herself. She had already left for her visit to the Pump Room this morning, bidding Theo good-bye with equanimity. Well, that was what Theo had been hoping for, after all. Now her mother must finally accept the fact that Theo and Debenham would never marry. She cast her mind back to that drive they had taken to the caisson, and wondered to herself if she had been mistaken about his intentions. Surely a man who had been about to declare himself to her would not take up with Julia so soon afterward.

But she was allowing her thoughts to run away with her again. She must focus on this present, happy occasion instead. She smiled warmly at Mansfield, and was surprised to be met with a frown. Debenham was certainly taking his time. Mansfield would be obliged to take his horses for a turn down the street unless—

The frown disappeared to be met by a smile. Here was the green and gold phaeton, making its way toward them. Now they could be happy again, Theo thought. Mansfield helped her into the phaeton, pressing her hand warmly before releasing it. Surveying her surroundings from high up in the air, she felt like a queen upon her throne and thought that at this moment she could not envy anyone. Debenham drew his horses up behind Mansfield's.

"Ready?" Debenham asked.

"Why yes, that is, I suppose you know the route."

"Take the road as if you were going to Phillip's Norton—you know the one, I s'pose—we will turn left at Hinton. You may follow us, after all. I don't s'pose you've had the horses out on the road yet. We'd better take it slowly so that you may be accustomed to them."

"I've driven them all over town," replied Mansfield, his color a little high. "And I daresay we won't see you after we leave town, for I mean to try their paces."

Debenham looked as if he would like to say something more, but instead he merely expelled a breath before adding, "Couplings are a bit long, aren't they?"

"It's how I like them," replied Mansfield, a little incensed. He strode to his carriage and took his seat. "We'll see you at Farley-Castle."

Debenham's face was expressionless. "Make certain to avoid the old road, then."

Mansfield said not another word, but picked up his whip and his reins, and gave a nod to the groom. The latter let go of the leaders' heads and scrambled to his seat in the back just as Mansfield started the horses and they began on their way.

Chapter Ten

How like Debenham it was to mar their happy mood at the outset. Mansfield, seriously irritated, had started off at a dangerous speed, leaving the others far behind. He was driving in a way that, although it was calculated to show his expertise, instead awakened feelings of nervousness in Theo. Seeing his scowl, quite an unusual expression for him, she dared not say a word for several minutes.

When he bowled around a corner at high speed, she could contain herself no longer. "Oh, please slow down," she begged, but met with no response. "That woman!" She gave a little shriek. "Oh, thank heavens, she hopped out of the way in time. *Dear* Quentin, please—" Here she gasped as he only narrowly avoided grazing the wheels of a carriage coming in the opposite direction.

Her words might have had some good effect, but unfortunately she negated it by adding, "*I* do not care what Debenham thinks, after all and—"

"Debenham!" He gave a bitter laugh. "Oh, I know, he's top o' the trees. He's the best whip in the kingdom. I should be *honored* he wanted to give me advice."

"Why, no—" Theo was beginning, shocked.

"Just because he was willing to introduce me to his friend, who happened to have a carriage for sale, I should defer to his judgment in everything. After all, no one taught me to drive when I was four years old."

Theo was becoming a little angry herself. "This is entirely ridiculous! If you would listen to me for a moment, you would realize that I think just the same way that you do. Debenham is *insufferable*, and has been ever since I have known him."

Mansfield was startled enough to check the horses a little. "Is that truly what you think—?"

"Of course it is. He is the most insulting, ill-mannered—"

There was genuine surprise on his face. "I thought . . . I thought when we met that you had a *tendre* for him . . ."

"For *Debenham*?" She could not contain her astonishment.

"Everyone seemed to think that you might—that you might make a match of it." For the first time, he looked a little embarrassed.

Theo had to laugh. "That was my mother's scheme, not mine. Do not tell me that it actually worried you!"

He shook his head and turned to give her that ardent smile that had become so necessary to see. "Of course not. It's only that's he's older, and—"

She smiled mistily back. "You are the only gentleman I have ever cared for—watch out!"

He turned to see the peddler pushing his apple cart, and with a quick correction of his reins, just narrowly avoided hitting him.

"Sorry."

"It's all right," said Theo with a carelessness that she was far from feeling. She added hurriedly, "We may talk at greater length when we are out of the city. There is so much traffic here, and the streets are so confusing."

Her words were unfortunately prophetic. From what Debenham had said, she was certain that the road they were to begin upon was the same one that had led them to Combhay. After they had left the city, they found themselves upon a steeply declining and rutted road that was nothing like the one she remembered from before.

"Confound Debenham! What does he mean by sending us out upon a cart track? I'll be lucky if one of my horses doesn't sprain a tendon."

It was dangerous work, but Theo had to let him know. "I am not sure that this is the road I have taken before," she ventured with some diffidence. "None of this looks familiar to me."

"Eh?" He stopped their jostling progress and looked about him.

"This might be the old road he mentioned—"

He shook his head. "Well, I don't see anywhere to turn around, so we've no choice but to go on. Since it's the old road, it should meet with the other, anyway."

That was true. Theo gripped the side of the carriage tightly as they began on their bumpy way.

She could be glad at least that they were now moving at

a slow rate of speed and that there were no obstacles for them to encounter. Her relief was to be short-lived. As they descended, they could see that they were approaching a village. Mansfield's face brightened. "We can ask directions here," he remarked confidently.

His words were to prove optimistic. As they drew nearer, they could see that the seventy or so houses that comprised the village were small, mean, and squalid. At the outskirts of the town, they were accosted by a group of beggars. Theo was forced to avert her eyes from the wretched spectacle, and to close her ears to their piteous wails.

Though the groom did his best to beat them back, exhorting them to stand clear, their thin, dirty hands caught at Theo's gown, and she could not help shuddering.

"Stand back! Stand back!" Mansfield had added his cries to the groom's, but the beggars followed them through the village. At last, seeing that there was no profit to be obtained from this quarter, the beggars gave up and let them proceed on their way.

"Theo, my dear—I'm so sorry you had to see that."

The groom spoke in a low voice.

"Johnson here says that this little village is the beggars' home. They stay here mainly to prey on the wealthy visitors during the season. Contemptible lot! I've no doubt most of them are charlatans. If their cases were truly unfortunate, they could seek relief from the parishes from which they sprung. I suppose begging is preferable to a little honest labor, however. There was quite a pretty little chapel there. Pity it is in the midst of all that filth."

Theo took strong exception to his words, but she held her tongue. Now was not the time for quarreling. He just was undoubtedly repeating words that he had heard before, and he was speaking in the heat of the moment. It had been an unpleasant experience, after all. It was probable that he felt even worse for having exposed her to it. She met his eyes and gave a little smile.

"It is all right now."

He smiled back, relief evident in his handsome features. "Yes, well, there's one benefit. See what a lovely view we have of Bath!"

Theo had never felt less like admiring a view, but now she did so, obediently.

*   *   *

The rest of the trip to Farley passed without incident. Mansfield meant to urge his horses, in order to make up for lost time, but Theo was able to protest with perfect truth that her nerves were too susceptible to stand for it at the moment. To his credit, he did not protest, but drove her at a sedate speed, which was a double relief for she now had begun to doubt his coachmanship. He had twice dropped the reins in trying to "loop" them, and had very nearly snagged his whip in a tree while attempting to catch it above his head. His horses fortunately seemed to be of a uniformly phlegmatic disposition. Theo had to be secretly grateful to Debenham for suggesting them. It was a pity that a superior equipage made for an inferior driver. If he had been content to drive along as quietly as he had in the gig, she thought they might have managed without mishap at all.

Fortunately, they found the turn at Hinton with little difficulty, and soon their carriage was climbing up a hill to the ruins of an abbey. All was not destruction, for there stood a church on the summit. Though Theo was no antiquarian, she might have liked to stop and visit the picturesquely situated building, but as they were undoubtedly late, she knew they must press on.

Near the bottom of the hill, lay what remained of the castle. There was still a strong arched entrance, fragments of thick walls, and two ivy-covered towers. The original chapel appeared nearly perfect. There was also a modern manor house, obviously constructed of material from the ruins of the abbey, but it was of less interest to her.

As they approached, Theo could see that Debenham had already arrived and was waiting for them. When they drew near, she noticed that under her blue silk parasol, Julia's pretty face was set in a pout. As soon as they had stopped, she came rushing up to them.

"Where have you been this age? La! We have been waiting here for an hour it seems, and John would not let me explore on my own."

As he hopped down, Mansfield murmured that Theo disliked traveling at high speeds. Julia sniffed.

"How poor-spirited of you, Theo! Why, I had thought we might have a race to see which of these—"

Mansfield was helping Theo down when Debenham strode up and frowning, interrupted her. "Where the devil have you been? And what the devil have you been up to!"

As much as she resented his tone, Theo could not help following his gaze to glance down at her ensemble. There were dirty handprints all about the hem of the white muslin dress, particularly on the left side, where the beggars had snatched at it. She turned her left arm to see that they were all about the outside of her sleeve also, where she was not able to notice them before. It did present a very suspicious appearance, and she blushed as she realized what Debenham thought.

By now Julia had taken in the same evidence, though fortunately she did not draw the same conclusions. "I vow, Theo, however did you become so smutty while riding through the country in a carriage? I—"

Debenham cut her off, silencing her. "Well?" he demanded of Mansfield.

The latter, by following Julia's remarks had at last realized the problem. He dropped his eyes. "I . . . I am afraid that I took that road you warned me about avoiding. Luckily, we came to no misadventure, but were only delayed a trifle."

The black brows met and bristled thickly together. " '*Only delayed a trifle*'—Good Lord! Do you mean to tell me that you drove a gently bred girl through that cesspool, and you haven't even the grace to be sorry for it!"

Mansfield's head drooped lower. Theo could not stand by and let Debenham ride roughshod over him. "The matter is entirely between Mr. Mansfield and myself," she told him evenly. "He has made his apologies to me. It was a natural mistake, and I do not see how the matter concerns you."

" 'You do not see how it concerns—' " For a moment she was afraid that he was going to explode with wrath. To her surprise, he drew in a deep breath instead and addressed Mansfield, "If you had taken my suggestion and followed me, you might have avoided all this. You might *think* before you act, at least once in your life. Miss Westmoreland claims she was not bothered by her visit to Holloway, but you might consider how easy it would be to cause her lasting harm."

Julia was bored by all of this friction. "John, may we go see the chapel now?"

He took out his pocket watch. "It is time to eat." He turned and strode off in the direction of his carriage. With a little sigh, twirling her parasol, she followed him.

Theo laid a reassuring hand on Mansfield's arm. "Quentin—" she began.

He shook it off. "He's right. It's time to eat. Johnson—unpack the basket."

The repast consisted of a cold game pie, a shoulder of mutton, cheese and bread, the fruit of the season, as well as the sorts of kickshaws that were Julia's delight. The meal was excellent, the view scenic, and the weather delightful. A few white clouds drifted across to provide occasional relief from the sun. The birds twittered happily in the trees. Theo was thoroughly miserable, Debenham more than usually taciturn, and Mansfield was sullen, though his appetite was unimpaired.

A squirrel, obviously tamed by visitors, appeared and proceeded to beg for scraps of bread. Julia delighted in throwing him bits and seeing him run off with them. Fortunately, Mansfield also seemed to enjoy watching this pastime. Soon he and Julia were competing with each other for the squirrel's attention. Having finished with her meal, Theo decided that her time might be best spent in attempting to tidy herself. Extracting a handkerchief, she rose, walked some little distance away to ensure a measure of privacy, and began attempting to brush the dirt from her gown.

She was a little startled when Debenham silently appeared beside her. He glowered at her for a moment, then abruptly said, "I'm sorry."

She shook her head, and began working on her glove. "I am not the one that you should apologize to—you should apologize to Mr. Mansfield."

His surprise was evident. "Why should I?"

How hard it was to keep from being constantly angry with him. "Because you were quite rude to him, and he was upset by it."

"I said nothing that wasn't true. Besides, he doesn't look as if he's suffering."

She followed his gaze to see Mansfield chuckling with Julia over the squirrel's antics. What a happy nature he had! Why another gentleman might have sulked the rest of the day.

"It's a mistake, you know."

Debenham's voice was low. She could just make out the words. "What did you say?"

Mansfield turned, and catching Theo's eye, smiled at her warmly. "Come look at this little fellow. He's the most audacious beggar you've ever seen!"

She smiled back, with equal warmth, disguising the fact that the word "beggar" brought back unpleasant memories for her.

"Never mind."

By the end of half an hour, both Julia and Mansfield having tired of their sport, the grooms were left to pack up the remains of the picnic lunch. Julia, now that her mind had been recalled to the subject, was all impatience to visit the chapel and examine its curiosities. The building itself was in good repair, evidently owing to the concern of the owner of the property.

It was not an unimpressive structure. As they entered, they could see that the nave was almost sixty feet long and twenty feet wide. On the north side was the chantry containing the old wooden pulpit, the immense granite altar, and some pieces of ancient armor. Approaching it, Theo could see a flat gravestone on the floor cut with the figure of a knight in armor, with an inscription running around it that commemorated Sir Giles Hungerford, one of the family who had owned the castle, and later forfeited their titles. On the south wall, a tablet monument dated 1585 attracted Theo's attention. She was about to call Julia's attention to it, but Julia was apparently preoccupied with the ancient table tombs, which were scattered about the chapel. Sculpted of stone, and occasionally gilt, these effigies were magnificent, though they were eclipsed by the monument that stood in the center. Composed of white polished marble and resting upon steps of black marble reposed the effigies of Sir Edward and Lady Margaret Hungerford. Even to Theo's inexperienced eye, it seemed that the work was particularly fine. However, it was evident that neither this monument nor the beautiful painting of the Resurrection upon the ceiling captured Julia's complete attention.

She had pulled out the guidebook her aunt had loaned her and was thumbing through it rapidly. "None of these look like what I—oh, here it is! We must go down into the crypt. I hope you brought the stick, Mr. Mansfield."

"I did, but I am most curious as to why we need it."

"You shall see. Now come, everyone."

Theo and Debenham obediently followed Julia as, Mansfield by her side, she descended into the chilly gloom of the crypt. When her eyes adjusted to the light, Theo could see a multitude of leaden coffins lying about the room.

"The pickled remains of eight of the Hungerfords," announced Julia triumphantly, quoting from her guidebook. Theo could not help shuddering, but Julia was all enthusiasm. "Now, let's see, which one is it? It says 'a perforation on the right shoulder,' but I wonder if he meant the body's right shoulder, or just on the right as you are looking at it. No, it's not this one . . . nor this . . . Ah, at last! Here it is!"

In response to her jubilant signals, the rest of the party joined her.

"The stick, Mr. Mansfield, the stick!" cried Julia in high excitement.

Just as curious as he was, Theo drew near. She could see that there was a hole in the leaden coffin.

"I hope this is long enough."

To Theo's utter dismay, Julia was putting the stick into the hole. Whatever was she doing? Now she poked it about, giggling slightly. As they watched, Julia extracted the stick, which was dripping with a thick, brown liquid. "It's the embalming fluid. The book says that the flesh is decomposed by the admission of air, but that the bones are still sound. You can feel them if you wiggle it about. Would you care to try?"

Fortunately for Theo, Mansfield stepped up for his turn. She felt an arm supporting her elbow and sagged into it. "I'll take you outside," muttered Debenham.

She could do no more than nod gratefully, and soon she was out in the bright sunlight again, gulping air thankfully. Debenham steered her to a stone, and she sank upon it. "All right now?"

"Yes. Thank you."

They said nothing further, and within a few moments Julia and Mansfield appeared from the depths of the crypt. "Didn't you wish to feel the bones?" Julia asked disappointedly.

"Miss Westmoreland had a trying experience this morning. Her nerves are still not recovered—"

"I just needed some fresh air," said Theo defiantly, not liking to have her weakness betrayed.

"Oooh, they felt horrible, though. Didn't they, Mr. Mansfield?"

He smiled good-humoredly at her. What a gentleman he was. He would never suggest that Julia had been disgusting. "Yes, they did."

"Isabel will be beside herself when she hears what she's missed," predicted Julia with confidence. Theo had never felt less fond of her.

It was Debenham who called everyone's attention to the time. If they were to return by a decent hour, they must leave.

Thankful for the suggestion, Theo assumed her place in the carriage. She was not even resentful when Debenham quietly suggested to Mansfield that they travel in close proximity, given Theo's past indisposition. It was irritating to have to be grateful to him, but she was.

None of the dreams that she had nourished for this expedition had come true. There had been very little of the lover about Mansfield today, but then, he had not been given much opportunity. There was not a great deal to be accomplished under the watchful eye of the groom, or with the other carriage just behind them, but Theo hoped that there would at least be some of those melting looks that made her heart flutter so pleasantly. What good did it do to be engaged otherwise?

All appeared well as they started off. Debenham had refrained from commenting upon the manner in which Mansfield's horses were harnessed. Mansfield himself, tenderly solicitous of her, refrained from indulging in tricks he had not mastered, and drove at a moderate pace. Her heart, which had been made heavy by the combined effects of the day, began to lighten.

They were perhaps two miles from the castle when disaster struck. Theo and Mansfield had been conversing pleasantly, with the promise of more personal exchanges to come, when the near leader, in swishing his tail at a fly caught it over the reins. Mansfield paled as he remarked it. He began pulling at the reins, further irritating the animal which faltered in his gait and began kicking, disconcerting the wheeler behind him. The whole team, uncertain, began to slow and veer from the road. Desperate, Mansfield tugged harder. The afflicted horse's ears were now pinned back, and he began to buck in the traces as he lashed out at everything about him. The carriage was rocking, and they were being pulled to the edge of the road. Theo, powerless to help, could only watch in fright.

The far leader, anxious to get away, pulled as hard as he could toward the other side of the road, dragging the other horses along with him. Mansfield rose in his seat, using all his strength in one last effort to control the team, but it was no use. Theo gave a shriek as the far leader gave one last tug, and the entire equipage tumbled over the side of the road into a ditch.

She was thrown from the carriage and landed heavily. It took her several minutes to regain her breath. When she at last was able to sit up, a dismal sight confronted her. The phaeton was tipped over on its side in the ditch. The horses, tangled in the harness, were neighing shrilly and making vain attempts to rise. She looked about for Mansfield, half afraid that a lifeless corpse would meet her eyes, but he was standing a few feet away, staring dully at the wreck, a handkerchief held to his forehead in order to stop bleeding from a cut he had suffered.

Where could she find help? She looked to the other side and saw that the groom was just beginning to sit up dazedly, as she had. It was as if her brain had ceased to function. She could not think what to do. Then, from the road above, she saw Debenham's face appear. A great weight rose from her heart. She would be safe with him. He would take care of everything.

He saw her and a surprising expression, which her confused mind could not interpret, crossed his face. He raced down the ditch to her, in great, bounding strides, his top boots tearing out chunks of earth as he went.

"Theo, my God! Theo, my dearest. Are you all right? Please the dear Lord, are you all right?"

She nodded, and with his arms about her, rose shakily to her feet. "Please," she whispered, "take care of those poor horses."

He nodded, yelled to the groom, and the two men went to the horses' aid. Debenham spoke in a low soothing voice to the pitching, rolling animals, whose eyes showed white with fear. He drew nearer, still using the caressing tone, and took the knife the groom handed him. With a few swift moves, the traces were cut and one horse was freed, then another. Mansfield at last seemed to come to life, exclaiming, "The horses," in an anxious voice. He went to take one of the trembling animals by the reins, which still dangled from them.

By now, Debenham's own groom had appeared, having tied his own horses, and was lending them aid. He examined the animals for injury while an anxious Mansfield looked on. All the horses by now having been released, Debenham called the other men to join them. With an effort, the four men managed to haul the phaeton back into an upright position. What a sad change there was from the elegant carriage of this morning. On the one side, spots of paint had been scraped off. There was a gash on the side of the box, and the twisted top had been torn and hung at a crazy angle. Debenham looked over the phaeton closely, testing it with a push here and there.

"It's basically sound, I think. Will, how are the horses?"

"The one's strained a fetlock, and there are some cuts and bruises, but by some miracle, I think nothing is broken."

Mansfield released an audible sigh of relief.

"Well, then . . ." He turned to Mansfield's groom. "Johnson, is it? How are you feeling?"

The man rubbed his skull ruefully. "I took a knock on the noggin, sir, but I'll do."

"Very well." He surveyed the scene around him, making his decisions. "Will, d'you think you can patch together enough harness to get this home?"

"Yes, sir."

"Very well, then. I'll leave you and Johnson here together to take care of it. You'll have to find somewhere to stable that lame animal or else bring it home at a walk. I don't know of an inn between here and Bath." He turned to Theo. "Miss Westmoreland can contrive to fit in the box with Miss Simpson and me. Mansfield, you may take Will's seat."

Mansfield shook his head determinedly. "No, I mean to stay here and help."

"You'd better come. These two will take care of everything. You'd better see that cut looked to." His voice was surprisingly gentle.

"Well, I—"

"I insist."

"But my horses—"

"They'll be fine. Come."

Reluctantly, Mansfield put a hand to his head and again wiped at the blood, which had slowed to a trickle. Following Debenham, who had taken Theo by the arm, he began trudging up the side of the ditch.

At the carriage, they found Julia full of concern. "Oh, my dears. How are you? I was dying to go down and help you, but John ordered me strictly to remain in the carriage." Her attention was first drawn to Theo, leaning heavily on Debenham's arm. "Oh, dear Theo, your pretty dress is torn—and what happened to your bonnet?" As soon as she caught sight of Mansfield, however, she lost all concern for the female involved in the accident.

"Oh, Mr. Mansfield. You are bleeding! Does it hurt dreadfully? What a terrible mishap! I hope you are not seriously hurt! Here, I will put a little lavender water upon my handkerchief—perhaps it will soothe your forehead."

He took the proffered handkerchief from her in a dazed way, mumbling his thanks, before taking the groom's seat. Debenham prepared to help Theo into the carriage. "Are you certain you're all right?" he asked in a low voice.

She was bruised, scraped, and dirty, and she knew that she would ache dreadfully in the morning, but she was not seriously injured and told him so. "Thank God," she thought she heard him murmur, but she could not be certain.

When he aided her into the carriage, Julia did not look well pleased. "Are you certain that there will be enough room, John dear? We are rather squeezed as it is."

"There is no help for it," he told her curtly.

She shrank back from Theo, then pulled a rug from underneath the seat. "*Dear* Theo, I know you will not mind wrapping this about your skirt. You became so dirty when you fell, after all, and this *is* my new dress."

They were crowded, but the rest of the ride would have passed comfortably enough, Theo thought, if it had not been for Julia leaning back every few minutes to ask Mansfield how he was. She was finally irritated enough to ask Julia if she wished for her to change places with him.

"Well, he *is* the one who is injured, after all, my dear and—"

"Enough," said Debenham. "She stays, Julia."

She drew herself up with a sniff. "Whatever you say, John dear."

The only thing worse about the ride was that Julia spent the rest of her time ingratiating herself with Debenham. Somehow the talk turned to hunting, and Julia was soon boasting of her exploits in the field and her fearless riding style. If Theo had been feeling less bitter, she might have laughed. Julia, who was terrified even to be near a horse, taking a fence? The picture was too ridiculous to even contemplate. Of course, Debenham apparently took her at her word, seemingly impressed by the imaginary feats that she was inventing. It made Theo sick to hear her. She only introduced the subject of horses because she knew it was Debenham's favorite topic. Of course, who had told her that? Theo could have kicked herself.

All this horse talk led to discussion of the accident and how it had occurred. Julia was quick to sympathize with Mansfield and to tell him so. It must be the most brutish, ill-tempered team of horses who had ever drawn a carriage. By the ride's end, she had convinced him that he was a thoroughly misused individual. He was ready to confront St. George and to give him a piece of his mind.

Debenham had exercised all his powers of self-control, but when they reached the Royal Crescent, Mansfield began to give him a share of the blame also, for helping his friend to saddle him with such an unmanageable team. The carriage was probably trouble prone also. Debenham could hold his silence no longer.

"You are not yourself. You'd best go see a doctor."

Mansfield looked sulky. "I'm not a flat. I know when I've been tricked."

Debenham stared at him icily. "You had the coupling reins too long, as I told you. Once the leader gets it under his tail, then the buckle holds it there."

"But it might happen to anyone."

"—And instead of letting out the rein once it was caught, you pulled up on it, which is certain to irritate the horse and cause an accident. You're lucky you were only ditched, instead of meeting another carriage. You could have been killed, and Miss Westmoreland with you."

"That's the point of all this, isn't it?"

Theo could bear it no longer. "Stop it right now! Debenham said it. You are not yourself. Well, neither am I. I need to go home."

"I am sorry. We will go."

A shadow crossed Mansfield's face. "I'm sorry, too, Theo. Debenham, I . . . I didn't mean what I said . . ."

"It's forgotten."

He kissed Theo's hand in farewell before making his way into the house. It occurred to her that it was the first sign of concern for her that he had shown.

Chapter Eleven

Theo's battered and bedraggled appearance evoked shock and concern when Debenham escorted her into her house. Her mother, who looked more pale and tired than Theo had expected, was given the brief details of the accident by Debenham, who with unexpected grace did not assign any particular blame to Mansfield. He would not stay, since Julia waited outside in his carriage, and he refused to accept their thanks. He took Theo by the hand and kissed it, commenting that he would see how she did in the morning. He bowed to her mother, and flattered a surprisingly anxious Peggy by adding that he knew Theo was in good hands.

Theo did not attempt to remonstrate as the two fussed over her. Peggy removed the ruins of her gown. It would be fit for little except gardening, and Theo no longer had opportunity for doing that. She refused all offers of food and tried not to notice their sympathetic gasps as they beheld her bruised, scraped body. Peggy sponged off the worst of the cuts and applied ointment to them. She offered to draw Theo a bath, and though it might have eased her aching limbs, she declined. What she wanted, what she *needed* most was solitude and rest.

Her mother could not be quite content with such inattention. Though Theo might not wish for the plaster of butter and parsley with which Peggy intended to soothe her bruises, she must be forced to accept some medical help. At last, the viscountess contented herself with bathing her child's forehead with lavender water, which she did for half an hour until Theo finally feigned sleep.

She was exhausted, still in shock, and utterly depressed. The emotions that she had been holding back so rigidly finally escaped and now she wept, with great racking sobs, which she did her best to muffle in her pillow. Mansfield had seemed to be her ideal of a gentleman. Now the blinkers had been torn from her eyes with violence. She had seen a side of him today that she had never seen before. How could she have been such a fool?

It took nearly an hour of crying before her shocked mind and spirit could begin to recover. Her first thought had been to break the engagement immediately. They had been deceived in each other. She was not in love with him, and clearly he was not in love with her either. A few more minutes of sober consideration brought a new problem to light.

If she broke off her engagement with Mansfield, she would be left with no suitor at all. She would be in a worse position than she had been when she arrived in Bath. There was her pride to be considered, for one thing. It was all too clear that Miss Bromley and others would assume that *he* had tired of *her* if they were no longer seen together. More important, though, her scheme would be at an end for rescuing her family from financial ruin. There were no other eligible gentlemen about. Mansfield had been her one opportunity. She, her mother, and her younger brother would have to continue as the Debenhams' pensioners. Her mind seized onto an even more horrifying possibility. If Debenham did marry Julia, what an uncomfortable position awaited Theo. Julia, already so fond of "lording" her situation over her sister, would certainly not be inclined to show Theo any mercy. To think of Julia being consulted about what she should be allowed for gowns horrified Theo. Abruptly, she forced herself to close that channel of thought.

There was no question of breaking off the engagement with Mansfield. She had been prepared to marry a hideous and aged man in order to save her family; she must consider that she was lucky to have found Mansfield. After all, he had also passed through a difficult day. He had waited all this time to obtain such an equipage and then almost lost it—to say nothing of the shock and the danger. He probably blamed himself more than Theo knew, and had undoubtedly been crushed by Debenham's words. She knew that he was fond of her: he had proven it before. Who could criticize him for being preoccupied? As for the rest, well, that was clearly Julia's work. He would never have taken on that self-pitying tone without her encouragement.

She tried to look at the situation more cheerfully. After

all, every human being had his or her faults. She had a great many herself, which probably surprised Mansfield as much as his had her. Their only real problem was that they had not known each other very well when they began this engagement. Their affection might grow with time: many married couples started out with less. She was tired and nervous and had been through a draining experience. Things would look better to her after a good night's sleep. She wiped her nose on her handkerchief resolutely, closed her eyes, and in a short time was unconscious.

When she awoke in the morning, the first thing she was aware of was pain. As she had expected, she ached in every part of her body. She gingerly raised herself to a sitting position in the bed, and discovered that her head was also aching. The optimistic frame of mind she had expected to materialize had failed to do so. In the gray light that filtered through the curtain from the clouded day outside, her future seemed every bit as bleak as it had the night before. "Break it off," a part of her urged. "The engagement has been secret from everyone. No one will think you fickle, and there will be no damage to your reputation."

She shook off these cowardly thoughts. Ending the engagement was not a possibility. She had seen that last night. Looking backward could not do her any good. Stifling an exclamation of pain, she rose and rang the bell for Peggy.

The servant, who appeared with unusual promptitude, was inclined to bully her and urge her to remain in bed, but Theo would not hear of it. When she saw that Theo was resolute, she finally submitted to her young mistress's wishes and helped her to dress, though she grumbled all the while. She threw open the curtains, and Theo saw that it was now raining. Perfect. It exactly matched her mood today.

To Theo's surprise, Peggy informed her that she might breakfast with Sir Francis, who was presently enjoying a cup of coffee in the drawing room. It seemed rather odd, but the only one who could answer her questions was Sir Francis himself. So after ascertaining that she looked as presentable as possible, Theo went downstairs.

He had ensconced himself in the green damask wing chair in the corner. He had the paper in one hand and a cup of coffee in the other, and he appeared entirely comfortable.

It struck Theo that it was hard to imagine a setting where Sir Francis would look out of place.

When she entered he sprang up, and though his eyes examined her keenly, he exhibited none of the fussy solicitude that was beginning to madden her. "So, you took a tumble, then, my dear? Your mother was inclined to fret, but I told her John said it was no worse than if you'd taken a toss at the Whissendine brook. You'll be aching for a day or two, but as long as nothing is broken, there is no need to worry." He helped her to a chair next to his and smiled at her.

She started to smile back but quickly put a hand up to her cheek. "I am afraid you are right. I am sore. Where is my mother?"

His smile disappeared. "She went to the Bath this morning, thinking it might do her good. She disliked leaving with no word of how you were faring, but I told her I would be happy to serve as her deputy."

"That is most kind—but why did she go to the Bath? I thought that she and the doctor had decided to discontinue them long ago?"

His tone was elaborately casual. "She has not been feeling as well as she might of late, and she thought it would do no harm to try them once again."

Theo was by now alarmed. "Is she ill? Has my mother had another attack? Please tell me!"

He shook his head and taking her hand, patted it reassuringly. "Of course not. She merely has been feeling . . . well, a little more tired of late. She would be distressed to know she caused you any worry."

The discussion was interrupted by the arrival of Peggy, who was bearing a steaming tray loaded with eggs, gammon, buns, kippers, and a pot of coffee. "Ah, just in time. Mrs. Chambers has been taking such good care of me this morning, I knew that you would not be neglected. Just a touch more, thank you," he said, holding his cup out to the proffered coffeepot.

After Theo had been served, Peggy retreated, giggling for the first time that Theo could remember. Apparently even she was not immune to Sir Francis's charm. He took a thoughtful sip of the coffee as Theo began to push the eggs about her plate in an uninterested manner.

He observed her in silence for some moments before venturing a comment. "My dear," he said at last with great gentleness, "I had promised your mother that I would see that you ate something this morning. I should hate to fail her."

"Oh." Theo obediently put a bite of eggs in her mouth, chewed them slowly without tasting them at all, and swallowed. With her fork, she began toying with the rest of the food once again.

The keen gray eyes were watching her closely. "Is something amiss?"

Oh, my word. How obvious had she been? "No, of course not."

He put his paper down and leaned forward in his chair. "You will forgive me for saying so, I am sure, but it appears to me that there is more wrong with you than simply having suffered a fall." She started to murmur another protest, but he stopped her. "You need not confide in me if you wish. I would only say that advanced age presents one advantage, in that I have been confronted by all sorts of problems in my life. I have found that talking about them is often the quickest way to sorting them out. I have a genuine concern for you, my dear, and should be happy to do anything in my power to help."

The food on her plate was swimming before her. She had dropped her head and now shook it quickly.

A corner of his mouth curled up ruefully. "I hope that that graceless son of mine has not been contributing to your distress in any way—"

"Oh, no." She could not let him think that. "Well, he was rather rude to Mr. Mansfield, but I cannot say it was unjustified." She struggled for words. "It is just—have you ever noticed that people have their faults as well as their virtues?"

"Eh? Oh, yes, of course . . ."

"Well, what I mean to say is that it is rather hard to see that at times—" Here she peeped at him shyly. "You . . . you have been married twice, after all."

Despite himself, his eyebrows ascended in surprise. "Yes?"

"Well . . ." She could not help blushing. "Did you not find that you had to focus rather on your wife's virtues, and ignore what you saw to be her faults?"

He was frowning at her, thoughtfully. "I . . . well, yes, I do suppose you are right, although I—" A thought occurred to him, and his brow cleared abruptly. "I think I see what you mean. Often you must look beneath the surface to see a person's virtues, for they may be obscured by his faults. How very true, and how perceptive of you, my dear. It is something that young ladies—and young gentlemen—very often fail to consider when they think about forming a union."

Theo could not help blushing at his words of praise. She had been thinking rather that a person's virtues, lying on the surface as they might be, tended to obscure his flaws, but she supposed that the principle was the same.

She would have been shocked to learn that Sir Francis interpreted her blushes in a very different manner.

There was one other matter to discuss, and he lost no time in bringing it up. Her mother had apparently been fretting over the obligation that they owed the Simpsons as well as the countess. She had decided to host a dinner party for them. "—Of which," Sir Francis said, "I am not all in favor, given her weakened condition at the moment. You know your mother, though, my dear. She insists and will not be convinced to do otherwise." He frowned slightly. "The best I have been able to do, is to try to convince her that she may host the dinner at my house and let my housekeeper and chef take care of all the arrangements. To have the dinner here would mean a dreadful squeeze—"

He was putting it politely.

"I will confess that she saw the force of that argument, at least, though your mother is dreadfully proud and cannot bear the thought of being beholden to me, either. The one problem is that I fear I may be called out of town in a few days, so we must have the dinner as soon as possible. The Bromley's ball is on Tuesday, so I thought we might have the dinner before it—"

Theo was happy to help, though it surprised her a little that the viscountess should balk at his offer of aid. It seemed to her that her mother had been only too happy to accept his support all along.

It was unlikely that she would have discovered the truth, except for the viscountess's weakened condition when she returned to the house. Sir Francis had departed some minutes previously. Lady Westmoreland always found the Bath draining, and this one had been no exception. After being put to bed, she shrugged off Theo's remonstrations. She said that since the doctor had suggested resuming them, she felt that there could be no harm in it. Theo was quite angry at hearing that the doctor had been to see her mother the previous day, but the latter pointed out gently that she could hardly have told Theo, who was miles away. She had not wanted to trouble her with it last night, either, when Theo was still clearly suffering from shock.

Arguing with Theo had wearied her further, and when her daughter brought up the dinner party, she was forced to agree to Sir Francis's terms before too much time had elapsed. Theo was just beginning to be pleased with her victory when she noticed a tear running silently down the viscountess's cheek.

"Mother! What is it?"

"It is nothing," said the viscountess, wiping the tear away. Seeing that she had not convinced her daughter, she added, "This dreadful weakness from the Bath—perhaps you are right, perhaps I should stop them."

Theo had seated herself by her mother's bed, and now took her hand. "You *must* tell me, Mother. What is the matter?"

The tear had been joined by others. "A handkerchief, please." The viscountess wiped them away fiercely. "It is so ridiculous—it is just that I would not have you exposed to any unpleasantness and . . ."

"What do you mean?"

"Sir Francis . . . has been so solicitous of us and so good . . ." The tears were flowing freely, and she jabbed at her face again. "Forgive me. It's just that—well, I should not wish him to suspect—I am most grateful, of course, but—"

"But what?"

"We have been so constantly together that I am afraid there has been some talk. For me to host a dinner at his house will probably increase it. And I have been out of mourning for only a year or so, after all. This is such a dreadful gossiping town!"

Theo hugged her frail mother gently. "You must not worry about that, Mother. Why, both of us know that it has been nothing but kindness on his part. Why should we care what the gossips say?"

"Yes, of course." Her tone was unconvincing, but Theo did not notice. This dinner party might serve another purpose. She might be able to find an opportunity to be alone with Mansfield. She had made up her mind. Since she was to marry him, there was no point in delaying. She would tell him that if he failed to inform the countess of their engagement, she would do so herself.

Mansfield was undergoing the same sort of physical suffering that Theo was this morning. She might have been reassured to know that his first thought, after concern for his horses and wondering how he was going to approach the countess about repairs to the carriage, was for her. He had treated Theo abominably: it had taken Debenham's words for him to see that. How surprising it was that she hadn't had a *tendre* for Debenham, when it was clear to see . . . Of course, he had to admit that she hadn't shown a great deal of concern for him, either, not as Miss Julia Simpson had done. She had seemed to comprehend his disappointment and anguish instantly, and— He shook his head, attempting to banish such disloyal thoughts. Theo was rather like a princess, or a queen, after all. It still seemed miraculous that she had accepted him, particularly given Debenham's attachment to her. Debenham, after all, was a far richer prize. There were no strings attached to the fortune he held. To have won her away from him was quite a feat. No, her esteem for him must be sincere—it must just be that she was not a particularly demonstrative person.

He sighed. And how basely he had treated her. A secret engagement. He was sure that Debenham had overheard. He could read the condemnation in those gray eyes every time he met them. And hadn't she accepted his judgment most placidly? What a trusting girl she was. She was right. He must tell his aunt, and he would . . . at least he would just as soon as the matter of repairs was finished.

Debenham himself would probably have been surprised to learn that he figured in Mansfield's thoughts. He had called upon Theo during the first part of the afternoon. Although bruised, she apparently had not suffered otherwise as a result of the accident. She greeted him with great good spirits, thanked him for the role he had played in rescuing them, and commented with drollery upon the picture she must have presented.

After visiting briefly, he rose to leave, remarking that he did not wish to tire her. She protested, but he clearly was set upon going. He explained that he had an errand to run for Miss Julia Simpson in town. For the first time, her brows joined in a frown.

"I am surprised that she asked you to discharge it for her."

He shrugged indifferently. "With such foul weather, she did not wish to venture out of doors. I was going into town anyway, so it was no trouble for me."

To use Debenham as an errand boy! What gall! She was angry, and was forced to remind herself that she could not resent what was done to *him*. It was not her concern, after all. She told herself that what she disliked the most was his passive acceptance of such a role. He should certainly value himself more than that.

By way of a distraction, she mentioned the upcoming dinner party, how much they appreciated Sir Francis's hospitality, and how sorry they would be to see him leave Bath. She added the hope that his trip would not be a protracted one.

For some reason, she had the impression that her words surprised Debenham. His trip . . . a protracted one . . . no, he did not think so. It was peculiar, but she could almost swear that his father had not told him of the trip before this.

It was a matter that Debenham took the first opportunity to discuss with that erring gentleman. Having dropped off the parcel for Julia, he returned to their house in Marlborough Buildings.

He strode angrily into the drawing room, while the water dripped from his many-caped greatcoat, forming puddles about the sadly muddied top boots. He found his father in shirtsleeves, wearing his spectacles, while on the table before him reposed little piles of hair of different lengths and colors, wool and feathers and threads of gold and silver as well as silk threads in more sober hues. He had some small, bright red feathers in his hand, and was just reaching for thread when he was distracted by his son's entrance.

He looked up at him above his spectacles. "Good afternoon," he said politely.

"Sir Francis—"

"If you will forgive me, I am in the midst of the operation, which is a most delicate one." He coughed delicately.

"If I may venture to make a suggestion, you might wish to remove your greatcoat before the carpet is utterly ruined."

Debenham knew better than to try to obtain a reply from his father when thus occupied. He gave a sigh, and yielded to the ministrations of the worried young footman who had appeared to remove his coat and boots. With his feet now comfortably encased in slippers, he called for a glass of port and flung himself down onto the sofa with a frown.

Sir Francis, intent upon his work, had taken up a hook and with the thread was carefully attaching the feathers to it. After several adjustments, he gave a sigh of satisfaction, tied the knot, and extracting a small, fine pair of scissors, began to trim the fly. When he had finished, he held up his work for his scowling son to admire. "A pretty thing, isn't it?"

Debenham, refusing to abandon his ill-humor, gave a snort. "D'you expect a fish to mistake *that* for a real fly?"

Not at all discomposed, his father twirled it gently in his hand. "I've a mind to try for grayling this summer. Something tells me I may wish for a holiday by August. These are *parakita* feathers, and the grayling is said to respond to them, though I've no doubt that I may do as well with a hawthorn fly, or an oak fly, or even a natural fly, if they're to be found, though of course it would not do to depend entirely upon them."

His son had risen and was examining the odd collection upon the table. At random, he picked up a ball of cream mohair. "And why not this for a fly?" he asked without any real curiosity.

"*Isabella*? No, it would do for March, but never for August. Although there are some that use it for the oak fly, along with bear's hair and black wool, but I prefer black wool with a gold twist and brown mallard's feathers for the wings." He looked up at his son ruefully. "I have never been able to interest you in the slightest in dubbing flies, have I?"

Debenham shook his head and regained his place on the sofa nonchalantly. "No, but then my fingers have never been as clever as yours for fine work."

Sir Francis put down his lure and removed his spectacles. "You have your own sort of cleverness." He regarded his son in thoughtful silence for a moment. "I must say I expected better. Have you been to see Theo?"

Debenham's face darkened. "Yes, I have and it was she who—"

"Was your reception warm? I should have thought so, from what I gleaned—"

Debenham shook his head puzzledly. "I don't know what you mean. If this is an attempt to distract me from—"

"No." Sir Francis leaned forward, suddenly intent. "Do you mean the girl was not convinced by what happened yesterday? I received the impression that she was."

Debenham's face was bleaker than his father had ever seen it. "There is no hope for me in that quarter, and there has not been since—but I do not wish to speak of it."

Sir Francis concealed his surprise and his curiosity. With an effort, Debenham wrenched the subject back to his father's offense.

"She did tell me, though, that you were planning to leave Bath and hoped you wouldn't be gone for long. I assume you meant to leave me a note at least?" His voice was scornful.

Sir Francis smiled at him in delight. "An excellent attempt, though you have not quite the way of it yet. Sarcasm always works best with a cool voice, I—"

By now Debenham was incensed. "When do you mean to stop treating me like a child? You intended to step in and take care of everything at the last by yourself. I was not to be informed, even though—" His anger choked him, and he could not continue.

His father studied him in an ominous silence. "I do not know where you came by that temper," he at last commented in a dry tone of voice. "I actually meant to discuss my plans with you today. Since it is apparent that the chase is almost at an end, I have decided to return to London and finish the work which you"—he inclined his head gracefully toward his son—"began. As I told you before, since I was the executor, I am the only one in a position to see that restitution is made, if possible. I know very well that you would like to be in at the finish, but had you considered that your own affairs are in a sad tangle at the moment? I do not mean for my son to be known as a well-breeched trifler, do you understand me?"

Debenham dropped his eyes and muttered an affirmative. Sir Francis continued, more gently. "There is another thing. Lady Westmoreland is doing rather badly at the moment.

I've no doubt the anxiety has taken its toll . . ." He pressed his lips together, "If she should . . . if she should succumb to another . . . another upset, one of us should be here." His son was about to speak, but Sir Francis cut him off. "*Theo* will need your help, like it or not."

Gray eyes met gray eyes. "Yes, sir."

Chapter Twelve

It was a beautiful day. In contrast to the rain that had marred the three previous ones, the sun was shining brightly and the sky was cloudless. It was the sort of late spring day that seems designed to affirm that life is a pleasant thing, and Mansfield was no more immune to its influence than anyone else.

He had reason to be happy. Although the matter had required great delicacy of handling, his aunt had been brought to see that the accident was of the sort that might happen to anyone, rather than being caused by recklessness on his part. From there it had been a quick trip to the coach builders, where he learned to his joy that there were no major structural problems with the phaeton. All it would require was some straightening out of various parts, and a daub of new paint here and there to make it as good as new. The repair bill would be too small to cause his aunt any anguish or to require further diplomacy. There was also reason to be optimistic about his horses, for his groom assured him that they would be right as rain by the end of the week.

To cap it all, the invitation had arrived from the viscountess, proving that she, at least, did not bear a grudge. Though he had not had a chance to talk with Theo in private since the accident, he had seen her at the Abbey Church and had expressed his sincere regret as well as his hope that she had suffered no lasting injury from the mishap. Angel that she was, she had not accused him of neglect or remonstrated with him about his coachmanship. He could read the unspoken message in her eyes, however, and he knew that she was right. It was time to tell the countess. There could be no better one. Lady Verridge continued to speak of Theo fondly. The carriage matter was settled. The dinner was tomorrow. There was nothing to prevent his informing his aunt of his intentions before then, and he would do so. First, however, he meant to visit Theo and tell her what he meant to do.

He had risen early and dressed himself with great care. The reflection in the looking glass confirmed his opinion. He was in good looks today. He made his way downstairs and breakfasted heartily upon cold roast chicken, neat's tongue, a potted pigeon, a crimped cod, as well as sausages, boiled eggs, rolls, and an apricot tart. He did not subscribe to the modern notion that breakfast should be a light affair consisting of perhaps toast or muffins and chocolate. Whatever Theo might think of his appetite, it served to ensure his popularity with the kitchen staff. The countess's chef had a particular fondness for him, for it was certain that young Mr. Mansfield would *never* send a dish back to the kitchen untasted. In fact, it was unusual for him to send back a dish unfinished.

This morning he was able to do the meal full justice, in part owing to the excellence of his spirits. He had already put his hat on his head and was just pulling on his gloves in preparation for his departure when their butler interrupted him.

"I beg your pardon, Mr. Mansfield, but your aunt has a caller."

His aunt was a notoriously late riser. To her physician's despair, she ignored the prescribed regimen that dictated that she should partake of the waters early in the morning, preferring to sleep instead. No one in Bath would think of calling upon her before eleven, and it was just nearing ten o'clock.

"Send him away," said Mansfield graciously.

The butler coughed. "I beg your pardon, sir, but the caller appears to be a *relation* of Lady Verridge's."

The unspoken message was clear. Mansfield would have to handle it. He removed his hat, concealing a sigh of impatience. "Very well. I will see him."

He crossed over to the drawing room, where a small, dark-haired man stood examining a painting of the countess. Quentin planted a pleasant expression upon his face and advanced into the room. It was always better to be conciliating. One never knew whether or not it was an important relation.

"I am afraid that my aunt has not risen yet this morning. May I be of service to you sir?"

At his entrance, the man had swung around and regarded him keenly. Mansfield had the momentary, uncomfortable feeling that those bright blue eyes were not impressed with what they saw, but now the stranger held out his hand in an affable manner. Taking a few limping steps toward Mansfield, he said, "If Lady Verridge is your aunt, then I'll be bound that you are my cousin Mansfield. Permit me to introduce myself. Major Alfred Boyce, 13th Light Dragoons, at your service."

Somehow the title did not surprise Mansfield. The other, despite his size had an air of command about him that pegged him as a military man, even without a uniform. The news that he was a cousin came as a shock, however, and a most unwelcome one.

Mansfield regarded the other closely. Boyce resembled him not at all. He was dressed conservatively in dark clothing of a military cut. In addition to being short, he was slender, and while not unattractive, would certainly not be described as handsome. His skin had been darkened and lined by exposure. In addition, he had to be some fifteen to twenty years older than Mansfield. There were already touches of silver in his hair. Mansfield did some quick calculations. Boyce's mother had been Lady Verridge's *older* sister. His own mother had been much younger than the countess. The disparity in age was about right. Mechanically, he murmured his own name and took the other's hand, wincing slightly at the firm grip. No dandy this.

Despite his obvious imperfections, there was something compelling about Boyce. He spoke, again in a friendly manner. "I am pleased to make your acquaintance. It is kind of you to receive me."

Mansfield murmured something polite, and indicated a chair. They both were seated. He offered the visitor refreshments, but the latter declined.

"I'm afraid that I've been eating too well since my return to England. I was invalided out in March. As soon as I could get about, I tired of cooling my heels in London and decided to seek out my relations. It was my mother's fondest wish that the rift between her and Lady Verridge might be repaired. I regret that it did not happen during her lifetime."

It was as if Mansfield were in the midst of a nightmare. For the only possible rival for his aunt's affections and fortunes to appear here now seemed the worst possible stroke of luck. And he had stated that his whole purpose for the visit was to improve relations with her. What could be more inopportune? Dazed by his ill fortune, Mansfield sat and docilely listened to his cousin.

Boyce had spent most of his life in the army, having been enabled to buy (through the good offices of his father's brother) a cornetcy at the tender age of seventeen. A good portion of his time had been spent abroad, though the last ten years he had been quartered all over England. For an ambitious young officer, war with France had come as a boon. He had caught a ball in the knee at some place called Campo Mayor and been forced to return to England. It was clear that he deeply regretted it, as his regiment had been engaged in heavy fighting since then. He mentioned some place called Bajadoz and another place where a battle had occurred more recently, called Albuera. Mansfield could only suppose that they were somewhere in Spain or Portugal. As he listened, it became obvious that despite the darkness of his prospects, there was one glimmer of light on the horizon. Major Boyce was clearly longing to return to the Peninsula. As soon as his doctors pronounced him fit, he intended to leave.

After half an hour's mostly one-sided conversation, the major politely took his leave of Mansfield, adding that he intended to call upon Lady Verridge later that day. Mansfield was left alone in the drawing room to ruminate.

His cousin was well mannered, not unattractive, an officer, and what was worse, a wounded hero of sorts. He was quick to turn conversation from his wound and how he had received it, but Mansfield thought that such modesty would likely only endear him further to the ladies.

To tell his aunt of his engagement now was tantamount to asking her to disinherit him. Theo would just have to understand that they must wait a little longer. A helpful footman appeared with his hat. Mansfield waved him away.

"I've changed my mind about going out today."

Despite all of Theodora's concern, the viscountess had been unwilling to consider putting off their dinner party. Once she had accepted Sir Francis's help, matters improved somewhat, for then it was not difficult to convince her to allow the servants to take care of the majority of the work. Theo herself was only too glad to run her mother's errands.

To her relief, her mother, while she did not appear to improve, at least seemed no worse than she had for the past few days. If only this party might be over with, then at least she could rest. With matters settled between Theo and Mansfield, too, she would no longer need to be concerned over her daughter's future. Neither would she feel under further obligation to anyone. She could not be beholden to Theo's fiancé's family, and Theo did not intend to place herself under further obligation to the Simpsons.

She might feel sympathy for Isabel, who though still accompanied by the taciturn Mr. Warwick, was outshone by the picture of her younger sister and her more magnificent beau. The feeling did not extend to a desire for her company, since Theo also must then endure the sister's. Theo simply could not stand to see Julia leaning on Debenham's arm, gushing all sorts of falsehoods into his ear. How little she had known the girl. If she had considered what a disservice she had done to Debenham, Theo might have experienced some shame, but as it was, she was too strongminded. She had plenty of difficulties of her own: other people's problems were not her concern. *She* could not help it if Debenham were too vain or stupid to discredit Julia's lies.

At any event, she did not have to suffer them overmuch, for preparations for the dinner party had taken up almost all of her time these past few days.

Despite her illness, the viscountess looked as lovely as ever in a becoming gown of watered gray silk. Theo, who felt the need of courage, had decided to wear her newest gown as a complement to their host. Upon his arrival in Bath, Sir Francis had decreed that she must have another evening dress and had refused to be countermanded. Theo herself could not regret it, for although the design was simple, the dress was a most becoming pale lavender in the finest gossamer silk. With a low square neck, short sleeves, and edged simply with white, it was far more striking than the elaborate confections that dripped with lace and beads. In such an ensemble, she must look suited to be the niece-in-law of Lady Verridge, and secretly she hoped that she would shine Julia down.

In spite of everything, she could not help but feel excited about this evening. If all went well, by tonight her engagement would be official. Perhaps the countess would even hold a ball of her own to announce it. Theo lost herself in happy daydreams, and only awoke when their carriage reached Marlborough Buildings.

Though they had arrived early, her mother wishing to make certain that all arrangements were in order, Sir Francis was already dressed and waiting for them. He came forward quickly to support the viscountess, and Theo could see how grateful her mother was for his arm. With his watchful eye upon Lady Westmoreland, Theo would not have to worry about her for tonight, at least.

There had been some slight alteration in their plans. Lady Verridge's other nephew had arrived unexpectedly in Bath. Although he did not stay with her, Sir Francis judged it impolitic to exclude him, and besides which he himself was slightly acquainted with the gentleman.

"You had been worrying over having an insufficient number of gentlemen here tonight—so I thought it well to include him."

Theo scarcely heard him. Her heart was too full. She thought it would take all of her cleverness to arrange a rendezvous with Mansfield. John Debenham, attired in his usual quiet way with a black tailcoat, white satin vest, and knee breeches entered the room and bowed to her. How grateful she was that he could not read her thoughts. He inquired about her recovery. The last thing she wished tonight was to be reminded of the accident.

"I am quite well—my injuries were trifling, after all," she said with as airy a laugh as she could manage.

"*Fortunately*—" he was beginning, but was interrupted by voices at the door.

Julia came bursting into the room in a cherry-red satin gown that was suited neither to her age nor her complexion. Having unceremoniously left her family behind, she latched on to Debenham's arm in what Theo thought was a particularly vulgar way.

"Dear John! I *missed* seeing you today most dreadfully. I must tell you what my sister and her quiz of a beau have been doing but hush—!" She silenced herself dramatically as Isabel, Warwick, and Mrs. Simpson came into the room.

Scarcely had all the pleasantries been exchanged before

another visitor was announced, a Major Boyce, and a small, trim man entered the room. At first Theo could not imagine who he was, and then she recollected Sir Francis's words about the countess's nephew.

Their host was greeting the gentleman warmly, and began introducing him to everyone in the room. When it was Theo's turn to meet the major, the piercing blue eyes seemed to survey her with something more than polite interest. She felt impelled to ask if they had met before, though this contingency seemed quite unlikely.

"Met before? No, I haven't had the pleasure," he replied disarmingly. Nothing altered in his face, but for some reason she felt that she had been quietly assessed.

Sir Francis soon guaranteed that the major would not lack for conversation the rest of the night by mentioning that he was only lately returned from the Peninsula. Everyone was full of questions, and Theo was pleased to see that even Julia's interest in Debenham was overwhelmed for the moment. Of course, it did no good, as Debenham was every bit as curious to hear the latest reports as everyone else.

It was perhaps unfortunate that Mansfield and the countess should have chosen this very moment to arrive. They entered the room to find Boyce in the middle of an admiring throng, who hung on his every word. The countess smiled with pleasure as she claimed this distinguished nephew's attention, and he kissed her hand gracefully. Theo, mindful only of Mansfield, observed that he looked rather preoccupied.

It was easy to maneuver herself into the corner by him. The rest of the party's attention was focused upon the major. She smiled invitingly at him, but he did not notice.

"Mr. Mansfield . . . Quentin," she whispered.

He looked down at her, a frown still creasing his forehead. "Ah, how lovely you look tonight, my dear."

She still had the feeling that his thoughts were elsewhere. "Quentin, I must talk to you," she said in a low voice. "I have come to a decision—"

He was studying his cousin, she realized. "He certainly seems to fascinate everyone, doesn't he?" he asked ruefully.

"Quentin—it is most important that you listen to me," she hissed. "I have decided that I will bear this secrecy no longer. You must tell the countess tonight or else I will."

He looked down at her, suddenly alive to her presence.

"*Now* would be the *worst* possible time! My aunt has appeared to be quite taken with my cousin these last two days. If she has any objections to our marriage, it would be the perfect opportunity for her to cut me off without a cent."

Theo had been understanding long enough. "In that case," she said in a low, cold voice, "our engagement is at an end."

"No!" He did not speak above a whisper, but his desperation was evident in his voice. "Do not speak so hastily. This is the last, the *only* possible threat to our future happiness. My cousin means to return to the Peninsula as soon as possible. It may be a matter of days. Once he is gone, we may safely approach my aunt. It is now, as they have just met and he has made such a favorable impression upon her, that there is any real danger."

Theo was tired of delays, tired of the secrecy. She looked away from Mansfield to the happy group on the opposite side of the room. Julia was whispering something into Debenham's ear, and he smiled and pressed her hand. Theo abruptly felt ill. "Very well. It will be as you say, but I do not intend to wait forever."

She would have been happy to speak with him further, but in another few moments Julia had run up to ask her archly what the two of them were whispering about so seriously. No real answer could be returned, of course, and Theo did her best to try to appear unembarrassed.

There was no opportunity for further conversation at dinner, either. Mansfield was seated on the opposite side of the table, between Isabel and Julia. Debenham, to Theo's right, was being engaged in conversation by the viscountess. To Theo's left was the major. He gave her an encouraging smile and asked how she did this evening.

She replied that she was well, and after asking about his own health and receiving a positive reply was at a loss as to how to continue. After another moment, she recollected his injury. Was it not very painful?

"I have a twinge or two from time to time, but it's nothing to speak of. I expect to be pronounced fit any day now." She felt that this last statement was pointed at her directly, and was aware again of assessing blue eyes, but she was unsure what he meant.

She knew she should be asking him all about the war, but she didn't know quite where to begin. "I am sorry—I am so ignorant, I could not even guess what to ask you. I know that we are at war, of course, but I have not read any of the dispatches and—"

He gave her a charming smile. "To be frank, Miss Westmoreland, there is no topic that bores me quite as much as the war. It is one thing to act and quite another to spend all your time talking about it. Tell me, have you heard the details of the grand fete the Prince Regent is planning?"

It was a subject much more to her taste, and she listened to his description with pleasure. In addition, he was able to put her au courant with various tidbits of society gossip. By the time they had proceeded to discussing the people and customs of the island of Jamaica, where he had been quartered some twelve years previously, she was quite comfortable and would have pronounced him to be a most entertaining companion.

Across the table, Mansfield and Julia seemed to be having no problem making conversation themselves. One of the things Theo admired most about Mansfield was his ability to maintain his spirits while in company. One would think, to look at him laughing at some sally of Julia's, that he hadn't a care in the world. She hoped that she was able to mask her disappointment equally well. It was preferable, too, to see Julia exercising her wiles upon Mansfield instead of Debenham for once. Mansfield at least was not susceptible.

Theo herself did not have speech with Debenham until the dinner was nearly done. The viscountess was engaged in conversation with Julia and Mansfield, while the major's attention had been claimed by his aunt. Debenham leaned over to speak in a low voice.

"Your mother is looking fatigued. Has she been ill?"

At a not-so-distant time, Theo would have taken his words as a reproach and fired up in her own defense. Now she interpreted them correctly as simply indicative of his concern. "Yes. I hope when this evening is done, I may persuade her to take a few days to be quiet and rest."

His eyes were still on the viscountess. "My father leaves tomorrow. Should you need me, just send a servant."

There was a depth of sincerity behind the simple words. Theo thanked him awkwardly. Despite all his faults, she knew that he was thoroughly reliable. She glanced at that dark visage and saw an inscrutable expression there. He was looking at Julia, who had just rapped Mansfield playfully on the arm with her fan.

Did Julia's flirtatiousness cause him pain? Despite the fact that she had hoped the girl would expose herself in this way, Theo suddenly felt the urge to spare Debenham as best she could.

"She is so high-spirited," murmured Theo, while wondering indignantly to herself why she should defend Julia.

"What?" It appeared that Debenham was not attending to her.

The dinner passed off as well as Theo could have hoped. She managed to repress her own sense of despair and to present a smiling face to the rest of the company. When the ladies withdrew, the countess singled her out in a marked manner as before, taking her by the hand and monopolizing her in conversation. Thankfully, the topic of the major had ousted her favorite subject, though she showed an unfortunate interest in discussing the details of his wound and the surgery it had necessitated. Theo did not know the major well, but she had the feeling that he would have wished for anything rather than to have the topic of his injury covered so minutely.

The other subject that seemed uppermost in the countess's mind was that of her companion, who at length, she had been forced to dismiss. "I gave her a nice pension, of course, my dear, but tell me, what am I to do? I simply must find a pleasant *young* lady to companion me—I am so dreadfully tired of old faces!—and I have not the least idea where to begin searching . . . Of course, I suppose *most* young ladies would find it *dreadfully* dull to spend their days with a tiresome old lady such as I . . ."

Theo was making polite protests to the contrary when her mother interrupted them. "I do not wish to cut our conversation short, but I am afraid that if we mean to be at the ball in time for dancing, we had better leave."

The ball was just possibly the most miserable affair that Theo had ever attended. It seemed that every ingredient imaginable was there to ruin her evening. First of all, there was her own disappointment to be borne. She had expected to be engaged by now. Instead, matters stood in the same intolerable situation as before, with no resolution in sight.

She might easily have wept with anger, but instead she was forced to present a smiling face to the world.

Next, she must endure the unbearable sight of Julia flirting outrageously with Debenham. Theo was surprised that her mother did not speak to her, but then Lady Simpson was notoriously lax. Theo could almost swear she had seen Julia's lips brush Debenham's ear when she stood on tiptoe to whisper to him. She had also overbalanced herself and half fallen against him in what Theo thought was a most blatant, vulgar manner. They had stood up for two dances in a row. It made Theo sick to see it.

Most odious of all, though, was Miss Bromley's condescension. She and her mother had obviously cast themselves in the roles of Bath's leading hostesses. Theo wished again that she might have avoided this ball, but her mother had been adamant. Since the Bromleys were making the effort to discharge their social obligations, the Westmorelands could not refuse the invitation.

Miss Bromley had greeted Julia in a warm manner. Theo had noticed before that she took pains to single out the younger sister. Theo herself was accorded the welcome of a social inferior. When she thought of how grateful the Bromleys had been for *her* family's invitations in the past, she could have screamed in vexation.

When Miss Bromley did bother to speak to her later on in the evening, Theo knew that it could only mean trouble. Dislike it as she might, she could not prevent the other from sitting down beside her and addressing her in a kindly poisonous tone.

"I do hope that you are enjoying our little fete, Theo. It is just a small affair, of course—" It was the largest private party Theo had attended since arriving in Bath. "—But fortunately everyone seems to be amusing themselves tolerably well."

It took every effort to simply keep her mouth shut. Theo could not force herself to murmur polite inanities.

"Particularly your friend Mr. Mansfield. *Julia* seems to be making quite an impression upon him." Theo did not have to look up to know where Miss Bromley's eyes were. Julia was waltzing with Mansfield, Theo having tired of the activity early on this evening. Theo could hear her shrill giggles floating across the ballroom.

"Can it be that she has stolen *another* of your beaux?"

Theo slapped her with all the force she could muster. No, she hadn't. Her hands remained in her lap, though they were clenched together tightly. Miss Bromley gave a low laugh. "I am only *teasing* you, of course. Dear Julia confided in me that we should expect an interesting announcement shortly. Lady Debenham. It sounds well, I think, don't you?"

Theo did not know whether she made a response or not, but eventually Miss Bromley tired of her sport and departed for the far more attractive prospect of flirting with the major. The latter had created quite a stir, for it was his first appearance at a large gathering.

Had she felt more herself, Theo might have sympathized with him, for he clearly disliked all the attention he was garnering. As it was, she could only sit as still as a statue, her smile, she hoped, frozen in place. She felt as if she had been struck a physical blow. Debenham and Julia to be married! It was her worst nightmare come true. She vainly wished that the report might prove false, but in her heart she could not doubt it. Even Julia would not boast of such a thing unless Debenham had made his intentions plain. They doubtless were only waiting to announce their engagement formally. Theo's head was beginning to pound.

She did not know how long she might have managed to sit like that, but fortunately her endurance was not to be put to the test. Debenham appeared by her side. "Are you ready to go?" he whispered.

How could he know what she was experiencing? She nodded her head, blindly.

"Good. Your mother's not feeling well. Sir Francis noticed it and asked if we might leave."

Placing her arm in his, he escorted her from the unbearably hot, noisy, and overcrowded ballroom. He made their apologies to their hostess, assuring her that they had enjoyed themselves thoroughly, which perhaps he had. Theo was grateful that all she had to do was to nod and smile. She did not trust herself to speak.

She did not contribute to the conversation during the carriage ride home, and she was glad for Debenham's taciturn nature, since he clearly did not expect her to talk. Her mother and Sir Francis conversed quietly, without their usual exuberance. It was a most curious, contrary feeling, that of wishing the carriage ride would end as soon as possible and yet dreading the moment when it would.

Fortunately, when they arrived, the gentlemen's concern was focused upon her mother, who was dreadfully pale. Theo escaped their observant eyes. Peggy was called and the viscountess settled. Theo offered to help in any way she could, but her presence was obviously superfluous. She trudged up to her room and began her preparations for bed.

She did not have long to wait before Peggy came upstairs to help her finish undressing. In her concern over the mother, the servant failed to notice the unusual expression of melancholy on the daughter's face. She finished her ministrations, and Theo was left alone with her own bitter thoughts.

A large tear slid down one cheek and then another, but Theo did not weep aloud. It seemed like years instead of months ago that she told Debenham she was capable of running her own life. What a fine muddle she had made of it! She crossed the room to find a handkerchief and wiped her eyes, but still the great silent tears continued to roll down her face.

It wasn't until Miss Bromley had told her that she realized the length, breadth, and depth of her mistake. She could not bear the thought of Debenham married to Julia because she herself loved him! Mansfield was nothing more than a pretty Capodimonte statuette next to him. She had judged by appearances and ignored Debenham's true worth. How could she have been so blind? And she herself had been the one to "give" him to Julia! The irony of it was overwhelming. She dabbed quietly at her eyes again.

And there was nothing to be done now. Even if she could have freed herself from her own engagement, Debenham would still be taken. He had asked Julia to marry him, and she had accepted. No gentleman would ever renege on an offer of marriage, and Debenham was a gentleman. The thought started the tears flowing afresh. Why had she ever let herself be convinced that all she had to do was marry a fortune to solve all her troubles? Her husband hunt, once successful, had been the beginning to the worst of her problems.

She dried her eyes again. She was committed now. Mansfield's feelings must be considered, even if her own could not be. How hurt he would be by her disloyalty: after all, despite the fact that he might not be capable of great depth of feeling, he had remained constant to her. She could not afford to throw away her one chance at a fortune. She might not love him, but she would try to be a considerate and dutiful wife.

Chapter Thirteen

In sharp contrast to Theo's misery, Julia and Mansfield were having a marvelous time at the ball. Since they had been abandoned by Debenham and Theo, there seemed no harm in partnering each other for another dance. It was a pleasure, as Mansfield had discovered that Julia not only was light on her feet, but also pleasingly pliable in his arms. His compliments on her dancing could not help but be returned with the utmost sincerity. The truth was that he would have been happy to dance with her again, but he also realized that it might occasion comment. Still, there seemed to be no need to forswear her company. Julia eagerly accepted his suggestion, and they found chairs together. Her mother, in her usual lax manner, smiled at them indulgently across the room, and did not attempt to intrude upon their conversation.

Julia giggled and hid her face behind her fan. "Oh, if only you knew what I am thinking!"

"What is it?" he asked with a gentle smile.

"No, no, I cannot tell you—it would embarrass me."

"Come now, you can't raise a fellow's curiosity and leave it unsatisfied—"

After arguing for another minute in the same vein, Julia submitted with another giggle. "All right then, but you will have to excuse my blushes! I was just thinking of the first time that I saw you here in Bath, and thought you were the handsomest man I had ever seen. If I had known then that I would dance *two* dances with you tonight, I declare I would have swooned away with joy!"

Mansfield was no less susceptible to flattery than the next man, perhaps more so since it had been so sadly wanting these past several weeks. It would not matter if he indulged himself with a little pleasant and much needed flirtation. "I do not see you swooning now," he pointed out playfully.

She giggled again. "No. Well I *know* you now, after all. You seemed like some sort of a god to me then, but now I know that you are a man, just flesh and blood like myself—"

Her voice dropped off abruptly. There was a sudden heat racing through his veins. Julia was looking at him hungrily, her lips parted slightly. If they had not been sitting in the middle of a crowded ballroom, he would have been tempted to seize her in his arms and kiss her.

My word! What was he thinking of? He was an engaged man. He extracted a handkerchief from his pocket and wiped his forehead delicately. Julia had dropped her eyes and blushed a rosy pink.

"It is so hot in here," he commented. "Shall we go in search of something to drink?"

Julia assented quickly.

"Certain that you have everything?" The deepset gray eyes stared anxiously at him as Sir Francis placed his top hat on his head and carefully adjusted the angle of it. He turned his head to smile at his son.

"I am always certain. It is one of my many virtues."

"And should you need protection, you have—"

"Dear me, what filial concern." He extracted a long, wicked-looking pistol from his traveling bag. "A new one, from a matched set I had made to order recently. Rather nice, is it not?"

Debenham snorted. "I am not talking about *that*. I am speaking of help—"

"Well, you are within easy reach of a messenger, are you not?"

There was an unspoken wish in that countenance. Sir Francis saw it, and as he began on his way out of the room, said gently, "If I can arrange for you to be present when we bag our bird, I will. You have done most of the work, and you deserve to be there."

There was no spoken word of thanks, only a tight gripping of hands.

"Take good care of the ladies." Sir Francis stepped out the front door, and sprang lightly up onto the step of the waiting post chaise.

When Theo visited her mother in the morning, she could not help but feel concern. The viscountess's face was drawn with fatigue and pain. Sir Francis's barouche had arrived to take her to the Pump Room, but Lady Westmoreland only shook her head at the news. She coughed, then gave her orders to Theo.

"Please send it back and tell the driver that I shall not need it today, and perhaps tomorrow. Let me see . . . just tell him that we shall send for him if we need it."

"You don't mean to visit the Pump Room?"

The viscountess coughed again, apologetically. "I do not feel quite up to it today. I think that perhaps you and Sir Francis were right, and that I overtaxed myself yesterday."

Theo stared at the handkerchief. There were flecks of blood on it. "You are ill. I will send for the doctor."

Her mother did not have the strength to protest.

When the physician arrived, the news was as bad as Theo had feared. He was reassuring to the viscountess, advising plenty of rest, strict attention to her diet, and leaving a mixture of white rosin and honey to help cure her cough. Once outside the room, his face became grave.

"I am afraid that all of my lady's activity, as well as this changeable weather has had an adverse effect upon her constitution."

"What may we do?"

"Follow the advice that I gave her. Make certain that she rests, although it will not harm her to walk about her room occasionally. Keep her indoors when it is damp."

"And what of the waters?"

"It is more important for her to have rest at this moment." He saw Theo's anxiety and sighed. "At all costs, we must do all we can to prevent her catching cold. She is exhausted, and weak, and it could easily develop into something worse."

After he had departed, Theo consulted with Peggy about her mother's care. One of them must always be there at mealtime to see that she ate. Together, they must keep her from wearying herself further.

In a way, it was fortunate that matters with Mansfield stood as they did. There was no point in seeing him at the moment or in trying to conciliate the countess. She might focus all her energies where they were most needed.

She thought of sending for Debenham, then checked herself. After all, what could he do? He undoubtedly was out taking Julia for a drive or a walk anyway. He, at least, should be allowed to enjoy himself.

If she was not giving a great deal of thought to her fiancé, at least it could be said that she was not occupying the premier place in his mind either. Last night's ball had turned the major into a celebrated figure in Bath, and the countess was reveling vicariously in what she saw as his triumph. At the Pump Room, Mansfield had been forced to listen to a catalog of all the major's virtues. Just as bad were all the acquaintances who came up to them, continuously it seemed, to congratulate the countess upon having such a distinguished nephew. The major himself was not present. Having no interest in a course of the waters, he found it incredible that anyone but an invalid should go there voluntarily.

He meant to have them for dinner tonight at the White Hart Inn, where he was staying, by way of repaying the countess for her dinner invitations. Mansfield was not looking forward to it at all. His prospects seemed as dark as they could be. He was left only with the hope that the major might return to action soon.

The countess had sent him to return her books to Duffield's. Even though a short drive, it would at least give him the chance to exercise his bays for the first time since the accident. Fortunately, the carriage maker had been able to repair his phaeton quickly. He had been happy to see that it looked just the same as when he had purchased it. He clucked to the bays, and set off in prime style on his way to Milsom Street.

It was coincidental that when he arrived at Duffield's, he found Miss Julia Simpson there, selecting from among the new novels. She greeted him most cordially, though he could not be insensible of the blush that stained her cheeks when she saw him. A conversation about the delightfulness of the ball was inevitable. After their business was transacted, it was only polite to linger in conversation and to remark upon the fact that she was unaccompanied. She wrinkled her nose.

"Oh, as to that—I came out with Isabel and her beau— but they were determined to go for a stroll in the gravel walk. It sounded deadly dull to me, and besides, they made certain to show that *I* was less than welcome, so I parted ways with them, and thought to stop in the library here before I went home."

"I am surprised that Debenham is not here with you."

"Oh, well—" She gave him an arch glance. "I do not live in his pocket, you know."

With his customary good manners, he offered to drive her home. Julia glanced out the windows and let out a little shriek of pleasure. "Do not tell me that your phaeton is repaired already. Oh, I am dying with eagerness to take a ride in it. Let me go see it."

She fled precipitately out to the street with Mansfield close behind her. Her exclamations upon the handsomeness of his equipage and the beauty of his horses had its inevitable effect upon Mansfield. It did not occur to him that Julia had been the one to criticize those very same horses. Instead, he wondered to himself, why Theo had been less exuberant in her praises. It wasn't every day that a gentleman purchased a new carriage. If she were truly a feeling sort of girl, she might have responded the way Julia had, who was standing beside it, practically panting in her wish to be driven in this marvelous conveyance.

What was more, driving Julia about, he found that she gave him confidence. Unlike Theo, who was always pointing out possible obstacles and dangers, Julia never criticized his driving, seeming to have unlimited confidence in his coachmanship, and openly admiring the way he handled the ribbons. When he tossed the end of the whip above his head and successfully caught the thong, she exclaimed aloud in wonder. She was forced to confess to him that Debenham, although boasting such a great reputation as a whip, did not perform half of these elegant little tricks and in fact, drove in such a quiet manner that she hardly noticed how he did it. The passage of days had not dulled the sting of Debenham's words to him. Mansfield's estimation of Julia's perspicacity soared.

They were having such a pleasant drive, it seemed a shame to cut it short. Mansfield impulsively suggested that they extend it long enough to drive up Beechen Cliff and just as impulsively, Julia agreed. Accordingly, as they left Bond Street, they did not turn to head for Laura Place, but proceeded along Patronage Lane to Westgate Street. As Mansfield negotiated the difficult corner that led to Stall Street, they passed the White Hart Inn. With all their attention on the traffic, they did not notice a small, dark-haired gentleman who had limpingly left the inn and turned onto Westgate Street. The gentleman stopped just as a break in the traffic enabled Mansfield to urge his horses forward, and he and Julia went on their smiling way. The major stared after them thoughtfully for a moment, but was recalled by an angry pedestrian who protested that he was blocking the way. He nodded courteously and proceeded down Westgate Street, and if it were possible to limp jauntily, he was the man who accomplished it.

In a short time, Mansfield's carriage had reached Beechen Cliff, and it became immediately apparent that it was insufficient as a destination. As they rattled across the old bridge, Mansfield sneaked a look at Julia, and could read in her face that she was experiencing the same sort of disappointment that he himself was. Why, if they simply turned left upon Claverton Street as soon as they had crossed the bridge, they could extend their trip further by continuing on to Claverton Down. To say that Julia was amenable to the suggestion was to understate the case. Her face was pink with happiness. A few of those golden tresses had escaped confinement under her bonnet and now waved gently in the breeze. She made a most attractive picture, and after staring at her for a moment, Mansfield forced himself to turn his attention back to the road. For perhaps the first time, he wondered if he hadn't perhaps acted just a little too rashly in proposing this trip. Oh well, it was too late now. He flashed her a wholehearted smile, and gave himself up to the pleasure of the afternoon.

Since Theo herself did not feel like heading out and about, it was in some ways a relief to be confined at home in order to help care for her mother. The one drawback was that not being a sedentary person, there was little to occupy her time. She had never taken to painting or drawing. Her musical ability was negligible, and in any case, they could not have afforded to hire a pianoforte. She was not a great reader, and there were no old and dear friends deserving of a letter. In fact, the only person whom she could think to write to was her brother, and such news as she felt able to impart to him took up only a sheet and a half of paper. Accordingly, with a great deal of resignation, she took up the detested embroidery once again. Perhaps, if she applied herself diligently, she might finish it by the end of the year.

She was greatly relieved therefore when Peggy entered and announced that they had a visitor. She was so grateful to be interrupted that she would have allowed anyone to be admitted. She was a little surprised to hear that it was the major.

She greeted him, glad that she had thought to wear one of her more becoming dresses today. In spite of herself, her expression must have seemed inquiring, for without more ado he explained that he had been sorry not to have bid them farewell last night. He had only just heard of her mother's illness, and he was calling to see how she did.

She invited him to share tea with her. He did not wish to impose, and he was somewhat concerned about the proprieties, but Peggy's watchdog presence must have reassured him. Theo, glad for this one diversion, did not intend him to escape, and he permitted himself to be gently overruled.

His long military career had ensured that a good part of his life had been spent in exotic climes. In addition to service in Spain and Portugal, he had been stationed in Barbados and St. Domingo (where he had very nearly died of fever), as well as in various parts of Ireland and England. It was an interesting life, rendered the more so by his powers of observation and his intelligence. In a few sentences, he could convey to Theo what it felt like to spend your days in the muggy heat of a jungle, relate an amusing anecdote about a personal mishap that had occurred while fording a Spanish river, or sketch a picture of days and evenings spent in great houses in (it seemed) almost every part of the country. Theo could have listened to him for hours, and she felt a pang of envy. Why was it that men were permitted to have such interesting lives while women must content themselves with staying at home and taking care of the sewing? She could not know all the gruesome details that he was sparing her, and indeed could not have guessed at them from his airy manner.

In short, he was such pleasant company that she was surprised when he extracted his pocket watch, consulted it, and announced that he had imposed upon her far too long today. Surely he could not have been here for over an hour already?

He took his leave most gracefully, telling her that he would be happy to be of service to her and the viscountess in any way that he could. He trusted that she would be feeling better by the morrow, and hinted that he might call again, to give Lady Westmoreland his good wishes in person. "—But perhaps I am making myself too familiar. For all I know, you may be wishing me at the devil at this very moment, and are simply too polite to say so—"

"Oh, no," Theo assured him quickly, with obvious sincerity. "I enjoyed your visit so much—and I know that my mother would like to see you also . . . as soon as she is well enough."

He bowed by way of reply and made his way from the room. She hoped he *would* come again tomorrow. Then she might look forward to at least one bright spot in her day.

Visitors today, like sorrows apparently, did not come single spies, for scarcely had she picked up her tambour work when another arrived. Perhaps it was Mansfield, concerned about the lowness of spirits she suffered from last night. Scarce had the fear arisen when it was replaced by a worse. The visitor was Debenham. She asked Peggy to show him in.

He strode into the room, and she thought to herself how irritated she once would have been at a man paying a call in boots and buckskin breeches. Now, of course, she wouldn't have cared if he had arrived in a pair of trousers! He apparently was in some haste, also, for he held his hat in his hand.

"I don't mean to detain you. I came to see how your mother does."

She urged him to be seated, and he lowered himself gingerly onto a little black-and-gilt Chinese chair. She reported the doctor's reading of the situation, and the black eyebrows met each other.

"It is a damnable time for my father to have left. He could not help it, though," he added hastily, lest she consider him to be blaming his father for the circumstance. "The coachman gave me your message as soon as I arrived home. I would have come sooner, but Sir Francis had left some matters for me to attend to—"

At least he had not been with Julia. She crushed the thought as soon as it arose.

"—Which would brook no delay. Had the doctor other recommendations?"

She was forced to admit not.

He rose. "In that case, my presence can only be a hindrance. The carriage is at your disposal—and hers, whenever she wishes. Ask the doctor if the water may not be brought warm to her from the Pump Room. I'll attend to it if it may."

He took her hand. "If there is anything else I can do, you have only to call."

How could a person's hand be so very warm and comforting all on its own? She could not look up to meet those eyes, but instead murmured something that she hoped was an appropriate response.

He bowed quickly over her hand, and in another moment he was gone. She raised her eyes, which were now full of unshed tears. How could she have overlooked all his virtues for so long? What a pigheaded fool she had been.

It was decidedly odd how matters, instead of straightening themselves out and becoming simpler, instead tangled themselves up further and became increasingly complex, thought Mansfield as he guided his tired team home from Laura Place. The whole outing today had started out so innocently. More a question of good manners than anything else. And really, there had seemed to be no harm in prolonging the drive to Beechen Cliff, and from there to Claverton Down. It had seemed to be so unexceptionable, too. Julia had admired the view greatly, and it would have been a shame not to give her a real ride in his carriage, as taken as she was by it. He cast his mind back, trying to remember when things had gone wrong.

Somehow the conversation had turned to horses. That he did remember. Julia had confessed that she had always harbored a terror of riding, ever since a pony had thrown her when she was seven years old. It was such a handicap to her. Everyone else rode. There were so many parties and excursions from which her fear excluded her. Why, when they had all met at the riding school that one time, for example. How she wished *she* might have ridden with the others, with him in particular, she admitted, as she pinkened. He had such an easy seat upon a horse. She supposed it must be different when one had ridden all one's life.

He in turn was forced to acknowledge that he was not as at ease upon a horse as it seemed. He was not at all *frightened*, of course, he simply did not enjoy riding those high-strung sorts of beasts others favored. It simply didn't make any sense to him. Why spend all your time fighting to keep the animal under control? A gentle, even-tempered horse was what he liked, and he wagered Miss Julia would, too.

Strain his memory as he might, he could not remember the exact turn the next few sentences had taken. He only knew that it had ended with his urging Julia to go to the riding school with him the next day in order that he might supervise a lesson.

"Oh, if only I might," she had said, blushing. "I am certain that I should be safe with *you* there."

It was at that instant that he had awakened with a rapidly sinking feeling in the pit of his stomach. What on earth *was* he doing? He was engaged to Theodora, that lovely epitome of a lady, and he could just imagine what she would have to say about this proposed expedition. It made him break out in a cold sweat to think of it. He did his best to retrieve his error.

"Well, I daresay that Debenham would enjoy taking you there himself instead. He's a bruising rider, they say, as well as a famous whip."

Julia had dropped her eyes. "I-I was not quite honest with Mr. Debenham. I gave him the impression that I could ride well already." She peeped at Mansfield from under her lashes. "I think that *you* could make me feel easier around a horse than Mr. Debenham, anyway. He is so brusque and he says such cutting things, I would be afraid to take a riding lesson in his company." She smiled a little smile, and his heart turned over in his breast.

It was settled that he would call for her at ten the next morning.

Sir Francis smiled gently at the thin, nervous gentleman seated on the elegant gilded Greek revival settee. He looked uncomfortable perched on the red satin cushions, and in an effort to appear less so, rested his hand for a moment on one of the arms, only to draw it back abruptly upon noticing that it was a lion's head.

"You were much too kind," commented Sir Francis. "I am certain that your day is a full one, and I would not have wished for you to waste such a considerable portion of it in waiting for me. May I offer you some port?" Seeing that his visitor was ready to decline, he added, "I am having a glass myself. Or I will have tea brought, if you prefer."

"No, thank you, Sir Francis."

He wished to put this visitor at ease, but clearly it could not be done. Sir Francis poured himself a glass of port and seated himself opposite the other, who was staring at him in a marked manner.

"Is there something wrong?" The other shook his head, but Sir Francis persisted. "Out with it, my dear fellow. What is troubling you?"

"Oh, sir. I would never wish to . . . it's just that . . . you see, I expected someone quite different after dealing with your son . . ."

"And we are nothing like, are we?" asked Sir Francis with obvious sympathy. "I am sorry, I know it must be rather a shock to you. But let us attend to the business at hand. You wrote that you had made some progress, which is why I am here."

"Yes, we have discovered where Oliphant's partner is— that is, the man we *believe* to have been Oliphant's partner in this business. We have made additional inquires and feel almost certain that it is the same man." His self-consciousness had vanished in his excitement.

"Excellent. If you will be kind enough to give me the address, then, I will not trouble you further with the matter."

"G-give you the address. Oh, no sir, I could not. I can just imagine what Mr. Thomas would say to that. No, Sir Francis, if you are still unwilling to turn the matter over to Bow Street, I will accompany you to the person's lodgings myself. Or I would be happy to go in your stead."

Sir Francis, like his son before him, saw that he was to be saddled unwillingly with an accomplice. He was too well-bred to betray his feelings, however, and instead merely said, "Thank you. You are too kind. I do not feel that it would be to our advantage to call in Bow Street at this late stage in the proceedings. If it is convenient for you, we will set out tomorrow to see this person. I hope he is not settled at too great a distance from here."

Mr. Sanders appeared even more anxious than before. "But sir, I would have you consider the matter well. The man lives in Stepney, and it is no fit place for someone of your station—"

"Stepney, eh? Do you know, I have considered that my life has been a full one up until now, but I never yet have been privileged to visit Stepney. It is obviously time to remedy the matter. Where is Stepney? East of here, I believe."

Since they were presently situated in Debenham House, a handsome mansion on Charles Street, Sir Francis was technically correct, but his words understated the case. Sanders coughed discreetly. "Yes, it is situated by the West India Docks. At one time, a part of his business was concerned with shipping." He stared anxiously at Sir Francis. "I would have you consider the matter well, sir. It is a most unwholesome part of the area and—"

Sir Francis stared him into silence. "As I noted before, I have lived a long and very *full* life. I daresay I am less easily shocked than you may imagine. I will bow to your expertise in this matter. Shall we take my carriage or make our trip in a rattler?" He saw the confusion upon his confederate's face and smiled gently to himself, adding, "—a hired hack, that is. What is your opinion?"

Chapter Fourteen

It was pitch-black night when the noise awakened Theo. Disoriented, she groped about her in the dark. The evening had been too warm to necessitate a fire, and there was no light in her room. The noises were coming from downstairs, and now a bell rang. It must be her mother. She felt around for her wrapper and throwing it about her, called, "I am coming Mother!" She put on her slippers and made her way downstairs cautiously.

There was a candle burning in her mother's room. The bed was empty. A chair had been knocked over. Her mother was at the window, leaning out, gasping for air.

"Mother!" Theo fled quickly to her side, but she could only help support her. It was frightful. She could hear a bubbling sound as her mother struggled to take in air. There was nothing Theo could do.

Peggy appeared in the door, shawl over her nightdress and cap on her head. "Send Patrick for the doctor," ordered Theo.

When Peggy returned several minutes later, in accordance with Theo's directions, she righted the chair and brought it over to the window. Together she and Theo lowered the viscountess gently into it. Lady Westmoreland's condition had not improved. She gasped for breath as desperately as ever. Theo was close to being frightened witless, but she told herself that she must remain strong for her mother's sake.

She closed the window, mindful of the doctor's warning about the damp, and fetched her mother a new handkerchief for the coughs that racked her. Peggy was beside herself. "Lord, Miss Theo, what will we do?"

"Pray, Peggy" was all the advice Theo could give.

It was probably only an hour that they stood like that, Theo stroking her mother's hair gently, or holding her burning hand as she wheezed. It seemed far more like a lifetime. Miraculously, the viscountess's respiration began to ease. She was breathing more slowly and taking in deeper breaths. At the same time, she started to shiver violently. "I am so *cold*," she said in a weak voice.

Theo and Peggy exchanged glances. Despite the window's having been open, the room was not at all cold. Theo felt her mother's hand again. It was feverish.

"We had better get her to bed," she said.

They had just accomplished it when the doctor arrived. Theo gave him an account of all that had happened, and he said not a word, but began to examine his patient immediately.

In response to his commands, Peggy fetched extra pillows, so that the viscountess was propped up into almost a sitting position. The servant settled herself beside her mistress in order to sponge her brow, while Theo and the doctor stepped in the next room to consult. The viscountess had lapsed into unconsciousness, but every now and then she moaned. It was almost more than Theo could bear.

"It is as I feared," the doctor told her briskly. "It is an inflammation of the lungs."

"Will she live?" It was an awful question to have to ask.

He polished his spectacles by way of a diversion before he spoke. "It is a grave illness for anyone. Given your mother's damaged heart and her weakened condition . . ." His voice trailed off.

"What can we do?" Theo would not accept his answer. She could not.

"If you can make her drink *cold* water, it would be the best thing to make her fever go down. Should it become even worse, to the point where she is terribly restless, you may plunge her into a cold bath also, but it is a dangerous remedy, and should only be tried when all else fails." He glanced at Theo, who was obviously expecting more. He sighed.

"If her pulse were stronger, I might bleed her, but it is too weak for that to be of benefit. There are those who would recommend treacle plasters to the head. It will do no harm in any case, I should think. You may continue to give her the other medicine for her cough. Do all that you can to see that she remains sitting. If she lies down, her lungs will fill and she will have another attack."

Theo recollected Debenham's offer. "A gentleman," she could not help blushing, "has offered to bring her water hot from the Pump Room every day if it might help her."

The doctor shook his head. "If the fever leaves her, it might be worthwhile. Until then, I prefer her to drink cold water."

She was waiting for reassurance, and he had none to give her. "Do all that you can to see that she rests as much as possible. The fever will likely remain for several days. If she has another attack, call me." The lines under his own eyes were drawn deeply by fatigue.

Theo had been brave for this long, but now her lip began to tremble. The doctor laid a kindly hand on her shoulder. "I know that Lady Westmoreland will not lack for vigilance or care. With God's help, she will come through this crisis."

"Thank you." She was no serving girl, she was the daughter of a viscount. She raised her chin proudly. She would be strong for her mother's sake. "I will call Peggy to see you to the door."

"There is no need. I will see myself out."

She returned to the bedroom, where her mother tossed and cried out restlessly. The enormity of the situation before her almost overwhelmed Theo. "You'd better go to bed now, Peggy."

The old servant started to protest, but Theo cut her off.

"You are the only other one I trust to nurse her. If the two of us are to do this by ourselves, one of us must rest while the other remains by her side."

Her logic was inarguable. Peggy left and Theo settled herself by the bed, reaching out now and again to sponge her mother's brow.

Promptly at ten the next morning, a claret-colored phaeton pulled up in Laura Place. It might be wrong, but Mansfield had given his word and he could not go back on it. Besides which, he was looking forward to helping Julia with her riding lesson. She was right, after all. Debenham probably would say something beastly to her and rattle her thoroughly, so that nothing would be accomplished. With all due modesty, he knew that he himself was the better man for the job.

Julia looked lovely today in a riding habit in her favorite blue with braid across the bodice and a most fetching slouch hat of chip. When Mansfield laughingly teased her that she was well prepared for one who never rode, she shook her head. "Dear Papa and Mama say that I should be well dressed for every occasion, so Mama insisted that I have two or three riding habits made up this year, even though she knew my predilections. Of course, if I come to like it, I am sure she will let me have more."

He was a little staggered by her words. "Two or three made up *this* year"—when she didn't even like to ride! He had always seen her well dressed, and come to think of it had never seen her wear a gown twice, but he never had considered the matter deeply before. The Simpsons's fortune must be staggeringly large.

The lesson went as well as anyone could have hoped. Although she admitted her trepidation, with Mansfield's gentle encouragement, Julia was persuaded to mount upon a gentle, elderly mare. As her confidence grew, she became bold enough to walk it about the ring once or twice, and finally ended by coaxing it into a gentle trot. Both the riding master and Mansfield pronounced themselves pleased by her success. Her cheeks glowed at their praises, but she gave full credit to Mansfield.

"Oh, if *you* had not been here with me, I am sure I would never have *dared*—"

"Nonsense."

"No, you made me feel that I could do it." She sighed. "I think if I continued, I might become even better at it."

"Well, you must." Both Mansfield and the riding master were in agreement on this point.

She shook her head, her ringlets bouncing prettily beneath the bonnet of straw. "Oh, I am sure that I could not. I would come, of course, but unless someone were here to make me get on the horse, I wouldn't do it. I haven't enough self-confidence, I suppose—"

Mansfield again assured her that she was wrong, but she only shook her head once more. "No, it was most kind of you to accompany me today, though I know it must be a dead bore for you—"

He protested that she was wrong.

"—But I could not ask you to take me again. It would be an imposition, I know."

The riding master, who had taken a keen interest in the conversation, saw an opportunity for future custom and thought to encourage it. He coughed politely. "Mr. Mansfield rides here on Thursdays and Saturdays."

Julia's eyes turned inquiringly upon him.

"That is right. I should be happy for you to join me," Mansfield heard himself saying.

Of course, she stated that she could not accept his kind offer, but illogically, he did all he could to convince her that she would not be obtruding upon his pleasures. It ended with an agreement that they should meet twice a week to ride. It was patent that Theo would not be happy, but after all, did she have to know? It was such a harmless thing really. He caught Julia's admiring eyes upon him, and could not help puffing up slightly with pleasure. He was entitled to some enjoyment from life. There had been so little, lately.

Theo could never remember having passed a more exhausting night. On top of the sheer labor, the anxiety she felt had taken a terrible toll. Her mother had remained restless and feverish the entire night. She tossed and turned so that it was necessary to rearrange the pillows every few minutes. Fortunately, as a result, the patient had not succumbed to another of the frightening attacks of breathlessness. Still, it was terrifying to know that all that Theo was doing had so little effect. She had tried the treacle plasters, but her mother had merely torn them from her head with a mutter. She had not been able to coax more than a swallow or two of water down her. Theo sponged her forehead almost continuously, but the viscountess was still burning hot.

Once or twice during the night, when the restlessness was at its peak, she had thought to call Peggy and try the cold bath to bring down the fever, but she hesitated. From what the doctor had said, it might prove to be the end of her mother, instead of a cure. Fortunately, the restlessness would abate again for the moment, rendering such a drastic step unnecessary.

The hardest thing for Theo was to listen to her mother's piteous cries. She often called for her daughter, and though unconscious, was quieted when Theo took her hand and spoke to her in a soothing voice. To Theo's surprise, the other name that she cried out was Sir Francis's. She had not realized how greatly her mother had come to depend upon him. Not all the comforting phrases in the world could soothe her. Like his son, Theo began to wish that Sir Francis had not chosen this particular time to absent himself.

When the morning light began to filter in, Theo realized with relief that it would not be long before Peggy came to take her place. As much as she wished to stay by her mother's side, she knew that she could not remain an effective nursemaid for long, as weary as she was. It was surprising that the conscientious Peggy did not appear immediately. She undoubtedly was tired, too. Theo would let her sleep a little longer.

The minutes ticked by. Theo was feeling very tired. The sun was up. It was most curious that Peggy hadn't arrived to take over her duties. Not liking to leave her mother, Theo rang the bell. There was no response. After waiting several minutes, she rang it again. The little maid, Molly, appeared.

"Where is Mrs. Chambers?" Theo demanded.

Molly looked frightened. "She's in her bed, Miss Theo, and she says she's to come here to help you, but she doesn't look good to me."

"Is she ill?"

"She *says* she's not, but . . ."

Theo's brain was too confused to try to puzzle out this enigma. "Stay here," she ordered. "I will go see what is wrong."

She found Peggy seated on her bed upstairs, struggling bravely to urge her legs into a pair of cotton stockings. Theo saw her face and went straight over to her.

"You are not well, Peggy. You must lie down."

"No, I must help you, Miss Theo."

Theo placed a hand on the servant's forehead. It was burning hot. "You cannot help anyone now. You are too ill."

"I am well enough." Having finished her task, Peggy attempted to rise, only to collapse on the floor. Theo took hold of her about the waist and helped her back onto the bed.

"You will only make yourself worse if you try to rise now."

Tears were beginning to flow down Peggy's face, a measure of just how weak she had become. Theo had never seen Peggy cry before.

"But I can't leave you to nurse her alone. You're too tired already, Miss Theo."

"Molly may help me—"

"That flibbertigibbet! She'll fall asleep or go into one of her daydreams and forget all about my poor lady—"

"I can nurse my mother awhile yet. You rest. Perhaps a little sleep will restore you."

Theo had no such optimistic thought, but she could not let Peggy know that. After a few more protests, the servant allowed herself to be convinced and lay back down upon her bed.

Theo went to her own room to change into the gown that Peggy had fortunately pressed the previous day. She then trudged slowly downstairs. What was she to do? No idea presented itself. She walked into the sickroom, and found it cool. Molly had opened the window.

"I thought my lady might benefit from some fresh air."

Theo raced across the room to close the window, and noticed that the viscountess was now lying prone upon her featherbed. She hastened to the bed to prop her back up with the pillows.

"It seemed to *me* that my lady being so restless, she might be more comfortable without all those pillows," added Molly, criticism implied in her tone.

Theo hardly trusted herself to speak to the maid. "You'd better go attend to your duties. See that Mrs. Chambers is comfortable."

Molly left sulkily, and Theo let out a deep sigh. The maid had managed to make a disaster of the sickroom in just a few minutes. Peggy was right. She could not be trusted to nurse the viscountess. Theo must handle it all alone.

There were those who showed concern for her welfare. The cook, upon being apprised of the situation, sent up a hearty breakfast, along with some broth for the viscountess, but Theo could coax none of it down her. Theo turned to her own breakfast and made short work of it. It was a wonder how a meal could restore one. She thought she would do, now.

As the morning went on, she forgot to even think about her own weariness. The main problem seemed to be her eyes, which ached. She could see in the looking glass that they were quite red. She tried wiping them with a damp handkerchief, but the relief it brought was temporary.

Every now and then, she simply had to stop and close them. It was upon one of these occasions that she heard her mother cry out again, and opening her eyes, realized that she must have fallen asleep for a few minutes. It was a frightening thought. As soon as she had taken care of her mother, she rang the bell for Molly. "Ask the cook to please send up a pot of strong tea."

It was just before eleven when Debenham arrived. Although she disliked leaving Molly with her mother, Theo gave her the strictest sort of orders and prayed that she would be all right for a few minutes. The thought of not receiving him never occurred to her. She had been longing to share her fears with him all night.

When she came into the room, he omitted the usual pleasantries, instead remarking in his abrupt way, "My dear girl! How pulled down you look. Is your mother worse?"

She might have been offended at his description of her, but instead she came forward to give him her hands. "She is much, much worse," she said quietly. "I am afraid—" A sob half escaped her, startling her.

He pulled her into his arms, patting her back in sympathy. "There, there, my dear. You are tired. That makes everything look its blackest."

It was the most comforting thing in the world. She was actually leaning upon that broad shoulder when she recollected herself and drew back. He saw her distress and handed her his handkerchief. She wiped her eyes.

"The doctor says that there is little we can do. The illness will simply have to take its course."

Debenham scowled. "He sounds a worthless fellow. There must be another we may consult—"

Theo shook her head. "No, he has been the best that we have found. Mother has often said how tired she is of the quackery of others. I am sure that he is telling the truth." She hesitated, then with a blush, added. "I am sorry that your father is gone also. My mother has been calling for him."

"I wrote him a letter last night, urging him to return," said Debenham thoughtfully. "It is just that he is engaged upon such a ticklish business . . ."

Theo knew she should have made some polite protest, but she was so wholeheartedly in favor of Sir Francis's immediate return that she could not. She recollected herself suddenly. "I cannot stay. I must return to my mother. I do not trust Molly with her."

His brows drew together again. "You are nursing her *yourself*?"

"Yes . . ."

"And you've been up all night doing it from the look of you. Where is Mrs. Chambers?"

"She is sick abed."

If possible, the eyebrows drew even closer together. "You can't do this alone, Theo. You'll only make yourself ill, too."

The tears started flowing afresh at the concern in his voice, and she was forced to apply the handkerchief again. "I have no choice—if you will excuse me now—"

"No." He spoke firmly. "I will help you." He began to strip off his driving gloves in a businesslike fashion.

"You help—oh, no . . . it would be most improper—" Theo was starting to stammer when he cut her off.

"Damn propriety. It's your mother's life we're speaking of." He saw her stricken expression and added more gently. "I shall keep that useless little maid with me, if it makes you feel any better. It's a temporary solution anyway. We'll send that manservant of yours out to find the doctor. Perhaps he can recommend a reliable nurse."

A nurse. Theo hadn't even considered the possibility. It would be frightfully expensive, but . . . She dismissed the thought for the moment. Debenham was thoroughly reliable, but would he prove adequate as a nurse?

He read the uncertainty in her eyes. "I've been up all night often enough with a sick horse," he said dryly. "You may give me the doctor's instructions—I *imagine* I have enough intelligence to follow them. If I have any troubles, I can have you awakened."

He left her no chance of making a reply, but instead headed for the viscountess's bedroom, Theo trailing along beside him, muttering inarticulate protests.

They reached the bedroom and found the patient tossing restlessly while Molly sat before the looking glass, admiring the picture of herself in one of her ladyship's caps.

Theo had no time to say anything, for Debenham's face contracted into a fierce scowl, causing the maid to gasp and snatch the cap from her head, replacing it with her own.

"Tell my groom to drive my horses back to Marlborough

Buildings. I shan't need him the rest of the day." Molly fled to obey his commands.

He said nothing further, but as Theo readjusted the pillows, he listened carefully to all of her directions. She was loath to leave the sickroom, but he did not permit her to linger.

"Go now. The sooner you are awake, the sooner you will be able to nurse her again yourself."

The combination of relief and strain was almost too much to bear. She made her way upstairs wearily, checking to make certain that Peggy was resting comfortably before returning to her own chamber. Too exhausted to cry, she fell into bed, welcoming the oblivion of sleep.

Mr. Sanders mopped his brow with his handkerchief, still obviously overcome by the effects of their recent journey. Sir Francis smiled at him. "Come, you cannot now refuse a glass of my port—it is excellent, you know—for you clearly have need of it."

His companion did not deny it, for he knew such denial would be useless. He had discovered to his dismay that Sir Francis had a great deal more in common with his son than one would ever suspect. Sir Francis poured the port and crossed over to hand him the glass, regarding him sympathetically.

"Do you know, Sanders, I think you have been leading far too sheltered a life if this sort of a little jaunt is enough to upset you."

Sanders took a sip of port, before replying acidly, "I thank the good Lord that I have never had occasion to visit such a . . . such a *place* before . . . except for that which I visited with your son. I most sincerely hope it will not fall my lot ever to do so again."

There was a twinkle at the back of Sir Francis's eye, but his face was grave. "Come, this is harsh. I would almost think you had not enjoyed yourself."

And what was all the more remarkable was that it had been patent that Sir Francis, like his son before him, had. The smell of the filthy, ramshackle hovel had been nearly enough to make Sanders sick. The odor of their unwilling, gin-swilling host had almost completed the job. He had been forced to hold a handkerchief to his nose almost the entire time just to control his stomach. Sir Francis apparently did not suffer from such sensitivity. Sanders shook his head disbelievingly.

Sir Francis adopted a soothing tone. "You must at least be pleased with our success."

"Yes." At last Sir Francis was talking sensibly. Their quarry had been most eager to cooperate once he had seen the gold coins Sir Francis produced. There had been some concern about the steps Oliphant might take for revenge, as well as the possibility that he himself might be dragged into the courts. Sir Francis had confessed that he did not mean to take legal steps unless absolutely necessary, considering that Oliphant would flee before then. He also had promised to book him passage to a foreign country. With these fears dispersed, the man was happy to sign a statement that detailed how the fraud was worked.

"I suspect you will not wish to delay any further," said Sanders, after taking one last sip from his glass and setting it down firmly. "I am ready to go confront Oliphant right now, if you are."

"Wait." Sir Francis gave a cough. "I suppose you will think it odd of me, but after waiting so long . . . my son did most of the work, after all. I am afraid that I was a bit rough with him before I left, but he deserves to be in at the kill, as it were. As much as I dislike cooling my heels in London, I think I should give him the opportunity to join us. If I post him a letter today, I should think he could be here in three days."

Sanders blinked. This side of the heretofore ruthless Sir Francis was most unexpected. He was a little too stunned to speak, but finally thought to say, "Shall I wait, then, for your lordship to contact me?"

The twinkle reappeared in Sir Francis's eyes. "Oh, yes. I have no intention of excluding you from our little spree, since you have aided us so faithfully all along. But come, won't you dine with me tonight first? I have a mind to sample some of that excellent duck at Grillon's."

The notion of dining in public with one so far above his own station caused Sanders to redden and protest inarticulately. This was one battle that Sir Francis would not be allowed win.

Really, thought Mansfield, it was singular how he continued to bump into Julia, not that he had any objections, of course. After finishing their riding lessons, he had returned her to Laura Place. They had taken somewhat longer than he had anticipated, but by making haste, he still had time to return to the Royal Crescent and change into appropriate attire in order to escort his aunt, in her carriage, to the Pump Room for her noon visit. They had been there perhaps fifteen minutes when he was surprised to see the Simpsons enter. Julia was looking lovely in a fresh gown of sprigged muslin. She affected surprise upon seeing him there also.

It was delightful to have almost an hour more to speak with her, the countess being occupied by a particular acquaintance who had not yet heard the details of how the major had been wounded. Mansfield hardly minded the major's existence when he was in Julia's company. He somehow found himself confiding that they were planning to attend the fancy ball at the Lower Rooms on Friday, and was pleased to discover that she, coincidentally, was to be there also. In spite of the rumblings of his conscience, he begged her for two dances, which she agreed to reserve for him. In response to his question as to whether Debenham would mind, she merely gave him an arch look and said that she did not consider Debenham.

He had been enjoying himself so hugely that it wasn't until they had made their farewells and he was riding home with his aunt that he remembered that Theo had been absent. It was odd for her and her mother to miss two days in a row at the Pump Room. Of course, they might possibly have been called out of town. It was no concern of his. Theo undoubtedly would explain when he saw her again.

When she awoke, Theo was startled by the half-light that came filtering in through the cracks in the curtains. She felt disoriented. Surely it must be morning—but something seemed wrong about it. Her head felt peculiar. She crossed to the curtains and opened them. It was clearly evening. Had she slept through the day?

As she thought about it, memory came flooding back to her. Her mother was ill, and she had left her in Debenham's care all this time! She glanced at herself. She had fallen into bed without bothering to undress, as a result, her gown was sadly wrinkled. With a quick shake of her head, she began to remove it. A gown was waiting for her, pressed. It was unlike Molly to be so thoughtful. She would have to thank her.

Despite the difficulty of having to dress herself, she was ready in a short time and hastily made her way downstairs. She peeped into her mother's room. The patient looked much the same as ever, moaning, and tossing restlessly. The difference was that a plump lady with a pleasant face beneath her cap sat beside the viscountess, bathing her forehead. Theo was about to announce her presence when this person spoke. "She's asking again, sir."

As if it were a cue, Debenham rose and made his way over to the bed. He was in his shirtsleeves and his face looked drawn and rather paler than usual.

"Sir Francis," moaned the viscountess.

"I am here," replied Debenham, taking her hand. "I am here."

Her eyes flickered briefly up at him. She gave a sigh and ceased her moaning for the moment, though Debenham continued to hold her hand. Theo thought it time to recall their attention from the invalid, so she coughed gently.

"I am awake now," she announced quite unnecessarily.

Those deep-set gray eyes met hers from across the room, and in them was a look of such warmth that her heart fairly exploded with happiness. "Your mother is the same. We have an excellent nurse here in Mrs. Tompkins, recommended by your doctor. I was fairly at a stand until she arrived."

The matter-of-fact words brought Theo's soaring hopes quickly back to earth. He was an old friend, concerned about her mother, nothing more. Each of them was engaged to someone else. She must not forget that. Besides, she had more important things to think of at the moment.

The nurse was smiling, pleased by his tribute. "Mr. Debenham is exaggerating. I'd not say he was born to be a nurse, but he was managing just fine before I arrived. He has a knack for quieting my lady, too."

Theo crossed to her mother's side, but could not help being aware of Debenham. How odd it was. In all the years that she had known him, she had never seen him in his shirtsleeves before. With that weariness and worry in his face, there was an air of vulnerability about him that she found most appealing. She turned her attention to her mother, who indeed did look much the same as when Theo had left her. She stretched out a hand to her mother's forehead and found it fiery hot.

Mrs. Tompkins spoke, "My lady still has a distance to travel before she's rid of this fever. I expect she'll be worse before she's better, but God willing, she'll come through this." She smiled at Theo reassuringly. "My lady has a lot to live for, and I've found that is often what makes the difference."

Debenham spoke again, "Mrs. Tompkins just arrived late this afternoon. She's to nurse Lady Westmoreland into the night. You may wish to return to bed and rest further."

Theo shook her head, and Mrs. Tompkins commented shrewdly. "Miss Westmoreland will want to bear me company for a while to see how I go on with my lady. There may be things I do that she would want me to do different. Or there may be things I do that she would like me to keep on doing."

"Well, you must eat anyway, Theo."

She was about to protest, but she suddenly realized that she was famished. "I think I will. Won't you join me, John? Shall we send a tray up for you, Mrs. Tompkins?"

The latter had begun to chuckle and now exclaimed, "Bless me, no!"

Debenham explained. "Your cook, a most industrious woman, sent us up a tray full of food scarce an hour ago." He attempted to stifle a yawn. "I mean to return home and rest myself." He hesitated for a moment. "Theo . . . would you wish me to send for your brother?"

The unwelcome thought had already occurred to her. She shook her head. "No, for Mother thinks his studies are of paramount importance. She would be most angry if . . ." Her voice trailed off.

He did not press her. "Very well. I'll be back as soon as I waken, of course."

"You will do no such thing," Theo had rarely spoken to him so strongly before, and his surprise showed in his face. "My mother is in good hands, as you yourself have pointed out, and Mrs. Tompkins and I between us will be able to care for her all night. It is foolish for you to exhaust yourself unnecessarily—" Her eyes softened. "—Though I can't thank you enough for all you have done."

He shook his head. "I've done nothing. I wish it were in my power to do more." He sighed heavily, and met the obstinate look in her eyes. "Very well. I'll leave matters in your hands, my dear. I expect you to alert me if your mother's condition changes." He pressed her hand, then bowed over it formally. "I'll see you tomorrow."

He nodded to Mrs. Tompkins and left. "What a fine gentleman," she remarked. There was that look of wholehearted admiration again. It was unfortunate for Theo that she now shared that feeling.

Chapter Fifteen

In obedience to Debenham's orders, Theo went to the dining room where she made a thorough assault upon a potted lobster and a veal chop. She was forced to refuse the pupton of apples that was offered her; she could see why Debenham and Mrs. Tompkins had laughed at the notion of eating again anytime soon. She also learned from the servants that the major had called this afternoon, and sent his wishes for her mother's speedy recovery. He was a most thoughtful gentleman. It struck her forcibly that his cousin Mansfield had not thought to call even once.

Feeling somewhat restored, she returned to her mother's chamber. There was no change for the better, but Mrs. Tompkins seemed to be taking good care of the patient. In the act of bathing the viscountess's forehead, the nurse still had time to smile at Theo as she entered. Finished with this task, she plumped the pillows and settled Lady Westmoreland as comfortably as she could. The viscountess moaned and turned her head from side to side restlessly.

"A fever often climbs when the sun goes down," commented Mrs. Tompkins, seating herself once again as Theo dropped noiselessly into the other bedside chair. "Dr. Mapleton said I might try giving my lady some of Doctor Boerhaave's fever powder, so she might rest, but it hasn't worked as well as I hoped."

"Sir Francis," murmured the viscountess. Mrs. Tompkins reached over to pat her hand. "There, there," she said kindly, "he'll be back soon." The words seemed to ease the patient for the moment.

The nurse turned back to Theo. "It's a pity your young gentleman had to leave. He has a rare knack for soothing my lady."

He was not her young gentleman. Theo opened her

mouth to say so, but closed it again. It little mattered what the nurse thought, anyway.

Mrs. Tompkins was continuing. "He was worn to the bone, though, I could see that. Still, for a gentleman he did a good job of nursing my lady. There's not many as might do so well. It's a rare man who'll bear others' sicknesses with patience, though their own . . . well, that's a different matter."

The drone of Mrs. Tompkin's conversation along with her own full stomach and the sleep she had missed were combining to make Theo drowsy. She blinked a few times, then looked at her mother. Was it her imagination, or was she resting more comfortably? Mrs. Tompkins had followed the direction of her gaze and, as if reading Theo's thoughts, nodded.

"Aye, the powder's taking effect. She'll sleep for a bit, anyway." She noticed Theo's heavy eyelids and added, "Why don't you take a bit of a rest, yourself?"

"Oh, no, I couldn't leave her—"

"You don't have to leave. You could just lie down on that little sofa over there. I'll be sure to wake you when I tire or if my lady needs you."

She had indicated the viscountess's elegant gilt and satin chaise longue, one of the few pieces brought from Westleigh. It seemed to beckon to Theo. "Perhaps I will," she said, barely repressing a yawn, "But only for a little while."

She later was to be glad for that sleep. It was sometime in the middle of the night when her mother's cries awakened her. She looked groggily up at Mrs. Tompkins, who was trying to hold the viscountess in bed and sponge her forehead at the same time.

"I was just going to wake you," she told Theo. "My lady is much worse." There was no desperation in her voice, but the serious expression upon that placid face sent a chill of fear through Theo. She rose and crossed quickly over to the bed, taking her mother's hand and murmuring to her in a quiet voice that everything would be all right. Her words had no effect. The viscountess was struggling with all her might to free herself from Mrs. Tompkins's grasp.

"I can't get my lady to hold still," confessed Mrs. Tompkins. "The powders aren't working now." She drew in her mouth grimly. "What I fear is that she'll lie down flat, as she seems to want to do. Then her lungs will fill up again, and we'll find ourselves in a hobble."

"Should we try the cold bath?" asked Theo anxiously.

She pursed her lips. "I don't like to do it, but I suppose we must."

Theo rang for Molly, and the bath was brought to the viscountess's chamber. After filling it with cold water, they plunged the patient into it. It was a difficult thing to do, particularly given the viscountess's protests. Theo could hardly stand to see her mother's teeth chatter so, but miraculously, the bath had an effect. Her temperature was dropping, one could feel that her forehead was cooler.

They had her out of the bath in a moment, though Mrs. Tompkins advised them to leave it in the room. The viscountess was soon dry and back in her shift in bed. She was so still that Theo began to worry.

"She has some relief now," Mrs. Tompkins told her. "Whether or not it will hurt her, we won't know for a while yet." She shook her head. "I wish that she was less troubled in her mind. That is what is doing the harm."

She yawned broadly as the little ormolu mantel clock chimed three. "I'm done for, myself. I think I'll have a wink on the sofa. Call me if you need me."

If Theo hoped that this was to be the turning point in her mother's illness, she was to be disappointed. Within the hour, the fever had begun to rise again, although it was not as severe as it had been. The night changed into dawn and then into morning as she went through the routine of mopping her mother's brow, administering cold water, and speaking calmingly to her. She was again near exhaustion when her companion woke. Mrs. Tompkins was quick to agree to Theo's suggestion that they breakfast, and soon Molly came staggering upstairs burdened down by an ample tray.

The maid was able to assure Theo that Peggy was doing better, her fever having subsided during the night. The old servant was anxious to help with the nursing, but Molly confided that she thought her too weak as yet.

"You need not concern yourself with that. I will have a talk with her as soon as I return upstairs," Theo promised. Molly was about to leave when Theo stopped her. "By the way, I meant to thank you for pressing my dress yesterday. I know it is not your usual duty—"

"Oh, Mr. Debenham asked me to do that. And I've pressed a fresh one for you today as well," confided Molly with a smile that assured Theo that there had been some financial recompense. She dismissed the servant. Debenham again. She could not dwell on him.

Scarcely had she made this resolution and turned her attention to a buttered muffin when the object of her thoughts himself appeared, looking remarkably fresh in his snow-white starcher, tailcoat, and inexpressibles. He looked as if he were ready to pay a morning call upon the Prince Regent.

"I'm sorry to wander in unannounced. I saw no one downstairs. How is your mother?"

"She passed a bad night. Have you heard from your father?" Theo was too tired to deal with anything other than the essentials.

"Not yet, though I expect I will soon."

"I think I'll step outside for a breath of air," said Mrs. Tompkins discreetly.

There was a great deal that Theo wished to say to him, and a great deal that she did not dare. Her poor brain was too tired to sort it all out. He sat with her companionably as she finished the last of her breakfast, and refused her offers for refreshment himself. He sent her upstairs with the promise that he would remain, in spite of her protests. He considered that both she and Mrs. Tompkins would need to conserve their energy in case her mother should have another equally bad night. What convinced her more than his words was the way her mother quieted in response to the sound of his voice. In pitch and timbre, it was not unlike Sir Francis's.

At the Pump Room, Mansfield was enjoying another pleasant flirtation with Julia. She had confessed that tonight he meant to come to the masquerade dressed as Venus, which he could only regard as a most appropriate role. He was about to tell her what his own costume would be, but he silenced him playfully, asking him not to spoil the surprise. "—For I am such a poor, drab little figure of a girl that you might scarcely notice me, but I am certain that I may easily spot you, for you are always the handsomest and most striking gentleman in the room."

Others might have caviled at her words, but it was not in

Mansfield's nature to do so. Instead he looked at her with a great warmth of affection. "You underrate your own charms without cause. I think it is the fault of these fashion periodicals. Indeed, most gentlemen object to stature in a woman. You must be aware that a petite figure such as yours seems the feminine ideal to me." It occurred to him too late that his intended, far from being small, was one of the tall elegant ladies he had just professed not to admire.

It appeared that there was nothing to check his happiness. In addition to the ball tonight, he had their riding lesson tomorrow to which he might look forward. It is not for bliss to remain long unclouded, however. The first inkling he had that all might not be well was when the countess called him over to her side to inquire fretfully where Miss Westmoreland and her mother might be. He responded graciously that he did not know, but it did not seem to allay her irritation.

"Haven't seen the gel since Tuesday. Something particular I have to say to her, too. Well, if you have news of her, please tell me. I wish to speak to her."

In response to Mansfield's unexpressed hopes, Theo did not appear with her mother at the Pump Room today. It seemed odd that his aunt would have been inquiring after her even though she seemed so fond of the girl. The countess rarely gave a thought to those not in her direct sphere of influence. It might have been taken as an ominous sign, but Mansfield chose not to let it bother him. However, there was another, more troubling circumstance of which he was unaware.

Julia's conquest of Debenham had done little to promote peace and harmony in the Simpson household. The subsequent attentions of Mansfield were making Isabel sick with envy. Julia had always been prone to give herself airs, and now she was unbearable. It was awful to think of her younger sister attracting two such eligible gentlemen.

Isabel was wont to remind her sister that Mansfield was but the nephew of a countess and not the heir to the title. She pointed out that Julia was throwing away a baronet with a very handsome fortune in favor of him. Julia merely tossed her head.

"Pooh!" she remarked. "When a gentleman is as handsome and distinguished as Quentin is, he needs no title to set him apart. I don't see why you say I've thrown anything away, either. Debenham has scarcely shown his face these past several days. He can scarcely reproach *me* for wishing to amuse myself a little."

Isabel was at her iciest. "Had you considered that Mr. Mansfield is the particular beau of our dear friend Theo, who *is* the daughter of a viscount. Do you imagine that you will replace that friendship easily when she learns what has occurred?"

"Nothing has occurred." For the first time during their conversation, Julia looked sulky. "Besides, I don't see that friendship should stand in the way of a romance. You would drop her acquaintance in a second if she were to come between you and your precious Mr. Warwick—"

"It is not at all the same—"

"—Besides, my *new* friend Miss Bromley says that he cannot help falling in love with me, so you see it is not at all my fault."

With these words she had flounced out of the room, leaving Isabel in a rage so intense that she was forced to vent it upon her unsuspecting fiancé. This usually phlegmatic gentleman was so startled, he almost thought to ask her if something was the matter. He decided against it, however.

Isabel was not one to take her defeats calmly. Accordingly, it was a jealous and angry pair of eyes that watched the progress of Julia and Mansfield's flirtation in the Pump Room that day. She was troubled by the problem of what she could do to thrust a spike into this budding romance. Upon consideration, all was made plain. She would go to Theo and tell her what was happening. Theo had been absent for several days now. It was Isabel's duty to tell her how matters stood.

She called upon Theo that very afternoon only to be surprised by the news that she was resting. Apparently the viscountess was suffering from ill health. She had never expected such an obstacle, and was not quite sure which steps to take next. Well, the viscountess could hardly be sick forever, after all. Her own father usually recovered from one of his attacks of the gout after a few days. She smiled brightly at Molly, "Tell Miss Westmoreland that I shall call upon her again tomorrow."

When Theo received the message that evening, she experienced no more than a passing surprise that Isabel should have called. She had been neglecting that friendship lately, she thought, but oddly enough, she felt no twinge of guilt. It was owing to her own weariness, she supposed.

She was brightened by the news that the major had once again visited. He was proving himself to be a thoroughly reliable gentleman. She enjoyed his company and could have done with a few of his humorous anecdotes now, but there was too much else to concern herself with at the moment.

She found Debenham and Mrs. Tompkins downstairs with her mother. The viscountess's condition had not altered for the better. She still moaned and tossed, but it seemed to Theo that her voice was even weaker than it had been. Mrs. Tompkins shook her head. "Such an illness would exhaust anyone, let alone my poor lady. I think that tonight will prove the turning point."

She did not say whether for good or ill. Looking at her mother's wasted form, Theo realized that she very likely lacked the strength to survive such a terrible night as the last.

She thanked Debenham quietly and urged him to leave. "I won't."

She was unprepared for his flat denial, but she made her arguments. "You are exhausted. You can be no help to us if you fall ill. There is no reason for you to remain."

"There is one reason." The viscountess was murmuring Sir Francis's name in a low voice. Debenham stood by her and took her hand. "I am here." The creases left her brow; her tossing ceased for the moment.

Theo shook her head. "But you cannot remain here all the time. Excuse us." She led him out into the passage and looked at him with great affection.

"I know that you love my mother. You must imagine how I feel. It is unbearable to have to leave her in the hands of a stranger—for me to be beyond her call. But none of us know how long this illness may last." Despite herself, her eyes began to fill with tears. "If . . . when my mother recovers, she will need us all to help nurse her back to health. There will be a thousand errands to run, and tasks to accomplish. I will not be strong enough to do it by myself. I will need you."

The look on his face was the bleakest she had ever seen. He was silent for a moment, as if trying to master his own emotions. "Very well, Theo. It will be as you say."

He turned on his heel and walked away. She wanted to run after him and stop him, but she knew she must not. In this instance, it was better to hurt his feelings if it accomplished her purpose. She turned and reentered the sickroom.

The days and nights had begun to blur together to her. There was a period of wakefulness and a period of rest. Although her mother's fever rose, it never ascended to the heights it had the previous night. She mentioned this as an optimistic prospect to Mrs. Tompkins, but the latter only pursed her lips and looked thoughtful.

Her mother was, inarguably, weaker. Theo almost wished that she would roll about and moan as she had before. She was paler than Theo had ever seen her. She seemed to have moments of consciousness where she knew Theo and was reassured to see her there. Her pulse was feeble, her breathing shallow.

Mrs. Tompkins had consigned the matter to the Almighty and gone to bed. The first gray light began to filter in through the curtains, and it seemed to Theo that her mother's life was ebbing with the night. For the first time, she forced herself to face that fact that the unacceptable was happening. She had done nothing except to vex and disappoint her mother. There would be no second chance, no opportunity to redeem herself. Though hope was dwindling, she began to pray. Tears rushed down her face as the thin hand she held slowly began to cool.

There was a tremendous racket downstairs. The knocker sounded angrily. Footsteps rushed about. Voices shouted. What could it be? The tread of boots sounded in the hallway. Sir Francis, looking more disheveled than she had ever seen him, appeared at the chamber door. His eyes were on her mother's face.

"Jane!"

He crossed the room swiftly, almost knocking Theo out of the way. "Jane!"

Now beside the bed, he put his arms gently around her mother's fragile torso and held her to him tenderly. "I am here. I am here at last, my dear."

He was too late, couldn't he see that? Theo's eyes were blinded by tears. She rose and took a few steps back, burying her face in her handkerchief.

"Jane, my darling. I've come at last." The scene was very nearly too horrible to witness. Theo choked back a sob.

"Sir Francis?"

The voice was weak, but it was undeniably her mother's. Theo lifted her face. The viscountess's eyes were open.

"Sir Francis?"

"I am here, my darling."

Her mother's head turned toward her. "Theo?"

She fled to her bedside, and took her mother's hand in hers. It was cool, not cold. "Mother?" She knelt by the bed, reaching out her other hand to feel the viscountess's forehead. "The fever has gone!"

"I feel so tired," murmured Lady Westmoreland, closing her eyes for a moment with fatigue. She opened them again. "And I am parched."

Theo rose and crossed the room to pour her a glass of water. Mrs. Tompkins had awakened now and like Theo before her, felt the viscountess's forehead and then her pulse. A smile spread across that plump face. "Her ladyship'll do, now."

Her mother was regarding the nurse with some wonder, so Theo effected hasty introductions. Sir Francis had removed himself discreetly to the foot of the bed, but as the nurse heard his name, she clapped a hand to her face.

"And to think of me standing here like a clot. Your ladyship may fancy some broth, and some toast to dip in it, and perhaps a nice cup of tea. I'm certain Miss Westmoreland will be so kind as to help me."

To her amazement, Theo found herself propelled out of the room by this forceful person. She turned to ask Tompkins what she meant by this behavior, but the latter only wagged her head and putting a finger to her lips, said, "Sssh!"

Theo glanced behind her into the chamber and saw that Sir Francis had taken a place by her mother's bed and was holding her hand.

"Best medicine in the world," opined Mrs. Tompkins, and she made her way to the kitchen.

Unsure what to do with herself, Theo was walking toward the drawing room just as Debenham arrived. Although he obviously had dressed in haste, he still managed to look neat.

"My father?"

"He arrived a few minutes ago. He is talking with my mother now."

"Talking *with* her?"

The tears began to slip down Theo's cheeks again. "Yes. The fever has finally broken. She is weak, but . . ."

She did not have to say anything else. Luckily, she was still clutching her handkerchief, and she applied it to her face.

"How—how wonderful!" His face was glowing.

The most natural thing in the world would have been for her to fall into his arms. Now that the crisis was over, it was as if there were an invisible wall between them. She had taken half a step toward him before she realized it. She must not touch him.

Debenham must have sensed it, too, for he made no move toward her. "Sir Francis posted here from London during the night. He only stopped at Marlborough Buildings to learn how your mother was. He wouldn't even wait for me to dress, but came straight here."

"Mrs. Tompkins thinks that his presence will be of the greatest benefit to her." Theo could not quite repress a blush at the words.

"Just so." There was a moment's uncomfortable silence.

"I am forgetting myself. Would you care for some breakfast? I daresay that Cook is preparing something at the moment."

"No, thank you." He hesitated for another moment, then spoke. "Theo . . ."

"Yes?"

"Because my father had to leave London so abruptly, there were some matters that he left undone. I must return there now to take care of his affairs."

"Oh." She was overwhelmed by a feeling of desolation. She had been relying on him so much. Of course, what did it matter? He belonged to someone else. She would lose him sooner or later.

"Theo, I . . ."

"Yes?"

He closed his mouth abruptly before opening it again, and somehow his tone seemed different. "Well . . . I shall not be so terribly long in London, after all."

"Oh." There didn't seem to be much else to say.

*   *   *

Really, the manner in which Mr. Mansfield and Julia had behaved at the ball last night was almost scandalous. No doubt they thought themselves protected by their fancy dress, but everyone at the assembly undoubtedly recognized Mansfield's tall figure, disguised or not. Besides which, they had been so bold as to dance together *after* the unmasking!

There would have been no harm in that in itself, except for the way they had acted the rest of the evening. Isabel had warned Julia that everyone would think she was fast, but Julia had merely laughed at her and gone on her way. She and Mansfield had actually danced two dances together in a row, a terrible breach of conduct. What was even worse was that the dance after unmasking was their third. If they thought no one kept count, they were certainly mistaken. Bath was a town in which gossip flourished, and they were providing it with plenty of fuel.

Anyone might have noticed them sitting on the sofa with their heads together for a half an hour at a time. Julia's blushes and giggles undoubtedly forced everyone to put the worst construction on matters. She was throwing away her reputation, and Isabel feared that it might tarnish her own. She mentioned as much to her almost fiancé, Mr. Warwick. He did not comment, but looked appropriately grave.

She had tried to convince Julia at least to break her appointment to ride with Mr. Mansfield the next morning. Julia had merely looked at her incredulously, saying that hardly anyone would see them together there, if that was what was worrying Isabel. She had added that since Isabel had often ridiculed her for being afraid of horses, she should be glad that Julia was learning to ride at last. When appealed to, Lady Simpson had only smiled and said in her careless way that Julia must do as she thought best. There would be no help from that quarter.

There was only one thing that Isabel could do. She must go talk to Theo as soon as possible. Theo could call Mansfield to heel and put a stop to all this. Isabel had a duty, as both a sister and a friend to tell Theo the truth.

Bolstered by righteous indignation, she thus was doubly frustrated to discover upon calling in Gay Street that morning that Miss Westmoreland was once again resting. She eyed the servant with acute suspicion and very nearly demanded to see Theo. Surely a less feeble excuse might have been thought of for denying her!

"I should have thought Lady Westmoreland would have recovered by now," announced Isabel in a hostile manner.

Molly, the only servant not otherwise occupied at the moment, bristled. "Her ladyship is as ill as can be, miss."

They glared at each other for a moment before Isabel was forced to concede defeat. "Very well. I shall leave my card, and you may tell her that I wish to speak to her on a *most urgent matter,* that is, if you can remember to tell her."

"I'll tell her."

Well, thought Isabel angrily to herself, if Theo lost her attractive and eligible suitor, it would be just her own fault.

When Theo arose, she was puzzled by Isabel's message. It seemed odd that anything else in the world could be considered an urgent matter, besides the question of her mother's health. Well, she would call upon Isabel when she had the time, but she was much too busy at the moment.

Her first act had been to visit her mother's chamber. Not surprisingly, Sir Francis was gone, though he had left a message that he would return. The doctor had arrived and made an examination. He smiled at Theo as she entered, and her heart leapt with hope. It could only mean that her mother was on the road to recovery. He confirmed her thoughts. The crisis was past. Her mother would remain weak and tired for some time. They must continue to keep her propped upright as much as possible. Care must be taken to protect her from drafts and damp. She must be urged to eat.

Theo heard all his instructions with a glad heart. He confessed that he thought her mother's recovery nothing short of miraculous. He smiled at the nurse. "Mrs. Tompkins told me that she thought her ladyship had a great deal to live for, and that is what made the difference. I am not certain that she is not right."

Theo had never seen a doctor to the door as happily as she did today. Mrs. Tompkins assured her that she was well rested, so Theo thought to have a bite to eat. It was late afternoon, past time for a nuncheon and not yet time for dinner. The cook solved the problem by offering to serve her tea.

Theo had just been settled in the drawing room with a

pot, some freshly made buns with a great deal of jam and butter, when the major was announced. She was only too glad to see him, and when he entered, offered to share her repast. He accepted, and Molly was dispatched to fetch another china cup.

His concern was for her mother, and he seemed to delight in the news of her recovery. "—Although, I might have guessed it from your appearance, Miss Westmoreland."

When asked to explain, he had some difficulty, but made a brave attempt, "I suppose it is in your eyes. The strain about them has disappeared."

Theo recollected herself and made polite inquiries about his own health.

"I am progressing very rapidly and hope to be rid of my cane soon. Then they will have no reason for keeping me in England."

Theo smiled. "We shall miss you when you leave. You have provided a breath of fresh air to our humdrum existences."

"I hardly know how to respond to such flattery."

"It is not flattery, it is the truth. But tell me, how does the countess?"

"She is well."

"Since I have been shut up here for four days, I am sure that much has happened. What are the latest *on-dits*?" she asked playfully.

It seemed she had said something to make him uncomfortable. "I do not go about as much as others," he finally said reluctantly.

She affected surprise. "What? No assemblies, no concerts, no visits to the theater?"

"My aunt invited me to accompany her to a fancy-dress ball last night at the Lower Rooms. It is not the sort of affair which I enjoy." It seemed to Theo that he was choosing his words with care. "My aunt assumed the role of Diana, which did not seem appropriate to me for either her age or station."

"Oh, dear." Theo could not quite repress a smile. "And how did you dress?"

He smiled. "I wore a domino." He gave his cane a little shake. "This precluded the possibility of disguising my identity."

"I shouldn't think so. Half of the persons in Bath use

canes." She gave him a sympathetic look. "But it must have been terribly dull, since you are unable to dance."

He had to laugh. "I will ruin any good opinion you hold of me, but I must confess that dancing hardly contributes to my enjoyment of an evening." His face grew more serious. "To be frank, I find it damnable—excuse me—to be cooped up at a frippery assembly when my comrades are more worthily occupied with keeping Napoleon at bay."

She could not help but honor him for his sentiments, and said so.

With practiced ease, he diverted the conversation into lighter channels.

She was again sorry when he took his leave of her, stating that he had imposed upon her hospitality far too long. He told her he would be happy to be of service to her in any way he could, and she could not doubt the sincerity of his tone. He promised to call again the next afternoon.

It was only after he had gone that it occurred to Theo that he had never mentioned his cousin once by name. It was rather odd, wasn't it? It seemed even more peculiar that four days had passed without Mansfield calling once upon his fiancée.

Chapter Sixteen

Her questions about Mansfield were to be dispelled when he arrived in person the next day. Although the viscountess was still a long way from being well, her condition had improved so dramatically that Mrs. Tompkins had persuaded Theo to sleep in her own chamber. The nurse would herself doze upon the chaise longue and so would be within the viscountess's call. She would wake Theo if she needed her, but from observing the patient with a practiced eye, she very much doubted that she would.

Her mother had added her persuasions to Mrs. Tompkins. Sir Francis had arrived and volunteered to sit a part of the evening with Lady Westmoreland. This arrangement was so evidently to her mother's liking that Theo did not have the heart to argue further.

Therefore, when Theo arose Sunday morning, she felt truly refreshed for the first time in days. After dressing, she went downstairs to her mother's bedchamber, but both the viscountess and Mrs. Tompkins were sleeping peacefully. Theo sent up a little prayer of thanks.

After breakfasting, she thought it might be time to write her brother Andrew and let him know what had occurred. After completing this task, she returned to her mother's chamber, where she found the viscountess awake and ready for her own meal. Peggy joined them shortly, looking pale, but otherwise herself. With such support, Theo was able to dismiss Mrs. Tompkins for the rest of the day. There were some matters the nurse had to attend to at home.

The only problem with Peggy's arrival was that she was a little too inclined to fuss over the patient. She was on the verge of making Lady Westmoreland uncomfortable, until Theo spoke to her, though in the kindest manner possible. Neither she nor her mother had the heart to dismiss the servant from the bedchamber. The day passed more peacefully than Theo could have imagined possible just a few days before.

It was in the early part of the afternoon when Mansfield was announced. Theo felt an unexpected dread. For a few days at least, she had not been forced to confront the fact that her future lay with this man. The crisis she had passed through, and Debenham's subsequent behavior, had wiped away the last vestige of any affection she held for Mansfield. She swallowed. He must not guess it. As she had seen so clearly before, she had little choice but to marry this eligible suitor. His feelings must be considered also. He had said he loved her. She must not disappoint him. After all, what did it matter whom she married? Debenham was engaged to another, and he was too much the gentleman to ever . . .

It was an unproductive train of thought, and she dismissed it. She looked in the mirror to make certain there was nothing amiss with her appearance. Her face was pale and grave. She tried to assume a more cheerful expression and failed. Ah, well. Perhaps he would attribute her lackluster spirits to the recent crisis.

She could not know it, of course, but Mansfield had been just as reluctant to see her. Without her about, he had been free to happily ignore his duty. The prospect of meeting her face-to-face had a most uncomfortable effect upon his conscience. He was engaged to Theo, after all, secretly engaged, in a rather dastardly fashion. He had never told the countess, and Theo had not reproached him, merely waiting with an angelic sort of patience and trust. He had not seen her for five days. What must she think of him?

Even worse, he was aware that he and Julia had been creating something of a stir, to which the countess fortunately seemed indifferent. Could it have come to Theo's ears? Was he to face a furious scene? He had never seen Theo in a temper. He hoped that she was not the sort of female to resort to violence. He recalled his friend Wigham, and how his mistress had once blackened his eye. It had provided amusement for the club for several months, so much so that Wigham had finally given up his membership. And Theo was taller and undoubtedly more powerful than the other.

He swallowed at the thought, trying to contain his apprehension. After all, Theo might not know. Besides, he could always respond that there was nothing to the rumors. One stolen kiss hardly counted, after all. At the memory, his eyes softened and his heart raced. Theo might be like a queen, but Julia was the most appealing armful he had ever encountered. Flesh and blood as she had said. More than that, she made him feel . . . well, he could not describe it, but she made him feel cleverer and stronger and wiser somehow.

Theo . . . now that was more like kissing an ice maiden. He shuddered a little at the thought. For the rest of his life, she would tell him how inferior his driving was, urge him to ride horses that would do their best to throw him, and remind him of all he had left undone. It was a depressing thought. Why had he ever proposed to her? He tried his best to cast his mind back and imagine why he had, but he could only attribute it to a passing madness. However, no gentleman ever drew back from an engagement. He was well and truly stuck. He heaved a depressed sigh and let the knocker fall.

His guilt returned with a rush when Theo entered the room. She had that patient resigned expression upon her face. What a cad he was! To have been enjoying himself to the hilt these past several days with Julia, and giving hardly a thought to Theo.

She greeted him quietly and taking a seat, indicated that he should seat himself also. He perched himself upon a chair at the opposite end of the room. There was a moment of uncomfortable silence before he thought to speak.

"I trust I find you well?"

"Yes, quite, though my mother has been ill for several days."

"Oh. I am most sorry to hear that."

How inane the man's conversational style was. How could she ever have imagined herself in love with such a block-headed fellow? Theo hoped she was smiling at him.

"I am sorry not to have seen you," she lied.

Quite unexpectedly he flushed, and in a most uncharacteristic way began to fiddle with his watch fob. "Oh, I've been busy, this and that, don't you know." He glanced at her. She still had that angelic expression. Perhaps it was better to confess part of the truth. "I've been giving that friend of yours, Miss Simpson, riding lessons."

"Isabel?"

"No, Miss Julia Simpson."

Good, she had restrained the guffaw that had threatened to burst out of her at the notion of his attempting to teach anyone anything about horses. "I am sure she is most grateful," said Theo demurely.

"Yes, well . . ." He fiddled even more with the fob. "I suppose you have things to do, so I'll be brief. My aunt has particularly felt the want of your company. There is to be a gala Wednesday night with a concert, fireworks, and illuminations, and she would like to invite you and Lady Westmoreland to dinner and then to accompany us to Sydney Gardens to see them. It is to be a small party only."

"I am not certain that my mother will be well enough to attend."

"Then we should be happy to have you alone. My aunt seemed to wish to speak to you about something." He did not meet her eyes.

"Have you told—?" Theo's heart was racing in fear.

"No." This was it. He must do the honorable thing, if he ever were to think of himself as a gentleman again. It was better to have it done. "I will tell her that night, if it is agreeable to you."

Theo's heart sank. Why she wished so to postpone this inevitable step, she could not say. She should be glad that he finally was showing a little backbone. "Very well."

If it did not strike Mansfield that his fiancée was lacking in enthusiasm, neither did she notice that his manner was far from loverlike. He did kiss her hand good-bye, but that was the extent of their contact. Had she thought about it, it might have seemed puzzling, but her preoccupation did not permit such thoughts. To be formally engaged to Mansfield! She hoped it would not hinder her mother's recovery. She would have to be careful to simulate overwhelming happiness.

Another caller arrived soon after Mansfield's departure. It was the major, who, observing a sudden weariness in her face would not stay, but again asked after the viscountess. What a pleasing contrast he formed to his cousin, who had expressed only the most cursory interest in her mother's illness. He wished aloud that he might take Theo out for a drive, but dashed his own hopes by adding that he imagined she would not wish to leave her mother now. Theo, regretfully, could not but agree. He ended by asking if she were to form one of the party at Sydney Gardens on Wednesday.

Brightening visibly at her affirmative answer, he commented that he would see her then and departed in a jaunty manner. It wasn't until he had gone that it occurred to her that he had discarded his cane.

The last visitor of the day was Isabel. Theo, by now disinclined to see anyone, toyed with the idea of having herself denied, but decided that it would be unforgivably rude. Isabel was admitted.

She flounced into the room. "*Dear* Theo, I have *something* of the *utmost urgency* to confide."

At the moment, Theo could not have been less interested. Isabel had not even inquired after her health or her mother's.

Isabel did not require a response. "Julia and Mr. Mansfield have betrayed you!" she announced dramatically.

For a moment a glimmer of hope shone in Theo's heart to be quickly extinguished. This was just more of Isabel's playacting. Julia had been lording it over her again, and she could not stand it. Isabel was waiting expectantly for a response. Theo rose and crossed over to close the door, hoping that the servants would not be too well entertained. "I wish you would keep your voice down, Isa."

This was not the reaction for which Isabel had been hoping. "*Theo!*" she exclaimed, properly scandalized, "Don't you even *care*?"

Theo heaved a sigh. "What is it that you wish to tell me?"

Isabel flushed at the indifference in her friend's voice. "It's Julia and Mr. Mansfield. They have been meeting every day at the Pump Room—"

Theo smiled. "Really, Isa—we all have met every day there."

"That is not all. They went for a drive together *alone*—" She could see that Theo was not taking this seriously enough, so instead of continuing with the more minor offenses, she decided to concentrate on the most grievous ones.

"And he danced *three* dances with her at the ball Friday night."

This sounded a little more promising. Considering it, Theo sighed and shook her head. The muttonhead was likely not keeping count. He had shown himself to be careless in the extreme. "I hate to say this, Isa, but they enjoy dancing together. He probably just preferred her company to Miss Bromley's for example. You mustn't get into a pet because he did not ask you."

"Get into a—" Isabel's horror was apparent. What on earth did Theo think? That she was making this all up out of spite? She swallowed back her anger. She must control herself. She was here to do Theo a favor. She must keep that in mind.

"If you had seen them making sheep's eyes at each other at the ball—"

"Oh, Isa, really—"

She persisted. "And there are the private riding lessons they are taking together. I suppose that means nothing to you either?"

"Mr. Mansfield told me about them today. I am glad that someone has been able to persuade Julia to mount a horse." No hope there either. Why would he have told her, if there were truly a romance between them?

Isabel's face could not quite achieve the shade of red known as beet, but it was making a fine attempt. "Well! Of all the ingratitude! I come here as your friend, simply hoping to help you, and you choose to disbelieve everything I say!"

"Oh, Isa, come down from your high ropes. I know that Julia undoubtedly has been most annoying, but you should not let her discomfit you so—"

"I never!" Her rage almost did not permit her to speak for a moment. "I came to give you a friendly warning—but obviously you prefer to blind yourself to the truth! There will come a day when you will wish you had listened to me, Miss High-and-Mighty! You'll be sorry—and *I* shall *laugh*!" She turned on her heel and whirled from the room.

"Oh, Isa, I am sorry, but really—" Her apology was not heeded. Theo might have pursued her, but she didn't see the sense in it. If Isa chose to be offended because Theo didn't believe her improvised drama, then there was little Theo could do about it. She sighed and went upstairs to join her mother instead.

Another arrival who could not truly be accounted a visitor was Sir Francis. Theo had to agree with Mrs. Tompkins's assessment. His visits seemed to do the viscountess more good than all the broth or powders in the world.

Her mother had seemed strangely hesitant to permit Theo

to join the countess's party by herself. Upon learning that Sir Francis was also invited, she quickly granted her permission, over his protests that it would be a sadly flat evening without her.

"But this way, you will be able to take care of Theo, so that I shan't have to worry about her." A look passed between the two of them, and her mother added, "Blame it on an invalid's fancies."

He leaned over to kiss her hand. "Your wish, as always, is my command, my lady."

She laughed, and Theo thought what a refreshing sound it was to hear after all these days of illness.

The next few days were quite unremarkable. To Theo's satisfaction, her mother, though still very weak, was continuing to improve. Sir Francis, at his most amusing, beguiled her leisure hours, popping in with the latest magazine, or to read her an account of the Prince Regent's fete, which had taken place June 19th. She could not help but be entertained by the description of the prince in his garish Field Marshal's uniform, which a wit had said must have both cost and weighed two hundred pounds. Most remarkable of all, of course, was the highly decorated stream of water that ran down the center of the table, and that was inhabited by live silver and gold fish. Sir Francis was able to add that a friend who had been there confided that the fish succumbed to mortality early in the evening, so that he was treated to the unappetizing sight of them floating upside down in front of his plate while he ate.

There was apparently no news from Debenham, or at least Sir Francis did not confide it. Perhaps it was best not to think about him at all.

Not wishing to leave her mother long, Theo was not able to distract herself with the diversions of the town. There was one other problem that occupied her mind, however.

From the moment that Peggy had reappeared, it had been obvious that there could be trouble between her and Mrs. Tompkins. Each woman had a different system of caring for the viscountess and to Peggy's mind, hers must necessarily take precedence. Her anger erupted when Mrs. Tompkins removed a plaster she herself had prepared, or threw out a posset that was her own special receipt. Peggy demanded that the nurse be dismissed, but Theo knew that the old servant was not yet up to the task of nursing the viscountess herself. Soothing words had to be spoken, placating promises made. The role of intercessor was an exhausting one, all the more so since the last thing Theo wished was to trouble the invalid with the problem. She could be grateful for one thing. For at least a small part of the day, the friction kept her mind from dwelling upon Wednesday night. It was most unfortunate that the night she should have been looking forward to with the highest excitement, instead awakened feelings of dread.

"I understand that congratulations are in order." The sharp black eyes beneath the wig surveyed the gentleman seated across the desk in an assessing manner.

Debenham shook his head. "No. If it were a true success, we might have been able to restore the Westmoreland's entire fortune, and perhaps that of others equally misused. As it is—" He shrugged. "—They will at least have an income and be able to reclaim Westleigh. Except for a few economies, they will have the life they once had."

The black eyes glittered. "And Oliphant?"

An unreadable expression crossed Debenham's face. "He sails for Jamaica tonight, without his booty. I should have liked to . . ." He fell silent.

"What of the remainder of his fortune?"

"A good part of it was spent. Some funds may be realized by the sale of his horses, his carriages, his homes, his gold plate . . ." Debenham was at his most sardonic. "I have given the authorities what information we obtained. They must do as they see fit."

Mr. Thomas leaned back in his chair, clasping his hands together. "Was Sanders reliable?"

"He was invaluable. You should have seen him reasoning with Oliphant. All I had to do was to level my pistol and look menacing. What a shrewd head he has, too. He was able to tell Oliphant practically to the penny what he had stolen. I could see the rogue's eyes fair popping from his head at the words."

"It took more than a threat to make Oliphant sign these papers."

Debenham merely regarded him enigmatically.

"Youth must ever be impetuous," said Mr. Thomas,

quoting himself. He sighed. "I might venture that there is somewhere that you wished to be yesterday."

"How perspicacious you are, sir, as usual." The two rose and shook hands.

"I hope that you will give my best regards to the ladies," said Thomas meaningfully, as he escorted him to the door.

"I will."

"And do not forget that your father must sign these papers that we prepared."

"I won't. Thank you."

Mr. Thomas smiled at him, adding mysteriously, "Good luck."

As Debenham left the office, he noticed Sanders standing just outside the door, and taking his hand, shook it heartily. "Thank you again. I hope I may call upon you if I ever find myself at a nonplus like this again. I know of no one I'd rather rely upon."

"You may. And I might say the same of you, sir."

He watched that powerful figure exit with genuine affection in his eyes. One always heard that the nobs were so huffy, but Debenham was an exception to the rule. Heaven knew that he himself was no tufthunter, but—

"Sanders."

"Yes, Mr. Thomas?"

"Will you please step into my office? There is the matter of your promotion to be discussed."

"M-my promotion, sir?" Sanders had never seen his rather severe employer smile before.

There was definitely something odd in the air. At first Theo had ascribed it to her own disordered nerves, but a calmer, more rational look at the situation had convinced her otherwise. It was not that the countess's manner had changed, far from it. If anything, she was even more affectionate and conciliating than previously. In fact, she went to such pains to single Theo out that Theo could not help feeling torn between discomfort and curiosity.

A wild thought had crossed her mind. Perhaps Mansfield had already told the countess? A look at his face showed her that he had not. Why then did Lady Verridge lavish such attentions upon her?

She had insisted upon conducting Theo upon a personal tour of the house, pointing out its luxuries with pride

"—For I do so feel that being *comfortable* is of the essence, do not you, my dear? I make certain that all of my people are comfortable. You may ask any one of my staff if their situations are not better than any comparable which they have held."

Quite startled by this suggestion, Theo had responded that she was willing to take the countess's word in the matter. "Good," replied the latter, not at all perturbed. "Now here is the bedchamber of my former companion, the one which I was forced to dismiss. Pretty, is it not? And you will see how convenient it is to my chamber, as well as to the kitchens. I have the same arrangement in all my homes. She never feared that she would have to walk long, drafty corridors in the dark, either, for I keep candles burning all night. Some would call me extravagant, but as I already mentioned, comfort is of primary importance to me."

Theo could not imagine what the point of this soliloquy was, though she obediently admired the bedchambers. At least the countess's taste in furbishings was good.

After their tour concluded, she supposed she should have been honored to be seated by the countess. It was refreshing to have Lady Verridge boast about the excellence of her chef, rather than reciting her many ills in her usual unappetizing manner. Theo felt quite conscious at being asked to try this or that, and also at the countess's pronouncements of delight when some dish met her particular fancy. Lady Verridge did set an excellent table, but Theo did not see why she in particular would be called upon to admire it.

She glanced at Mansfield several times during all these proceedings, but he seemed to be avoiding her eyes almost deliberately. Of course, it was difficult to tell, since his attention, as usual, was focused almost entirely upon his food. When she did catch his gaze with a question in her own, he could only shake his head. He had no more idea than she did why she had merited this particular treatment.

The major was there also, and to her relief also seemed openly puzzled. It was not just her imagination at work. When they met hers, his eyes held the most droll expression, and once or twice she had been forced to conceal her smile with her napkin.

Of all the guests, Sir Francis was the only one who seemed completely incurious. He repasted thoroughly and flirted capably with the countess as well as the lady on his left. He smiled at Theo reassuringly, giving her a little heart.

After the conclusion of dinner, their hostess again singled Theo out, insisting that since Lady Westmoreland was not present, she should keep a close eye on Theo herself. Accordingly, she announced that Theo was to ride in her own carriage with herself and Mansfield. She squeezed Theo's hand and added in a whisper, "I have something particular to discuss with you, my dear, and I wish to do so privately. I know you are as fond of my nephew as I am, and since this matter concerns him also, you will not mind his presence there."

Theo was given no room to object. What could be on the countess's mind? Was she husband-hunting for her nephew? Theo would not put it beyond her. What an irony *that* would prove to be.

Sir Francis managed to catch Theo's ear as they were waiting for the carriages. "I will be there as soon as you arrive, my dear. Should you need me, I will be happy to be of service." His words comforted her while at the same time her doubts grew.

It wasn't until they had been settled in the carriage and it had begun on its way, that the countess resumed her talk. Having insisted that Theo sit beside her, she took the girl's hand and patted it.

"This is not so very bad, is it? A fine dinner, a comfortable carriage to ride in, and all sorts of entertainments waiting for us?"

"Indeed not, my lady. I am most honored—"

"Tush. It is *you* who honor *me*, my dear. Wouldn't you say so, Quentin?"

He murmured something inaudible, and tried to struggle farther into a corner of the coach.

"And this is how my life is. Despite my illnesses, I prefer not to be a recluse. There are parties here, as you have seen, and in London and often in the country, too, aren't there Quentin?"

He replied in the same fashion as before, but she did not seem to take it amiss.

"And I am not one to exclude a companion from such festivity, like so many others I know. No, as my companion you might enjoy a most interesting and varied sort of life—"

Was Theo hearing aright? Was Lady Verridge actually offering her a *position*? She glanced at Mansfield who was making a small strangled noise in his throat and gradually turning purple. Evidently the countess had not consulted him about this plan.

"Since you and my nephew rubbed along so well together, it was evident to me that you might fit very easily into my household. And naturally with a staff the size of mine, your duties would be rendered light. No, I need young eyes to help me with my sewing, read the paper to me, help prepare my medicines—for it is of the utmost importance, you know, that the materials be fresh and that precisely the right quantity be compounded—I was forced to send my last companion to five different apothecaries before she could find satisfactory emetic tartar! So many of these rascals, you know, will adulterate with chalk or magnesia, so that one doesn't know exactly how much one should take. I have been forced to send as far away as Bristol before—"

There seemed to be no question in her mind that Theo would accept the position. Theo had flushed with a combination of anger and humiliation. That Lady Verridge should think this a fitting position for her, a viscount's daughter!

"I beg your pardon, my lady. I am sorry to interrupt, but will not be your companion."

"What?" The countess stared at her in perplexity, still retaining her hand.

Theo decided that she might have phrased things more tactfully. "I have misled you if you thought that I was searching for a position—"

The countess patted her hand, reassured. " 'Searching'—of course not. I should not have wished to take you on if you had, my dear. I would be happy to discuss—"

Theo could not believe that Lady Verridge still continued to willfully misunderstand her. "Lady Verridge, I have no interest in being your companion. I do not know how to make it plainer. My own mother suffers from ill health, and would not leave her—"

The countess dismissed this with a wave. "Oh, you may easily hire a nurse to attend to *her*. I daresay someone on my staff could recommend one—"

Theo's anger was developing into rage. She withdrew her hand from the other's. "I am obliged for your hospitality, and I do not wish to be rude, but I will not be your companion. Our affairs are not yet so desperate that I must enter into servitude. I suggest that you consult an agency of some sort. Perhaps *one of your staff* might recommend one."

Lady Verridge had never met with sarcasm in her existence, and it confounded her sufficiently to deprive her of speech for a full fifteen seconds. "Well—such ingratitude! I am most greatly displeased with you, Miss Westmoreland. I thought out of the kindness of my heart to offer you a way out of your difficulties, and instead you fling my words back at me." She sniffed in her resentment. "If you imagine that you will be invited to the Royal Crescent to dine again, you are greatly mistaken." With these words of bitter triumph, she contented herself. By an exercise of supreme will, she managed to keep from confiding to her fellow travelers the sudden twinge she felt in her back, which was undoubtedly the first sign of a truly serious disorder, and instead preserved a frosty silence all the way to Sydney Gardens.

Theo had looked at Mansfield for help, but there was no reassuring smile, no grave shake of the head, nothing that revealed his concern for her. In fact, he appeared to be wishing that he could simply evanesce. It might have served as an excellent opportunity for another man to leap in the face of the countess's anger and declare his undying affection for her, but apparently it was not Mansfield's sort of cue. They rode like three wooden puppets to Sydney Gardens.

The illuminations were really quite pretty, and even the countess seemed somewhat soothed by the sight of them, as well as the sound of the orchestra. Sir Francis, true to his promise was waiting there for them. With great discernment, he took the countess's arm and led her off in the direction of the concert, flattering her into a pleasant mood with some of his more outrageous compliments.

Theo was left alone with Mansfield, who offered her his arm mechanically and began to lead her in the same direction. Some minutes passed. They were well out of the servants' hearing when it occurred to Theo that Mansfield did not mean to say anything at all.

"Are you simply going to take me to the concert as nothing had occurred?" she demanded.

He gave a heavy sigh. "I do not see that there is anything

else that we can do. My aunt is in a very fractious mood.
It would be most inopportune to inform her this evening."

"Most inopportune?" Theo had to halt in her tracks and
stare at him in disbelief. Had she honestly allowed herself
to become engaged to this pigeon-brained, this clodpated
imbecile? "Are you honestly so thickheaded or are you
merely afraid?"

He gazed at her, offended. To answer in the affirmative
to either suggestion seemed hardly flattering to him.

"She'll *never* be reconciled to our engagement. We will
have to present it as a fait accompli. She will have to know
that we mean to marry despite her!"

Now she was throwing French at him. It was an unequal
battle and he knew it. He tried for a placating tone. "I hope
that you may be wrong, Theo dear," he began ponderously.

"A sapskull," she muttered.

He was a little daunted, but he persevered manfully.
"Your anger is understandable, but you must realize that
my own fortune is negligible. Without the countess's goodwill, we could not afford the little luxuries which make life
worth the living. I think, given another several weeks, or
perhaps a month or two, that—"

This was it. Theo no longer cared about her future in any
way except for the proviso that it must not be spent with
his well-favored idiot. "That is all."

"What?"

"We have given it enough time. Our engagement is at an
end."

Had he really heard those marvelous words? "Theo, you
cannot mean this," he said stupidly.

For some reason, his words caused Theo's rage to boil
over. "Yes, I can. Is it possible that both you and your aunt
are hard of hearing? Our engagement is at an end. It is
finished. It is over. It is through. Do you understand me?"

"Please, keep your voice down," he commented ner-
ously. Though it was becoming dark, the altercation had
attracted the interested attention of several passersby. At
once made aware of their curious stares, Theo felt the urge
to flee.

"Oh, go away," she urged Mansfield, trying to keep from
bursting into tears.

"I cannot *leave* you, Theo," he pointed out reasonably.

"Go away, I say. Go away!"

It was a difficult situation. As much as he had not appreciated the words that had been hurled at him this evening, he was grateful to Theo for releasing him from their engagement. And, as a gentleman, he could not simply abandon her in a public place in the dusk. His problem was solved when Sir Francis materialized at his elbow.

"Your aunt is looking for you. I will take care of Theo." Crushed, she took the arm he held out to her.

"Good-bye, Theo," said Mansfield. She could not reply, but Sir Francis bid him farewell and asked him to make their excuses to the countess.

She could not meet Sir Francis's eyes, could not bear that sympathetic gaze upon her. She felt the veriest fool alive. She remained silent as he located his coachman and had his carriage brought around.

"I will take you home," he said kindly.

"Oh, no. I would not wish you to miss—" Her voice cracked. She fumbled with her reticule, but was forced to accept the handkerchief he offered instead.

There was a part of her that would have liked to confide in Sir Francis, but pride kept her from doing so. What would he think? He preserved a tactful silence for the first part of the ride home. When he finally spoke, his voice was gentle.

"I could tell from your face that something unpleasant had occurred upon the carriage ride to Sydney Gardens. If you wish, you may feel free to talk to me about it, and it will never go any further. Or if there is anything I might do for you, you have only to ask, my dear. I have always felt as if you were my own daughter."

His understanding was too much to bear. "Oh, Uncle," she sobbed. Soon he was patting her on the back and murmuring soothing words to her.

When the first flood of emotion had abated, she confessed what had occurred. He seemed neither as surprised or as shocked as Theo would have thought. She confronted him with it.

"I know that Lady Verridge's offer took you aback, my dear. Your mother, however, had a good idea of what her plans were from some things she had let slip from time to time. Her hope was that you would not be so terribly disillusioned as you are."

He pressed her hand comfortingly. "You must realize that

it is no reflection upon *you*. Lady Verridge is simply one of those selfish people who are not in the habit of thinking of anyone else in more than a superficial way. And of course the possibility she suggested is not one that would ever be considered for a moment—I hope you realize that."

His words reassured her, but there was a great deal more that she could not confess to him. She must tell her mother of her secret engagement, and let her know how very foolish and wicked she had been.

Chapter Seventeen

Although it was not yet nine o'clock, Theo was certain that her mother would already have fallen asleep. She would have to live with this guilt for one more evening. After thanking Sir Francis in what seemed to her to be an inadequate way, she began trudging wearily toward the staircase. She was surprised to hear a faint voice call out, "Theo?"

It came from the direction of her mother's chamber. She tiptoed over to it and found her parent awake in bed, reading. "How was—?" The question died on the viscountess's lips. Instead she held her arms out mutely, and Theo rushed into them, the tears flowing freely once again.

"Leave us Peggy," said Lady Westmoreland in her quiet but authoritative way. The servant, despite her curiosity, obeyed without a murmur. The viscountess stroked Theo's hair tenderly.

"Oh, my dear. I have been so afraid. I knew that this would wound you terribly. It must have been the most unpleasant sort of shock."

Theo shook her head and drew back to gaze with brimming eyes at her mother's face. "No, Mother. You don't understand . . ."

Her mother frowned. "I thought that Lady Verridge must have asked you to be her companion."

"She did, but . . ." Theo let out a sob.

Her mother drew her into her arms again. "It is all right, my dear. Whatever it is."

The words only made Theo weep the harder. Several more minutes passed before she recovered herself. Drying her eyes with the handkerchief her mother offered, she met the viscountess's eyes bravely. "I have been engaged, secretly, to Mr. Mansfield."

Despite herself, Lady Westmoreland's delicate eyebrows rose. "You have?"

Theo shook her head again. "I knew how wrong it was, but I still did it. He was so handsome, and so eligible, and I didn't realize what a tremendous blockhead he is."

It was a true test of motherly affection, but the viscountess managed to keep the corners of her mouth from curving upward. "You must tell me all about it," she said gravely.

With this invitation, Theo provided a full and detailed accounting of the entire history of her romance, from its auspicious beginnings to its ignoble end. Her mother quite naturally considered Mansfield's behavior to be despicable, and Theo was forced to remind her that undue excitement was not good for her.

"I knew that you had a *tendre* for him," admitted the viscountess, "and that was why I was so afraid about this evening. I knew that you imagined that Lady Verridge had far different plans for you." She placed a loving hand upon her daughter's. "She thinks of no one's welfare but her own, you know. Sir Francis had remarked to her that you seemed to have captured Mr. Mansfield's attention, and she merely responded that he was forever falling in and out of love, and that it never amounted to anything. She was completely indifferent as to whether you might be injured."

Lady Westmoreland drew herself up slightly. "I must share in the blame for this, because I took her at her word—"

"Oh, Mama—"

"No, I did, which I should not have done. My illness prevented me from chaperoning you as I should have, also. But I could tell that he was not the sort of gentleman who would ever make you happy, and I thought that in time, you would come to see that, too. He . . . lacks depth."

She looked at her daughter questioningly. "I must confess, too, that I thought that my plan had been working these last few weeks, that you did not seem as fond of him as formerly . . . ?" The silence finished her question.

Theo flushed. "You are wondering why I didn't break the engagement before tonight." She could not meet her mother's eyes. "The truth of the matter is . . . although I was strongly attracted to Mr. Mansfield, and did fancy myself in love, before I understood what it meant . . . I thought that with the countess's inheritance, we might repair our own fortunes . . . return to live at Westleigh, and restore it for Andrew . . ."

"Oh, my dear." Her mother's eyes were now as bright as her own. "I'm afraid that was most impractical."

"I know that now." Theo heaved a sigh. She looked up into her mother's eyes again. "And because I have been so very foolish, I have ruined all possibility for future happiness."

Her mother squeezed her hand. "My dear, it is not as bad as all that. Your reputation is hardly ruined, after all. You were chaperoned on every outing." She brightened. "And obviously Mr. Mansfield would have even less interest in this . . . this episode's being made known than you do. I understand that he is utterly dependent upon the countess and from what you have said, this news would be certain to infuriate her." She thoughtfully refrained from adding that Mr. Mansfield had already demonstrated his spinelessness. "I feel certain that someday you will find a kind and honorable gentleman with whom you may share your heart. If your attachment is sincere, he will understand about a youthful mistake." She smiled sunnily at her daughter.

Theo gazed at her mother with disbelief. Was it possible that her mother, who had been so perceptive, so understanding, so omniscient all along, still failed to guess where Theo's true anguish lay? Perhaps it was better this way. Her sorrow would only be doubled if she knew.

"I am aware that it all looks very black to you now, but I promise that after a good night's sleep, your prospects will seem much brighter to you."

She was suddenly looking very weary, and Theo realized what a toll this must have taken upon her. She threw her arms about the viscountess impulsively. "I love you, Mother."

"I love you, too, my dear."

For the first time in weeks, Theo found that she was able to enjoy a good night's sleep, but the rest of her mother's prediction failed to come true. The countess's proposition did not smart quite as much as it had the night before, and it was a relief not to be engaged to Mansfield, but otherwise, things seemed no less gloomy than they had the previous night.

She had thrown away her one chance to marry a fortune, possibly her one chance to marry at all. Bath was not teeming with wealthy, eligible gentlemen, after all. There would never be a return to Westleigh: she knew that now. Her brother would have nothing but a title with which to make his way in the world. Possibly he might marry some antidote with a fortune behind her, but that would be years in the future, anyway.

She deliberately diverted her mind. There was no point in wishing things undone. She must strive to appear cheerful, if only for her mother's sake. Nothing mattered besides the fact of her mother's recovery. She must hold on to that.

Peggy was there to help her this morning. There were no reproaches from the servant about disturbing the viscountess or about young ladies who chose to while away the entire day in bed. She had thoughtfully pressed Theo's handsome mull gown and dressed her hair with particular care today. Though not a word had passed between them the previous night, Theo knew it was an attempt to raise her spirits, and she thanked the servant.

When she made her way downstairs, she found that her mother was napping, and she partook of her breakfast in solitude and silence. She hardly noticed what she ate.

She was about to bite into a bun when a visitor was announced. Major Boyce had arrived and wished to speak with her. The matter was of some importance.

She did not wish to speak with anyone today, not even with such a sympathetic friend as this, and especially not upon a matter of importance. She was dreadfully tired of matters of importance and did not wish to hear any more about them. She sighed. If she were to begin being courageous, today was as good a day to start as any.

When she entered the drawing room, she was surprised to see the major in uniform. He wore a handsome coat of blue with light buff facings, worn over pale buff breeches and a shining pair of hussars. It was less striking than the gorgeously braided uniforms worn by the hussar regiments, but its more severe style became him well, and Theo was properly dazzled. He was pacing about the room in an agitated fashion, his limp hardly obvious. When he saw her he smiled, and no longer seemed a magnificent and somewhat intimidating stranger, but rather one whom she had come to think of as a dear friend.

He crossed over to her, holding out his hands. "My dear! How are you?"

She returned the smile as he took her hand in his and

kissed it. "I am well, thank you, but I hardly need inquire about you. I see that your wishes at last have been fulfilled."

"I am to report to London today. With luck, I may be able to sail within the week."

Theo felt a pang. "We will feel the want of your company, but I cannot wish that matters were otherwise. Please, won't you be seated? Would you care for tea?"

He shook his head as they both took their seats. "Thank you, but I am afraid that my time is too limited today." The blue eyes surveyed Theo for a moment, keenly. "My purpose in coming here today is twofold. First, I learned from Lady Verridge what had occurred yesterday, and since she is my relation, I wish to apologize for her conduct."

Theo's cheeks began to pinken. "Really, it is not necessary."

"She is a vain and foolish woman, with a great deal too much notion of her own consequence. I found her in a rage this morning because Sir Francis had gone to take you home, without taking leave of her himself." A grim smile hovered at the corner of the major's mouth. "She had been fancying him to be a beaux of hers, preposterous as it may seem."

Theo was given no chance to respond, for he continued furiously. "It was as nothing compared to my own anger when I learned that . . . that *puppy* Mansfield had practically abandoned you in the Gardens—that if Sir Francis hadn't appeared—by gad! I gave my cousin a piece of my temper. Not only did he fail to inform my aunt of your understanding and defend you from her attacks, but then to run off in such a cowardly fashion—"

Theo's face was red now. "Our understanding—how did you know of that?"

The major looked conscience-stricken. "My unruly tongue! I do apologize. I promised never to let a word of it escape my lips."

Her nerves were too agitated to permit her to remain in her chair, so instead she leapt up and began to pace. He was too much the gentleman to remain seated. "It is of the utmost importance that you tell me. Dear heaven! I thought my unhappy secret safe from the world." She turned with a sudden thought. "Could Mansfield have—?"

"He is a coward, but not altogether base. No, actually"— He looked a little uncomfortable, but proceeded on—"well, to explain it from the beginning, it was Sir Francis who first involved me. I had become quite bored with convalescing in London, and happened to meet him one day at my club. We had known each other before, of course, and upon my mentioning my kinship to Lady Verridge, he seemed much struck. He said that I might do him the greatest sort of favor since his niece was in Bath, on the point of becoming engaged to my cousin, whom he considered to be no more than a young coxcomb as well as completely ineligible. He suggested that my appearance here might make my cousin anxious about his inheritance and disincline him to pursue the romance, for fear of incurring my aunt's wrath. I was happy to oblige him, having wearied of London life."

He dropped his eyes for a moment, consideringly. "I am afraid that I was a trifle harsh with my cousin, whose nerves must be of the weakest. I was dressing him down about how he had betrayed you when the young idiot, thinking I divined all, confessed about your understanding. I unleashed all my guns then." One corner of his mouth flickered upward suspiciously. "I don't suppose he'll be telling anyone else."

He caught Theo's eyes. "Needless to say, neither shall I."

"Thank you." A thousand thoughts were reeling through Theo's brain. *Sir Francis* had been responsible for the interference, then. She might previously have denounced such cold-blooded manipulation, but she had to be glad of the result. It would have been a nightmare to be married to Mansfield and also to have been forced to listen to the countess's constant complaints. She gave a little shudder at the thought.

There was more that the major had to say. He took her hand, anxious to claim her attention. "Miss Westmoreland."

"Yes?"

"As I told you, I had *two* reasons for coming here. First, I wished to apologize for my family's behavior. Second . . ." He swallowed. "I wish to ask you to grant me the honor of your hand in marriage."

Theo stood too shocked to speak.

"I know that I am not as handsome a fellow as my cousin, nor so polished, nor so . . ." despite himself, his lip curled. ". . . fine. I am, however, possessed of a comfortable living, and dependent on no one for it. It is possible that I may raise to an even greater position with this war—" Here he shrugged. "—Though, of course, I might be killed. I know that nothing can ever compensate you for my cousin's betrayal, though if I were convinced that you were still attached to him, I would not ask you now. I like you better than any lady I've met. I think we rub on well together, and I see no reason why we should not be happy. I know that this may seem sudden, but you can understand the need for haste. We will need a special license, of course, and I expect you will wish to remain with your mother here while I am abroad, but—"

He was offering her one last hope for a comfortable future. As his wife, she would never face sinking to the role of a paid companion or a governess. He was attractive (more so than his cousin, she now thought), he was intelligent, and he was kind. He knew about the engagement, and he didn't particularly care. This was the sort of man her mother had predicted might appear. If she refused him, it could be her last hope.

"Oh, no." She could not help interrupting him. She could listen to no more.

"Eh?" He was more surprised than she had been.

"I mean, I am most honored by your offer, but I could not consider becoming your wife."

He gave a rueful grimace. "I have been too abrupt, haven't I? They breed decisiveness onto a soldier and it does us so little good off the battlefield." He looked into her eyes, sincerity shining from his own, "I would not hurry you. If you prefer to think it over today or tomorrow—I can wait. If you wish for a long engagement, I will marry you upon my return."

"No." It pained her so to give this honorable gentleman distress, but she knew it was kinder. "I mean that I cannot marry you at all. I find you admirable, amusing, an excellent companion, but I cannot marry you. You are too fine—and you deserve someday to marry a lady who loves you with her whole heart." Her eyes were full.

It was clear that he had never expected this blow. "Your heart is given to another?" he asked, with pardonable incredulity.

She dropped her eyes. "I know that someday, someone will make you very happy." She bravely raised them to smile at him again, "And I fully expect to hear that you have become a general."

For a moment he merely regarded her quietly. At last he spoke. "I suppose there is nothing else to say, then."

She shook her head in confusion.

"I hope that you may find happiness with this gentleman."

She shook her head. "I cannot."

"Then I hope you may find it elsewhere." He bent over her hand. "I would be obliged to you if you would give my regards to Lady Westmoreland."

"I will and I am sure she sends hers to you, also."

"Then, farewell." He hesitated at the doorway, and unexpectedly flashed a smile at her. "Wish me luck."

"Good luck." She smiled tearfully back as he left her.

Mansfield had awakened with a heart as unclouded as the day outside. He had come out of things much better than he might have anticipated. Though the countess was in a foul mood this morning, he had not particularly fallen from her good graces. Most important, though, he was free from his obligation to Theo, as free as if nothing had ever occurred. The best part was that he now might spend as much time as he wished with Julia, as much as was not taken up by his aunt's demands, in any event. What he wanted most was to spend every waking moment with Julia. The realization shocked him. Could this be love? He resolved to call upon her this morning and put his feelings to the test.

His happiness suffered a severe setback with the arrival of his cousin. First of all, the major apparently had some one to pick with the countess, if Mansfield was any judge of what those upraised voices meant. It was inconvenient. Since she was already out of temper, it would probably take hours of work to soothe her.

Mansfield was even more taken aback when the major ambushed him in the hallway, and pulled him into the drawing room.

"Ah, cousin. I have a few words I wish to say to you."

He had not liked the way the major's eyes glittered then, and he had liked it even less after his cousin got started. His cousin had rung a peal over him, making him more and more uncomfortable as he went along. What business was it of the major's anyway? Theo had been *his* fiancée. When the words slipped out, he knew he had made a mistake. His cousin's wrath descended upon him more furiously than it had before. He might never have suspected that he was the lowest scab alive, but his cousin had spared no pains to make the matter clear to him. He was thoroughly sulky by the time the major finished. What did he expect Mansfield to do about it now, anyway?

The major had said that he would take matters in hand and with a few more open threats, had departed. Mansfield glared after him angrily. It was that uniform that had intimidated him, he knew that now. If it hadn't been for that one unforeseen circumstance, he would have been happy to give the major a piece of *his* mind. There was just some sort of authority about a man in uniform. Why he himself would probably look splendid in one.

Julia could not but agree. He would look magnificent in one, particularly one of those hussar uniforms with all the gold braid. But she hoped that her darling Quentin would never really seriously consider becoming a soldier, of course. It would frighten her to death to think of him in deadly peril every minute. And if he should be wounded . . . She nearly swooned at the thought. No, he must not consider it. Besides, she could not bear the thought of his leaving. He must promise her that he would not.

It was not hard to exact such a promise. He had done the right thing by coming here. Julia was just the one to restore his troubled spirits. She had resented the major's interference even more bitterly than he had. And how dare the countess take out her atrocious temper on such a lovable nephew? He was much too good to her, he really was. She would not stand for such treatment, even for a minute.

He sighed. "I *must* endure it, though. I would have no income if not for my aunt's generosity. I cannot do anything without her approval . . . even marry."

He sneaked a glance at her and was pleased to see that she had pinkened in that charming way of hers. "You cannot choose your own wife?" she asked, toying with the ribbons on her dress.

"No, but if I could . . ." He lacked the boldness to say it, but just then her eyes met his in perfect comprehension. "Oh!"

And then she was in his arms, just as soft and yielding

as he had often remembered. When their lips parted, she looked at him, her blue eyes wide open. "I love you."

"I love you, too." He could not help it.

It was Julia who gave their conversation a more business-like turn several moments later. "You know, my dear, if you married me, you should no longer have to depend upon Lady Verridge. I have eighty thousand pounds coming to me upon my marriage."

"Eighty thousand— Do you mean that you would marry me?"

"Of course, you silly man."

They were preoccupied by their own form of celebration when the door opened and Isabel poured into the room, trailed by her almost fiancé and her mother. "Well!" she exclaimed in horror and disbelief.

Mansfield leapt to his feet. "Mrs. Simpson, your daughter has done me the honor of consenting to be my wife," he said, bowing gracefully.

It was left to Warwick to have the final word. "Thank God!"

Isabel turned to glare at him.

It had taken Theo's nerves some time to recover from the painful interview of the morning. She had thought to confide in her mother, but the viscountess was still asleep and she did not wish to wake her. She went upstairs with half a notion of resting, but not surprisingly, sleep eluded her.

She took a stroll about the room. What a dramatic turn events had taken the past few days. It would be difficult to settle down into a dull routine once more. She picked up a novel that she had borrowed from Duffield's, but put it down again. Reading could not interest her now. Well, there was always her embroidery. She made her way downstairs.

The sound of raised voices attracted her attention. She found Peggy and Mrs. Tompkins arguing in the hall. She managed to soothe the two combatants before she thought to chastise them for leaving her mother unattended. "But Mr Francis is in there," replied Mrs. Tompkins, as if it were explanation enough.

Theo would obviously have to wait for her tête-à-tête. She could not stand to remain housebound any longer. She informed Molly that her company would be required and then went upstairs to fetch her bonnet. Perhaps her feelings would be relieved somewhat by a brisk walk.

She strode blindly down Gay Street, the little maid hurrying to keep up with her. She had no particular destination in mind, she simply walked. She had just reached the corner and turned down George Street, when a familiar carriage entered her line of vision. She continued walking. It was a green and gold phaeton, somewhat the worse for dust.

She raised her eyes to the driver. Debenham. She continued walking mechanically, right up to the point where Debenham pulled the carriage over. "Take 'em Will," he shouted.

Hardly had the groom seized the reins he had been handed, before Debenham leapt down to Theo's side.

"Did you have a nice trip?" she inquired.

"Good Lord! I've a great deal to say to you, but it can't be done here." He took her unresisting arm and fairly towed her back to her house. He pulled her into the drawing room and dismissing Molly with a quick shake of the head, closed the doors.

"I've the best sort of news possible, my love—"

Did he say "my love"?

"You and your mother and your brother have no further worries. I—well, my father and I, with help from other discovered that your father did *not* lose all his money, a we thought. He was swindled out of it, and we found the swindler—and though we could not get all the money back—there is plenty for you to return to Westleigh to live whenever you want—and there is plenty for your brother' education—and for a hunter—and for gowns—and for, well not for everything you wish, but still—"

He had never said so many words at one time before She burst into sobs.

"What on earth is this?"

"Y-you have been working on this all this time . . ."

"Well, I tried to tell you the first time I went to London, he said practically. "But you wouldn't listen."

"Oh!"

"Theo, stop that!" He seized her wrists, so that she n longer could bury her face in her hands. "Don't you se what it means? You don't have to marry that dashed Man field fellow—or anyone else—for his fortune."

"M-marry," she stammered, looking at him in confusion. "But how did you know?"

He snorted. "I saw you setting your hook for him. Besides, I heard him ask you that night at the masquerade."

"And you didn't tell anyone?"

"What do you take me for?" His resentment was plain.

"Oh, John. What can I say?"

"Well, you don't need to say much, but you can stop sighing and shut off the waterworks."

Despite herself, she smiled, and drawing the handkerchief from her reticule, applied it to her eyes. "You did not have to worry. I ended the engagement last night, but it was over long before that."

Debenham exhaled in relief. "Well, thank God for that. There's no obstacle now. Theo, you'd better marry me."

She should not have been surprised that his proposal would also be curt. She looked into his eyes questioningly and was flooded by a feeling of warmth.

"I can't live without you, don't you see, and I dashed well am not going to let anyone else marry you."

"Oh, John!" A well-bred young lady should have returned a negative reply, though one that might encourage hope. For once, breeding deserted her. Her actions left him no doubt as to the nature of her reply.

Her embrace was returned with equal warmth. Theo had not thought such happiness possible. An unwelcome thought intruded. She drew back, horrified. "But John, what of Julia?"

"What of her?"

"You are engaged to her."

His eyebrows drew together. "I never!"

"But Miss Bromley said—"

"You should know better than to listen to that female's rubbish."

It was a shock. She was still trying to digest this information. "But Julia is in love with you. She must have expectations—"

He gave a snort. "In love with me—ha!"

Theo looked at him curiously. "But she seems so fond of you—and you of her. I was surprised when you seemed to take such a sudden liking for her but—"

"You made it clear you weren't interested in me. She was."

"But you said they were beneath me . . ."

"So they are, and would be even if their father were a duke." He shook his head. "But what did it matter, when you belonged to Mansfield?"

"I felt just the same when I heard that you also were . . but what of Julia?"

"She never cared for me, never cared for anything but becoming Lady Debenham. I did not intend for that to happen, you may be sure." He frowned. "After the first day or so, she wasn't even interested in that. She didn't mean to desert me unless she had another eligible fellow on the line. Luckily for me, Mansfield obliged."

"Mansfield?"

"Yes. My dear girl, if you hadn't been cooped up here you would have heard. They're the talk of the town. Bets are being laid as to the date."

"Then you didn't really think that I would marry him?"

"I didn't know. You're devilish stubborn sometimes. Dash it, Theo. What a hobble you put us in. Taking care of yourself indeed. I'm going to keep a close eye upon you after we're married."

Married. What a delightful verb. "Yes, John," she responded obediently.

They were about to return to more important activities when the door suddenly opened.

"John!" It was Sir Francis.

He nodded.

"I trust that this means the business is complete?"

He nodded again.

"Good, although I suppose it will look like self enrichment. Jane has finally consented to marry me. She's afraid that there will be a scandal, though as I've explained to her, we are not actually related. As soon as she is better I mean to take her to Scotland anyway until the talk dies down. Excellent fishing in Scotland, too, and there's a physician that Mapleton recommends . . ."

"Congratulations." His son was shaking him by the hand.

Sir Francis eyed Theo with more hesitation than he had ever shown. "I hope we may have your blessing, also, my dear."

"But of course." What a surprising day this was turning out to be. "I am so happy for you . . . and her. I saw when he fell ill that what she needed most for her happiness was ou."

"Of course, you and your brother will both always have home with us, my dear."

"No, she won't."

"Eh?"

Debenham put his arm around Theo and drew her to m. "Her home will be with me. I hope we have *your* essing."

"My word! This is fast work." He surveyed them both ith affection. "Do you know, it suddenly occurs to me that have forgotten something in the other room. If I go look, am sure I will remember what it was."

"Obliged to you, sir." As his father shut the door, ebenham pulled his fiancée into his arms, proceeding to monstrate that in certain situations even a taciturn man ay be eloquent.

Mingled in with this wild happiness was a sensation of lief. She had been afraid that she did not like kisses at , but she was discovering that she had been mistaken. ho could ever have expected such a delightful sensation? e must remember to mention it to John. She must . . . hat was she to remember? Ah, everything else was so important, after all.